Praise for

Highland Press Books!

THE CRYSTAL HEART *(by Katherine Deauxville) brims with ribald humor and authentic historical detail. Enjoy!*
~ Virginia Henley

* * *

CAT O'NINE TALES by Deborah MacGillivray. Enchanting tales from the most wicked, award-winning author today. Spellbinding! A treat for all.
~ Detra Fitch, The Huntress Reviews

* * *

HIGHLAND WISHES by Leanne Burroughs. This reviewer found that this book was a wonderful story set in a time when tension was high between England and Scotland. She writes a well-crafted story, with multidimensional characters and exquisite backdrops of Scotland. The storyline is a fast-paced tale with much detail to specific areas of history. The reader can feel this author's love for Scotland and its many wonderful heroes.
This reviewer was easily captivated by the story and was enthralled by it until the end. The reader will laugh and cry as you read this wonderful story. The reader feels all the pain, torment and disillusionment felt by both main characters, but also the joy and love they felt. Ms. Burroughs has crafted a well-researched story that gives a glimpse into Scotland during a time when there was upheaval and war for independence. This reviewer is anxiously awaiting her next novel in this series and commends her for a wonderful job done.
~Dawn Roberto, Love Romances

* * *

~ Best Selling Author, Maggie Davis,
AKA Katherine Deauxville

* * *

INTO THE WOODS by R.R. Smythe - This Young Adult Fantasy will send chills down your spine. I, as the reader, followed Callum and witnessed everything he and his friends went through as they attempted to decipher the messages. At the same time, I watched Callum's mother, Ellsbeth, as she walked through the Netherwood. Each time Callum deciphered one of the four messages, some villagers awakened. Through the eyes of Ellsbeth, I saw the other sleepers wander, make mistakes, and be released from the Netherwood, leaving Ellsbeth alone. There is one thread left dangling, but do not fret. This IS a stand alone book. But that thread gives me hope that another book about the Netherwoods may someday come to pass. Excellent reading for any age of fantasy fans!

~ Detra Fitch, Huntress Reviews

* * *

ALMOST TAKEN by Isabel Mere is a very passionate historical romance that takes the reader on an exciting adventure. The compelling characters of Deran Morissey, the Earl of Atherton, and Ava Fychon, a young woman from Wales, find themselves drawn together as they search for her missing siblings.

Readers will watch in interest as they fall in love and overcome obstacles. They will thrill in the passion and hope that they find happiness together. This is a very sensual romance that wins the heart of the readers. This is a creative and fast moving storyline that will enthrall readers. The character's personalities will fascinate readers and win their concern. Ava, who is highly spirited and stubborn, will win the respect of the readers for her courage and determination. Deran, who is rumored in the beginning to be an ice king, not caring about anyone, will prove how wrong people's perceptions can be. ***Almost Taken*** by Isabel Mere is an emotionally moving historical romance that I highly recommend to the readers.

~ Anita, The Romance Studio

* * *

Ms. Burroughs easily will captivate the reader with intricate details, a mystery that ensnares the reader and characters that will touch their hearts. By the end of the first chapter, this reviewer was enthralled with ***HER HIGHLAND ROGUE*** and was rooting for Duncan and Catherine to admit their love. Laughter, tears and love shine through this wonderful novel. This reviewer was amazed at Ms. Burroughs' depth and perception in this storyline. Her wonderful way with words plays itself through each page like a lyrical note and will captivate the reader till the very end. The only drawback was this reviewer wanted to know more of the secondary characters and the back story of other characters. All in all, read HER HIGHLAND ROGUE and be transported to a time that is full of mystery and promise of a future. This reviewer is highly recommending this book for those who enjoy an engrossing Scottish tale full of humor, love and laughter.

~Dawn, Love Romances

* * *

PRETEND I'M YOURS by Phyllis Campbell is an exceptional masterpiece. This lovely story is so rich in detail and personalities that it just leaps out and grabs hold of the reader. From the moment I started reading about Mercedes and Katherine, I was spellbound. Ms. Campbell carries the reader into a mirage of mystery with deceit, betrayal of the worst kind, and a passionate love revolving around the sisters, that makes this a whirlwind page-turner. Mercedes and William are astonishing characters that ignite the pages and allows the reader to experience all their deepening sensations. There were moments I could share in with their breathtaking romance, almost feeling the butterflies of

love they emitted. This extraordinary read had me mesmerized with its ambiance, its characters and its remarkable twists and turns, making it one recommended read in my book.
~ *Linda L., Fallen Angel Reviews*

* * *

REBEL HEART by Jannine Corti Petska - Ms. Petska does an excellent job of all aspects of sharing this book with us. Ms. Petska used a myriad of emotions to tell this story and the reader (me) quickly becomes entranced in the ways Courtney's stubborn attitude works to her advantage in surviving this disastrous beginning to her new life. Ms. Petska's writings demand attention; she draws the reader to quickly become involved in this passionate story. This is a wonderful rendition of a different type which is a welcome addition to the historical romance genre. I believe that you will enjoy this story; I know I did!
~ *Brenda Talley, The Romance Studio*

* * *

BLOOD ON THE TARTAN is the powerful tale of a little known ugly time in Scotland, where raw, fighting Scottish spirit gathers itself to challenge injustice. In Catherine Ross and Ian Macgregor the reader is treated to a rare romance and love triumphant as they fight for Scottish honor.
~*Robert Middlemiss, A Common Glory*

* * *

RECIPE FOR LOVE - I don't think the reader will find a better compilation of mouth watering short romantic love stories than in RECIPE FOR LOVE! This is a highly recommended volume – perfect for beaches, doctor's offices, or anywhere you've a few minutes to read.
~ *Marilyn Rondeau, Reviewers International Organization*

Legend says that if you wish with all your heart upon the rare blue moon, your wishes were sure to come true. Each of the heroines discovers this magical fact. True love is out there if you just believe in it. In some of the stories, love happens in the most unusual ways. Angels may help, ancient spells may be broken, anything can happen. Even vampires will find their perfect mate with the power of the blue moon. Not every heroine believes they are wishing for love, some are just looking for answers to their problems or nagging questions. Fate seems to think the solution is finding the one who makes their heart sing.

BLUE MOON MAGIC is a perfect read for late at night or even during your commute to work. The short yet sweet stories are a wonderful way to spend a few minutes. If you do not have the time to finish a full-length novel, but hate stopping in the middle of a loving tale, I highly recommend grabbing this book.
~ *Kim Swiderski, Writers Unlimited Reviewer*

* * *

Legend has it that a blue moon is enchanted. What happens when fifteen talented authors utilize this theme to create enthralling stories of love?

BLUE MOON ENCHANTMENT is a wonderful, themed anthology filled with phenomenal stories by fifteen extraordinarily talented authors. Readers will find a wide variety of time periods and styles showcased in this superb anthology. *BLUE MOON ENCHANTMENT* is sure to offer a little bit of something for everyone!
~ *Debbie, CK²S Kwips and Kritiques*

* * *

NO LAW AGAINST LOVE - If you have ever found yourself rolling your eyes at some of the more stupid laws, then you are going to adore this novel. Over twenty-five stories fill up this anthology, each one dealing with at least one stupid or outdated law. Let me give you an example: In Florida, USA, there is a law that states "If an elephant is left tied to a parking meter, the parking fee has to be paid just as it would for a vehicle." In Great Britain, "A license is required to keep a lunatic." Yes, you read those correctly. No matter how many times you go back and reread them, the words will remain the same. Those two laws are still legal. The tales vary in time and place. Some take place in the present, in the past, in the USA, in England... in other words, there is something for everyone! Best yet, profits from the sales of this novel go to breast cancer prevention.

A stellar anthology that had me laughing, sighing in pleasure, believing in magic, and left me begging for more! Will there be a second anthology someday? I sure hope so! This is one novel that will go directly to my 'Keeper' shelf, to be read over and over again. Very highly recommended!

~ Detra Fitch, Huntress Reviews

Brides of The West

A Romance Anthology

Highland Press Publishing

A Wee Dram Imprint

Brides of the West

An Original Publication of
Highland Press Publishing - 2008

Satin and Snakeskin © Michele Ann Young
Gray Wolf's Bride © Kimberly Ivey
The Chances Are Bride © Billie Warren Chai

Cover by Deborah MacGillivray

For information, please contact
Highland Press Publishing,
PO Box 2292, High Springs, FL 32655.
www.highlandpress.org

ISBN: 978-0-9800356-4-3

PUBLISHED BY HIGHLAND PRESS PUBLISHING

A Wee Dram Book

Dedication

My story in this Brides of the West Anthology is dedicated to my husband Keith; after all, he did drag me West when we first married.
He is my best friend, my greatest supporter, and my hero, and without him I would not be able to create my fantasy world or have so much fun in my life.

Michele

~~~

For my husband and best friend, Jeff. You are my one true love, my soul mate, my support and inspiration in all that I do. Thank you for believing in me all these years and for never letting me give up. I couldn't have made it this far without you. This one's for you, baby.

Kim

~~~

My story, *The Chances Are Bride*, is dedicated to my loving husband, Henry Chai, who has stood by my side for twenty-seven years and gifted me with two beautiful sons, Jonathan and Gideon. With love.

Billie

Table of Contents

SATIN AND SNAKESKIN

Michele Ann Young

Texas 1867

"**M**ove a muscle, lady, and your days of breathin' are over."

The deep voice pierced the fog of Tess' doze along with her numb buttocks, her parched throat, and the sweat trickling between her breasts. The lock of a weapon clicked.

She froze.

And she'd thought things couldn't get worse.

Slowly, not daring to breathe, she opened her eyes and stared at a pair of dusty snakeskin boots planted five feet from her rocky perch. Her gaze climbed lean, long muscular legs encased in black pants, skimmed a belt slung low on narrow hips, and encompassed a broad chest clad in pale blue soft cotton. She paused at the wide-set shoulders steadying the rifle pointed at her chest.

Not a comforting sight.

From beneath a large black hat, eyes the shade of a clear winter sky and equally cool, stared unblinking along the dull gleam of the barrel, his lean cheek and hard jaw pressed against the stock.

Mouth dryer than the Texas dust she'd been chewing on for days, she swallowed to create moisture. "Here. Take my money," she croaked and reached for the satchel at her side.

"That does it."

Tess squeezed her eyes shut.

The explosion shattered the silence. Her ears rang. Small objects peppered her arm, thigh, and temple. The acrid taste of gunpowder hit the back of her throat.

Something long and soft flopped on her legs, twisting and writhing, glistening gold and black.

A snake. She leaped off the boulder, shuddering and brushing at her skirts. "Ooo," she shrieked. "Get it off me."

The creature slid off the rock onto the dirt and laid still, a limp sand-colored coil with black diamonds running along its length. Dead. And headless.

She shuddered, her heart pounding as if she'd run a mile.

The rifleman hooked the toe of his boot beneath the disgusting thing and flicked it ten feet into a patch of dry scrub. Another kick disposed of the remains of the head. "Rattler."

Feeling as damp as if she'd fallen into a steam bath and just as breathless, she glared at him. "You scared me half to death. Don't you know better than to fire that thing so close to a person?"

He tipped his hat back with one finger.

Her breath hitched as she caught the full effect of the sun-bronzed square-cut jaw, firm lips and straight nose. Her insides gave a twinge of approval.

Mercy. Since when did the sight of a pretty man set her afire?

He narrowed those gorgeous blue eyes, a furrow forming between straight dark brows. "Don't you know no better than to sit out here on a rock?"

Tess shook her head. "I'm waiting for someone." Her bridegroom.

A strange feeling churned in the pit of her stomach. The only thing in sight from this crossroads, where the stagecoach had dropped her, to the hazy blue horizon was this man and the gig he'd driven up in while she slept.

Impossible. She was prepared for fat and bald, or old and ugly, anything as long as he was kind. Never would she have dared to imagine this epitome of rugged male beauty.

Tender and delicate, tendrils of hope unfurled deep inside her, like seedlings after a spring rain.

She pushed back the sticky wisps of hair at her temples and straightened her bonnet. What a sight she must look after three days travel and goodness knew how long waiting in the hot sun.

He removed his hat revealing thick, slicked-back, dark hair, his expression nonplussed. "Ma'am." The deep timbre of his voice sent a shiver down her back. "Are you the widder-woman, Mrs. Dalton?"

"Yes," she managed in an awed whisper.

He ran a slow glance from her head to her heels. "Ah, hell." He banged the dust off his hat on his thigh. "What was Tom Wilkins thinkin'?" He shook his head. "Honey, this just ain't gonna work."

The tiny shoots shriveled, blasted by the chill in his eyes. Tess swallowed what felt like ten hats worth of dust. "You mean you really are..."

"Jake Redmond, ma'am."

The name on the contract nestled in her bag. Her heart sank slowly to her shoes. One look and he knew he didn't want her. It hurt, but she wasn't exactly surprised. No man ever gave her a second look after they took in her bony form. All twigs and bristles, her mother always said. Pete had only married her for a share of her family's saddle-making business.

"I see," she squeezed from her dry throat.

He glanced out to the never-ending scenery of grass and stunted trees then back, as if hoping she might improve with a second look. The rifle swung from one large strong suntanned hand. "I'm sorry, ma'am. You've been dragged all the way out here for nothin'."

His slow drawl seemed to stroke her skin, made her want to purr like a cat and roll her shoulders. It certainly took the sting out of his words. But, damn his arrogance. If he had to buy himself a wife, he couldn't be much of a catch.

Get a grip, Tess. Life just took a new turn. Come to think of it, she hadn't wanted to get married in the first place. She'd wanted to get to San Antonio to find Albert. And she had. Almost.

She stared him straight in the eye. "I'm not refunding the cost of the ticket."

His angular jaw dropped. "No, ma'am. Wouldn't dream of askin' you."

Just as well. She'd lost all her money in New York. "You will pay my passage to San Antonio. You owe me that."

The tan on his cheekbones reddened. "Yes, ma'am." He squinted up at the sky and then back at her. "The stage comes on Wednesday."

"Not until Wednesday? Four days from now?" Her legs felt weak, and she sagged against the rock, remembered the snake and leaped back.

He watched like she was some sort of wild animal. "Yes, ma'am."

"Wonderful."

"I beg your pardon, ma'am?"

Tess stared at him, then realized she'd spoken out loud. "I said, wonderful, Mr. Redmond. First, you were late and then you take me in instant dislike. If you had been on time, I could have continued on to San Antonio. Instead, I find myself stranded in the middle of nowhere. Hence, wonderful."

She grabbed her battered leather satchel by the strap and started down a road trampled into ruts and baked hard by the sun. "Good day, Mr. Redmond."

"Where are you goin'?"

She didn't bother to turn around. "San Antonio. Since I am saving you the cost of a ticket, you should be delighted."

"Damn," he muttered. He caught up with her and blocked her path, his rifle slanted across his body. "It's fifty miles to town."

She gazed into those gorgeous sapphire blue eyes and wanted to cry from disappointment. What on earth was the matter with her? Marriage to a stranger was the last thing she wanted. Six weeks ago, she thought she'd never make it off the streets of New York and today she was within fifty miles of Albert with no need to make the ultimate sacrifice.

This latest reversal should have her dancing for joy, not feeling as if she'd lost a shilling and found a penny.

"Excuse me, Mr. Redmond." She gestured for him to stand aside. "If I am to arrive in San Antonio today, I think I should...make tracks. Isn't that what you people say?"

His jaw tightened. "Us people?"

"Yes. Texans. The farmer on the stagecoach said it all the time." She mimicked the slow drawl of her traveling companion. "We gotta make tracks if we're gonna get there tonight." She sidestepped him.

He cut her off again. She narrowed her eyes and heard the blood of temper rush in her ears. "Stand aside, sir."

"You can't get to San Antonio before dark, ma'am. I'm sorry, but you'll have to come to my ranch. I'll bring you back to catch the stage on Wednesday."

Oh, so he didn't want her as a bride, but he wanted to take her home. Did he think she was green? "No." She walked around him.

The sun beat down on her back, sweat trickled between her shoulder blades.

"Ma'am?" he called out. "Mrs. Dalton? Watch out for the snakes."

Instinctively, she shuddered and glanced back, uncertain.

He nodded.

She dropped her bag and placed her hands on her hips. "Are you trying to scare me? I think you are the only reptile here."

His chiseled features turned to granite, blue sparks seemed to shoot from his eyes. Clearly she'd disturbed his infuriating calm. "It won't do you no good to argue, Mrs. Dalton. I ain't lettin' you walk to San Antonio. That's final."

Her stomach did a slow lazy roll of appreciation. God, but the man looked gorgeous when roused. And blast him, he was right. She might be angry enough to claw his eyes out, but she wasn't stupid. Fifty miles was like walking from London to Dover. She wouldn't try it in England, where she knew the country and its hazards. She'd be lucky to make fifty yards in this heat without dissolving into a puddle and soaking into the dust. And she didn't want to walk in the dark. Dash it all. She had no alternative but to accept his hospitality. On her terms.

"Lay one finger on me and you'll talk in a high voice for the rest of your life," she said.

He recoiled. "A Texas gentleman wouldn't dream of touchin' a lady agin' her will."

"Gentlemen don't leave their brides standing at the altar," she muttered.

If he heard, he didn't show it. He waved his hat in the direction of his gig. "This way, if you please."

Jake watched her narrow shoulders sag as she realized her predicament. She picked up her bag. The resolute cast to her generous mouth sent a twinge of guilt straight to his gut, where tears would've left him cold. Not having a way with words, and afraid he might say something he might regret, he grabbed for the small leather satchel that seemed to be the sum total of her luggage. She clung to it as if she thought he planned to rob her. The strength of her momentary resistance surprised him. He gave it a jerk and she let go.

He strode ahead and dropped the bag in the back of the buggy. He turned to help her, but she'd already climbed in like a cat up a tree. He unlooped the reins and joined her on the seat. With a click of his tongue he turned the horse homeward.

"How far is it to your farm?" she asked.

"Five miles north, and it's a *ranch*."

"Is there a difference?"

He stole a look from the corner of his eye to see if she was being mean, but her thin face held no malice and her green eyes were bright with nothing but curiosity. "Farms are itty bitty things with fields and crops and fences. A ranch is a big open hunk of land with free range steers."

"Steers? Is that what you grow?"

"It's what we *raise*. Cattle for beef on a hundred thousand acres."

She looked completely unimpressed. "No cows or horses?"

Why the hell did he give a cuss what this scrawny scrap of a female thought of his ranch? "I got a cow for milk and I got horses for work. I got some chickens, too. But I raise cattle."

"Oh."

A silence filled with the sound of grinding wheels and clopping hooves stretched out. It must be his turn to ask a question. Cuss it, he hated small talk.

"Where are you from, Mrs. Dalton? Seems like you ain't from around these parts. You got one of those eastern accents."

"I'm from England. London."

It figured. Even if she was a mite taller than most women, she reminded him of a porcelain doll he'd seen in a shop window. Pale and fine boned and delicate enough to break at a touch. That white skin of hers would fry in ten minutes in the sun. If he wasn't mistaken, her nose was already pink and covered in freckles. Worse yet, she didn't have enough meat on her to survive a cold day in winter. Tom Wilkins must have thought it was a fine joke to send him a woman who needed tendin', instead of one who could take her share of the work. Damn his no-good hide to hell and gone.

"Can you cook?" he asked.

"Yes."

The little pause before she answered added fuel to his rage. A liar and a city woman. No woman dressed like her would know how to cook. Only the Calico Queens who worked in the Dry Gulch Saloon wore the shiny silky stuff she had on. Gals who spent their days lazing around when decent folks were at work and spent their nights helpin' cowpokes out of their hard earned cash for a roll in the hay. He'd had his fill of that kind of woman.

And like a softheaded fool he'd offered to feed her and take care of her for the next four days...and three nights. Three nights of a woman under his roof that he couldn't lay a finger on and he wouldn't be able to see straight. He'd have to join Uncle Raven and the boys in the bunkhouse.

Another stolen glance at her out of the corner of his eye, showed little more than the tip of her nose around the brim of her straw bonnet. He'd seen enough back there at the crossroad. All skin and bone and enormous green eyes in an angular face, she reminded him of a half-starved cat. She wouldn't last a week out here. She sure looked as if she wanted to scratch his eyes out when he'd up and told her the truth. She'd thank him later.

Jake hauled in a deep breath and let go a long sigh. No doubt about it. The boys and Uncle Raven were sure gonna be fit to be tied when he gave 'em the bad news. Hell, he was disappointed himself. He'd been so damned hopeful at the thought of a helpmate to share his troubles and his toil, not to mention the vision of a soft willin' woman in his bed at the end of the day. There was nothin' soft about this one.

Nothin' except a full soft mouth that begged to kiss and be kissed.

Nor did she have the hard-eyed look of a saloon girl. She reminded him more of a prickly pear, with spines that got under a man's skin. And a soft, honeyed center. Curse it to hell. Had what happened to Bill taught him nothing?

Oh yeah. He'd sure like Tom Wilkins to eat his knuckles next time he saw him in town, 'cept it would add to his troubles.

"Circle Q is just up ahead," he said.

"Circle Q? That is a strange name for a village."

"It's the name of my ranch. There ain't no villages here 'bouts. The nearest neighbors are five miles down the road."

She turned to face him, eyes narrowed and as suspicious as a cornered barn cat. "Are there really lots of snakes out there?"

He cursed the urge to smooth her hackles and gentle her sharp tongue and nodded.

She gestured to the range at large and then pointed to the rifle he kept close at hand on his other side. "Is that why you carry a gun?"

Jesus. City women didn't know a thing about country life. "I bring it for the rabbits mostly. They make good eatin'."

She grimaced. "In London we buy our rabbits from the butcher."

Why wasn't he surprised? Perhaps if she understood what he'd been looking for in a wife, she wouldn't be quite so mad about his rejection. "It's the woman's job to skin 'em."

"Are you planning to hunt now?"

"If I see game, I shoot it. But we're here." He couldn't help the ring of pride in his voice as they passed between the posts with the board emblazoned with his brand swinging overhead.

To Tess, adrift on an ocean of dry grass interrupted by the odd flash of a green bush, the long, low buildings seemed to float waves of heat. No trees softened their hard outlines. No flowers offered a welcome. Not even any cows, or steers as he called them. Just the three clapboard buildings. The one with the chimney and the covered porch must be the house. A large barn stood a short way off with a split-rail fence out back and a smaller building at right angles, also with a chimney. A henhouse? Or storage? Maybe a smokehouse? It didn't really matter, since she wasn't staying, so she swallowed her questions.

As they drew closer, she caught sight of a figure in the entrance to the barn. A squat bow-legged man who drew back into the shadows the moment he caught her gaze.

"Who is that?"

His firm lips flattened into a straight line. "One of the hands."

She frowned. "Do you mean he works for you?"

"Yes, ma'am. He won't bother you none. Takes his food with us. Sleeps in the bunkhouse."

That must be the small building with the chimney. They pulled up in front of the house. Tess glanced over at the barn, but the man had completely disappeared. Mr. Redmond jumped down and tied the horse to a hitching post in front of the porch steps. He came around to help her down, his large hands filled the hollow of her waist, his breath cooling her suddenly fiery cheek. The space between them crackled like air tensed for a storm. He set her well clear of his body as if he'd felt the charge, too, and grabbed her bag.

"This way, ma'am."

She followed him up the two steps and across the wooden porch. He ushered her through a plain-boarded front door into what must be the parlor. The brown armchairs needed covers, if not replacing. The plank floor was clean, but pitted from boot heels. The windows were bare of drapery and the only picture on the wall had faded to an indeterminate blob. It had been a long time since a woman had laid a finger on this room.

"The kitchen is through there," Mr. Redmond said, jerking his chin to the back of the house. "Your room is down the hall."

Tess headed down the short passage and pushed open the door at the end. She halted, amazed. The window, floor to ceiling and two feet wide, looked out across the barren landscape to the horizon. "Oh, my."

Mr. Redmond came up behind her. The view no longer held her attention. Her skin shimmered with the heat of his body at her back. His manly scent invaded each intake of her breath while the sound of his breathing filled her ears.

"It's the only bedroom I have." He sounded almost defensive.

"The view is...spectacular." She glanced at the double bed and the rail across one corner holding what were obviously his shirts and pants. "Where will you sleep?"

"I'll take the couch." The words shot at her, as if he feared she'd invite him to share.

She swallowed her chagrin and managed a swift smile. "You are very kind to offer me such generous hospitality, Mr. Redmond, when clearly I am a disappointment."

"It's the least I could do." He twisted his hat in his suntanned hands. "Ma'am?"

She tilted her head in question.

"Do you think you could call me Jake? Everyone always called my daddy, Mr. Redmond, and I ain't so comfortable with it. Not as a general rule."

The telltale hint of red in his cheeks appeared again, barely noticeable in the dark bronze of his skin. It made him seem less hard, less sure of himself, just a little less perfect. She nodded. "Why not? After all we have to spend the next couple of days together. I'd prefer to be called Tess than ma'am, too. It sounds a bit like the Queen, don't you think?"

"Yes, ma...Tess." He grinned and tossed her bag on the bed. It was the first time he'd smiled since she'd met him. A thing of beauty, all flashing white teeth and crinkles at the corners of sparkling eyes. He went from merely strikingly handsome to unbelievably gorgeous. Her heart did a stupid little jump.

Mercy, she had to stop reacting to him this way. He'd made it perfectly plain he had no interest.

"I'll fetch in a pail of water for you to wash. There's a jug and a bowl in the kitchen you can use. Me an' the boys generally swill down at the pump out back. The outhouse is behind the barn."

Heat rushed to her cheeks at the personal turn in the conversation.

He strode out of the room clearly glad to be gone.

She removed her bonnet, stripped off her cotton spencer and felt a little cooler. She dabbed at the sweat marks on her best gown with her handkerchief. It was probably ruined. She should have known better than to dress so fine in the ramshackle place New York City had turned out to be. A bowl of cool water sounded like heaven with dust of half of America coating every inch of her skin. A bath would be better, but that didn't seem to be an option. She strolled down the passageway and peeked into the kitchen.

A scrubbed pine table surrounded by four ladder-back chairs sat in the center of the wooden floor. A Dresden-blue painted dresser stood against one wall and a surprisingly modern-looking cooking range against the other. Through the window in the back door, she caught sight of her host. Even at this distance, those long lean legs encased in black and his strong forearm working the pump handle made her breathe a fraction faster. "Don't look," she muttered. "You are a respectable widow, not an impressionable girl." She pulled out a chair, sat and folded her hands in her lap.

An unexpected sadness washed over her, a sense of loss. Pure girlish foolishness. Something she had long ago put behind her. She had no reason to feel downcast. All in all, the whole adventure had turned out very well indeed, and after such a shaky start. Having spent most of the journey wondering how she would explain to her bridegroom an urgent desire to visit San Antonio immediately after she was married, she really ought to be relieved.

Her stomach clenched. What if Albert had left San Antonio for California as he'd hinted in his last letter? All she held dear depended on him returning to England before Mother ruined everything. Fate could not be so cruel. Could it?

Boots thumped on wood. Seconds later, Jake flung open the back door and stomped in with the pail swinging from one hand. He glanced at her neckline. Her skin seemed to heat as if branded. While his face remained blank, his gaze skittered away faster than water bounces off hot fat.

Tess willed herself not to sigh. She didn't have the

kind of bosom that made men's eyes light up any more than she had the kind of face that made them look twice. It mattered not one whit that this man found her lacking, even if her insides jolted each time her gaze drifted his way, which it did with unnerving frequency.

Jake poured the water into a bowl on the table and fished out a jar of soap from the dresser.

"Nice cooking range," Tess said to break the awkward silence. "Is it new?"

He grimaced. "Ordered it special from out East."

For the bride he no longer wanted. Idiotic and from nowhere, tears misted her vision. She blinked them away before they could spill over. It was exhaustion, nothing else. She gestured to the bowl. "Thank you."

"You're welcome." He hesitated. "I hope you'll excuse me, but I've chores to do. Cattle and such to check. Can you do for yourself until supper? Perhaps rest up awhile?"

"Of course. I'll be fine."

She thought with longing of the large bed in the other room, imagined how he would look stretched out beside her. Felt heat rise in her cheeks. "I'll be fine," she repeated.

He looked unsure, but clattered out of the kitchen all the same. The sound of the front door opening and closing signaled his departure.

Unable to resist, Tess tiptoed into the parlor and, careful to stay out of sight, peeped out the window. He leaped up onto the gig with loose-limbed athletic grace. Seconds later, the vehicle disappeared into the barn. She sighed. The only man she'd ever met who made her heart pound like a blacksmith's hammer and he didn't want her.

But he had asked if she could cook. Perhaps that was one way she could pay for her lodging.

Jake urged Copper into a trot, the back of his neck itchin' like he was being watched. Sweat. It had to be sweat. The dark shadows inside the barn offered respite from the afternoon sun, its rich manure and fresh hay smells balm to his black mood.

He unbuckled Copper's traces, whistling through his teeth, watching his hands do work they'd done a hundred times before, trying to ignore the anger eating away at his gut like acid, steeling himself for the questions.

Footsteps shuffled out of the dark.

Uncle Raven wandered to the other side of the buckboard and released the leather straps. Together, they pushed up on the buggy until it rested on its tail with the shafts pointing upwards.

"So?" Uncle Raven said. "She came."

Jake finally lifted his head to look at the old man. Braided grey hair framed a leathery face the color of mahogany and fell to his bony shoulders. He'd worn his eagle feather for the first time in a long time Jake noticed. "She ain't stayin'." Jake slapped Copper's rump. "Move it, boy."

The lines around Uncle Raven's mouth and corrugated lips deepened. He cocked his head, his black eyes glinting like the bird he was named for. "Why?"

Trust the old man to get straight to the point. "You saw her. You watched us from the barn. She's a city woman. I'll spend all my time panderin' to her and she'll break like a twig."

"Or bend like a willow. Old saying of my people—"

"It's done. Over. And they're my people, too." He led the horse into his stall, removed the bit and the bridle and hung them over the rail. Buck, his bronco, whinnied a greeting from the next door. What a waste of a day. He'd needed to ride out to the east end of his property and take a look at his beef. Instead he'd set himself up for a fall.

"Ask the medicine man for advice," Uncle Raven said, handing him a currying brush and setting to work with a comb on Copper's tail.

"No."

Uncle Raven blew out a noisy breath. "What about Little Hare? She's a nice girl. You're better off without an ugly white woman."

A burst of anger clouded Jake's vision. He glared over Copper's withers. "Did I say she was ugly? No, I didn't."

"Skinny, then."

"Damn it, you're twistin' my words. Where're the boys? I thought they were with you."

Uncle Raven raised his eyebrows. "All right. Change the subject. The boys went to Mrs. Drew's for a haircut."

"Dang it. Have y'all gone woman crazy? Those boys never get a haircut unless I tie 'em to a chair."

"No need to shout. I thought it would give Mrs. Jake time. Damned handful, those boys. Send 'em back East to their mother."

He glowered at Uncle Raven. "The boys need wide open spaces, not gettin' into trouble in the city." And their mother didn't want 'em.

"Why did you bring the woman here?" Uncle Raven prodded again.

Jake reined in his anger and shook his head. "I couldn't very well leave her standin' at the crossroads until Wednesday."

"Why not take her into town."

"I might, tomorrow. It's too late today."

He forked some hay into Copper's manger and checked his water. "Help me saddle Buck. I'm goin' to check on a calf I saw wanderin' by itself this mornin'."

"I'll come with you. I don't want to scare your city woman. We'll be back before the boys."

Jake nodded slowly. What the hell had he been thinking? He couldn't bring a woman here. It wouldn't matter who she was, it would never work, not with his family ties.

Moisture trickled between Tess' breasts. She fanned herself with her hand. "Plaguey thing," she muttered at the stove. "Whoever said ladies didn't sweat, but merely gently glowed, has never been to Texas in July."

At any moment she expected to find she'd melted into a sticky mess on the floor. And to make it worse, she was talking to herself again. She dabbed at her face and neck with the handkerchief she'd dipped in water. It didn't help. Nor had sunset. If anything it felt hotter.

The back door crashed back. Two blond lads of around ten and twelve hurtled in. The *A Bride for All* mail order catalog agent hadn't said a word about Jake being a widower, or a father. Tess offered them a smile.

"Hey," the taller lad said. "You the woman what's come to marry Uncle Jake? At last, we'll get a decent meal around here. I'm starvin'.". The pair dove for the table, pulled out a chair each and grabbed for a bowl and spoon. Their hands were filthy and their faces weren't much better.

Nephews, not sons, and rude ones at that. Boys were boys no matter which country they lived in and she'd lived around them all her life.

She raised her brows. "Good evening, gentlemen. I'm Tess Dalton. Whom might I have the pleasure of addressing?"

"Matt," said the big one.

"Dave Redmond," said the younger, wiping his hands on his pants.

She put her hands on her hips. "Surely you don't expect to eat at my table covered in a day's worth of dirt?"

The younger boy slid to the edge of his chair. He stopped at a glare from his brother.

"Uncle Jake don't make us wash up," Matt said with a try-it-on-for-size sideways glance from hazel eyes full of resentment. "Do he?"

Dave hunched into his shoulders and avoided her gaze. "Nope."

"Uncle Jake may not, but Tess Dalton does."

When they didn't move, Tess reached across and rapped Matt on the knuckles with the wooden spoon. Not hard enough to hurt, but enough to make him take notice.

"Ow." The lad jumped to his feet, fists clenched, face scarlet. "Just because you get to marry Uncle Jake don't mean you can tell us what to do. I told him havin' a woman around here would ruin everything."

The boy sounded so angry Tess considered backing down. The kind of manners Jake expected from these lads wasn't her concern. In a few days she'd be gone.

"You ain't our mother," the little one said, ranging alongside his brother, a world of hurt in his voice and in his eyes. They were the same bright blue as Jake's.

Now what in the world had happened to his mother to make him look so wounded? She softened her tone, which she knew sometimes sounded sharper than she meant. "Well, and here I heard Texas gentlemen were the most polite in the world." She raised a brow. "And here you are with your hats on in the presence of a lady and covered in more dust than my mother's parlor after the maid's day off."

Dave whipped off his hat and nudged his brother with his elbow. The skin of his forehead was clean compared to the rest of his face and pink with embarrassment. His short dirty blond hair looked as if someone had taken a knife to it.

Matt glowered, but removed his hat. He had brown hair, the color of oak and just as short.

"Boys," she said with a smile, "if you want stew, you need to wash. And if you need to wash, you need to go outside to the pump. But if you prefer to go hungry, that's your choice."

Dave looked longingly at the pot on the stove and then at Matt.

The back door swung open.

The boys spun around.

Jake. No mistaking the boots, or the mile long legs ending in lean lithe hips on the threshold. Tess let her gaze slide up his length and mentally licked her lips at the sight of his muscular torso and the chest solid enough to rest her head on, before coming to rest on Jake's sinfully handsome face.

He removed his hat and jerked his chin at the boys. "What's going on?"

"I just met your nephews. They are on their way out to wash up for dinner."

Jake inhaled. A slow smile spread across his face,

changing it from sinful to dangerous to all womankind.
Tess' stomach did a little flip.

"Dang," Jake said. "You really cooked? I smelled it
from out there and thought it was wishful thinkin'."

What had he expected her to do? "It's only stew. I
found the meat in the larder along with some
vegetables. I hope you don't mind?"

"Mind? Hell no. Let's wash up boys." He frowned.
"Why are you in here in all your dirt, anyhow?"

Matt stared at Tess as if expecting her to tattle.

She headed for the stove. "So that's four of us for
dinner, then?" she asked Jake.

"Five. Uncle Raven will join us." He bolted out the
door.

She frowned. He hadn't mentioned an uncle. Was
this the boys' father?

She busied herself filling five bowls with good
helpings of stew.

It didn't take long for the men to return. Scrubbed
clean of their dirt, and with damp hair, the young lads
looked almost angelic. Jake looked good enough to eat.
A trickle of water coursed down his cheek and into the
faint haze of stubble on his lean angled jaw. Tess briefly
wondered how that drip would taste licked right off his
tanned skin.

Damn. What was the matter with her? She'd been
married. She knew all about men. But Pete had been
nowhere near as attractive as Jake. Elderly, kind and as
boring as a Sunday sermon, Pete had saved her from
spinsterhood and given her life a purpose, even if they
hadn't had the children she longed for. This man would
drag her straight to hell. And he wouldn't have to do
much dragging.

A few steps behind Jake came a short man with
bowed legs and wearing a checkered shirt. A large
brown hat shadowed his face and long grey hair
straggled out from beneath it. He doffed his hat and
held it against his chest, his black eyes watching her
cautiously.

The lantern swinging from the beam above the

kitchen table cast his slanted eyes in shadow and emphasized his high cheekbones and beak of a nose. The way his mahogany skin stretched tight over his lean features, he looked like a death's head.

Tess swallowed a gasp. This must be an Indian. The stories she'd heard of these savage people sent chills down her back. It was the first time she'd felt cool for more than a week. She backed up a step.

"This is Uncle Raven." Jake's voice sounded harsh. A muscle in his jaw flickered and jumped as if he would like to say more, but couldn't think of the words.

"I don't bite," the old man said, his carved face splitting to reveal brown stained teeth.

"Uncle Raven lives here," Jake said flatly.

This native was his uncle? She looked from one to the other, seeking a resemblance. Jake glowered at her.

She stuck out a hand. "Nice to meet you, Mr. Raven."

The old man wiped his hands on his leather buckskins and shook it in a firm warm grasp. "Raven," he croaked. "Just Raven, ma'am." He shot Jake a glare from beneath lowered brows. "I'm not really an uncle."

These Americans certainly believed in informality.

Jake must have given the two boys a lecture on manners outside, because they went to their chairs, but remained standing behind them, waiting for her to sit."

She smiled at them. Dave smiled back. Matt curled his lip.

Jake pulled out a chair for her at one end of the table and she sat. He strode to his own chair at the opposite end.

"Texans are polite," Dave said.

"So they are," Tess replied as the men took their seats in a clatter and scrape of wood against wood.

Fork in hand, Jake looked at Dave enquiringly.

"We were talking about local customs before you came in," Tess explained.

Matt glowered, but said nothing.

"Is it your custom to say grace before a meal?" she asked.

"Yes," Jake said.

"No," chorused the boys and Uncle Raven.

"It is now," Jake growled. He bowed his head and said a few word of thanks.

"Eat up," Tess said.

"Finally," Matt said under his breath.

For the next little while the only sounds were those of enjoyment. The odd 'pass the bread,' a bit of slurping from the boys and a very contented sigh from Uncle Raven as he put down his fork.

"Would you like some more?" Tess asked.

He pressed a hand to his stomach. "I'll burst if I eat another bite."

Jake leaned back, a sensually satisfied cast to his mouth. "Thank you," he said. "That was a real nice surprise."

Tess' heart swelled out of all proportion to the praise. She liked to cook, but Pete's chef had rarely allowed her in the kitchen. "You are all very welcome."

"If you cook like that," Dave said, "I don't mind if Uncle Jake marries a girl."

Jake stiffened.

Tess felt her cheeks go red. "Er...your uncle and I are not going to get married."

Dave's eyes widened to the size of his bowl. "But that means—"

"It means she ain't stayin'," Matt said. "Right, Uncle Jake? That's what you said outside to Uncle Raven."

"You are right, Matt," Tess said. "I am just visiting. I am going to catch the stagecoach on Wednesday."

Dave's shoulders slumped. He stared at the table and said nothing.

A heavy silence filled the room.

Sweat ran down between Tess' shoulder blades in what felt like a torrent. "My word it is hot."

"Always hot in summer," Raven said.

Now there was a conversation stopper. "Not in England," she said with a raised brow.

The air in the bedroom weighed on Tess like a wool

blanket. She threw back the sheet and turned on her side peering into the shadows cast by the lantern. Amidst the shadows and patches of light, she pictured Jake's square jaw and lean cheekbones, the brilliance of his eyes. Foolish shadows. She sighed. Never had she seen a man so handsome. A sweet ache blossomed deep in her core, her pulse picked up speed and her blood ran hot. Just what she needed. More heat.

She flopped over on her back. Dash it, where was the breeze of earlier this evening. Why did the cool night air seem to trap the hot air inside the house?

What-might-have-beens swirled in her restless mind. Her cooking, him returning home of an evening and gazing at her with that seductive smile before his hands came around her waist and pulled her close. She still felt the imprint of those hands on her waist as if he had branded her when he lifted her from the gig. What had he called it? A buggy?

And children. A whole host of boys with dark hair and blue eyes around the kitchen table looking just like their tall handsome father...

Enough. It wasn't going to happen. She kicked the sheet off the bed and rolled on her other side, praying for a cool breeze from the window. A faint breath of air kissed her cheek, cooled the sweat on her brow. She was halfway tempted to strip off her nightgown. Mother would be horrified. Or perhaps not. With the new man in her life, Mother seemed oblivious to everything, particularly anything Tess had to say. If only Albert would give up his foolish notions of striking out on his own and come home everything could be comfortable again.

She punched at her pillow. Blasted heat.

Perhaps if she opened the window more... She swung her legs over the side of the bed and padded across to the pale break in the dark wall. She found the casement ajar just a fraction and flung it wide. To her surprise it opened all the way to the floor. It was a door. And beyond it a balcony.

Cautiously, she stuck her head outside. It wasn't a

balcony, so much as an extension of the porch. It must run around the corner to the front door. The boards out here felt wonderfully cool beneath her bare feet.

The thought of cool night air on her parched skin seemed to grab her throat with longing. Dare she? What about snakes?

She quelled a shudder. Drat it. Was she going to be intimidated by a creature no wider than a stick and half as tall as she? Surely snakes didn't come near houses? They lived out *there*. She glanced at the moon-drenched landscape with the twisted limbs of mesquite standing like tormented guardians of the wilderness. Snakes slumbered on rocks in hot sun. Jake never said anything about them slithering around at night.

One step at a time, maintaining gliding contact with the rough wood planks beneath her feet, she headed for the railing. Like the trail of a silent rocket, pinpoints of stars emblazoned the sky, only fading into inky black to the west, where the colder light of the moon over-powered their twinkle.

"Oh my," she breathed.

"Beautiful night, ain't it?" a deep voice said. Satisfaction thickened the deep drawl to the texture of rich cream.

Jake. Her vision adjusted. Leaning against the railing, his solid bulk blacked out the brighter sky, a shadow outlined in sequins. She wasn't the least bit surprised, she realized with wry amusement. Even if her mind hadn't told her he would be here, alone in the dark, her wicked body had known it on some deep primal level. The pulsing desire that had been a low hum in her blood from the moment she looked into those indescribably bright blue eyes now filled her ears with a wild drumbeat.

Oh my. This time, she kept the thought to herself.

"Good evening, Jake," she murmured. "I hope I did not disturb you."

A long low chuckle emanated across the dark divide between them. "I came out for a breath of cool air and a *seegar*."

He pronounced it with such sensual appreciation her toes curled into the wood.

"Don't stop on my account. I love the scent of tobacco."

He took her at her word, because a moment later a match flared with the pungent smell of phosphorus. It lit the hard lean angles of his square face along with the slender cigarillo clenched in strong white teeth as he inhaled. The cigar glowed red. His long slow exhale of pleasure blew out the match and turned her insides to porridge.

The aromatic smoke curled around her as if forming some invisible link between them.

"Would you care to set a spell?" he asked.

"Set a spell?" Did he think she looked like a witch? Was that the reason for his instant dislike?

"I—"

"I can pull the bench up to the rail if you like."

Chairs. She squeezed her eyes tight for a second. He meant sit for a while. Sometimes it was as if these Americans spoke a foreign language. "Yes. I would like that very much." More than she really dared admit, despite the little skip of her heart.

His shadow moved, disappeared. Wood scraped against wood and a thump vibrated the planks beneath her feet. "There you are, ma'am. I mean, Tess." The smile she couldn't see came through loud and clear in his voice. Her heart clenched in foolish longing and she found herself blinking back moisture.

Gaining her composure with what she hoped was an inaudible sniff, she slid one hand along the rail for a guide until her foot encountered the seat's solid leg. "Thank you."

"You're welcome." He lowered himself onto the other end and swung his booted heels up on the rail with a deep sigh of contentment. "I reckon I favor this end of the day."

She ought to be looking at the stars, at the beauty of nature, but sight of his muscled thighs in tight black pants held her fixated. Oh great heavens. If she could see him... She glanced down at her nightgown and was relieved to discover that while a shaft of light from her room fell across him, she remained cloaked in the deeper shadow of the porch.

The silence lingered comfortably along with his cigar smoke. Now, sitting still, she could once more feel the breeze on her face. It fluttered her gown around her ankles. Delicious. Cooling.

"Have you lived here long?" she asked.

"All my life."

"It is..." She struggled for a word to describe her awe. Big did not seem nearly expressive enough. "Magnificent. Grand." She laughed softly. "Beautiful."

"Different to where you come from? England?"

"Very. I lived in London, near Cheapside. You can barely see the sky for smoke and chimney pots."

"Don't sound like my kinda place."

Not in her wildest dreams could she imagine this loose-limbed cowboy in a top hat and a starched white cravat. "I like it there," she said firmly. Exactly who did she hope to convince?

"Then what brought you all the way out here to be married?"

She hesitated, unwilling to reveal too much of the truth. Her body might ache to throw itself into his arms instead of sitting all prim and proper on the chair at his side, but she had no reason at all to make him a gift of her trust.

"It's a long story," she said. "And of very little interest."

The husky, almost scratchy, timbre of her voice set Jake's blood alight in a ribbon of fire every time she opened her mouth. Listening to her, inhaling the smell of his soap on her skin laced with her uniquely female scent was almost as good as sex. Almost.

Hell. He'd been semi-aroused since the moment he'd seen her dozing in the sun. But her avoidance of his question piqued another kind of emotion. Curiosity. A desire to know her better. Something he rarely felt about women anymore.

"I've got all night," he said.

Again she gave that low hoarse chuckle with its sharp edge. Blood rushed to his groin as if he was sixteen instead of going on thirty. If this continued, his balls'd be bluer than Uncle Raven's warpaint by morning. Cuss it, he'd have to make a trip to the privy to take care of the matter before he tried to sleep with her not four feet from his head. And in his bed, no less. Dammit.

"It really isn't a very interesting tale." She gazed out into the night. Against the lamplight, her profile looked sharp, pointy, nervous, like a fox or a wild cat with its claws barely sheathed.

"You don't look old enough to be a widow," he said speculatively.

Her head shot around to look in his direction as if she sought his expression. Could she see his face in the shadows? He thought not, but kept it noncommittal.

"I married young. My husband was an older gentleman. A friend of the family. A businessman interested in putting money in our family business. It seemed like a good arrangement at the time." She spoke quickly, then paused as if expecting his comment.

"Not so different from a mail order bride," he said, feeling just a mite uncomfortable.

"No," she murmured. "Not so very different, except that I had known him all my life. He was a good, kind man. It was the perfect solution to some money problems my parents had at the time."

"What happened to your husband?"

"Influenza. Two years ago. It killed a few people in our neighborhood, mostly the very young and the elderly, including my husband and my father. I did my best to care for them." She sounded almost angry.

"Do you have children?" Lord A'mighty, she didn't look strong enough to bear a child.

"No. Sadly not."

Regret filled those whispered short words. The ache of sympathy in his chest surprised him. But women from the East were notoriously fickle. For all that Bill's wife protested her love, she'd hated the way child-bearing changed her life.

"So what did make you decide to come all the way out here, instead of marryin' one of those fine London gentlemen?" he asked.

She drew her feet up onto the seat, cradling her shins with her arms, resting her chin on her knees. He visualized the slim legs and firm round bottom he'd seen moments before through the cotton fabric of her gown outlined by the lamplight spilling from her room.

"I thought it would make a change."

The slight hesitation told him she was lying. That saddened him. It weren't none of his business, and she could just have said that. For some reason, against all logic, he felt...disappointed. Left out.

He drew on his cigar. It no longer tasted good. Hell. Surely by now he was used to the sensation of exclusion. He'd lived with it all his life.

"I'm sorry I was not the wife you were seeking," she said, sounding crisp and practical and yet he thought he heard a note of regret in those husky tones. Or was it merely politeness?

"You sure seemed relieved when I said so," he replied.

She raised her head a fraction. Wisps of hair that the moonlight painted black instead of russet, haloed her tiny face. He sensed her full soft kissable lips curving into a smile, even though he couldn't see them.

"To be honest, I wondered what sort of man needed to buy a wife."

He winced. The curiosity went both ways it seemed.

"The *Bride for All* folks surely mentioned the short-age of women in the West. Suitable women," he amended, mentally discarding the kind of women available to him.

"Do none of the other ranchers around here have daughters?"

"Some. Their kind set their sights a good bit higher." They all knew. His father had made sure the moment he found out. They'd been looking down their noses at him ever since. "And there ain't one of them I'd offer for." She didn't need to know the cold hard facts. She was leaving. Let someone in town tell her, then he wouldn't have to see her scorn.

"You are a choosy man." The small catch in her voice seemed to express an acre of hurt. It was wishful thinking putting thoughts in his head, he decided. She was far too calm to be upset and she'd definitely been pleased when he'd said it wouldn't work.

And yet something didn't feel right under his skin. He'd been too blunt, maybe. "It ain't got nothin' to do with you personally. My rejection." Shit. That sounded bad. "I mean a woman like you ain't cut out for this life. I expected someone stronger, more..." Hell the stiffness of her body indicated he was digging himself a hole as deep as the Grand Canyon. "Substantial." God. That sounded as if he was only interested in tits. And she had lovely breasts, palm sized, like peaches. "Older. To take care of the boys. They are a couple of scallywags at the best of times. Old Tom Wilkins knew my needs."

Her chin dropped back on her knees and her long loose hair fell around her shoulders, veiling her face. "You are a good uncle to them."

"Family comes first." It always had. And he wasn't about to risk it for a bad case of lust.

"I understand," she whispered.

And strangely he sensed that she did. Tension oozed out of his shoulders.

"I am used to boys, though," she went on. "My father had a gaggle of apprentices in his workshop and I have a younger brother."

He swallowed. "Are you suggestin' you want to stay?"

"Oh, no. Not at all. The sooner I get to San Antonio the better."

The evidence of her desire to leave was undeniable and cutting. He curled his lip. "Are you lookin' to *A Bride for All* to give you another contract?" He found he didn't like the idea one little bit. Naw. Stronger than that. He hated the idea.

"No. I don't think so."

The relief sparking through him kindled anger. At himself. Dammit. It didn't matter what she did after she left here. He dropped his feet from the rail, stood, flicked his stogy onto the boards and crushed it beneath a boot heel. "I'll take you to town in the mornin'. I need to pick up some supplies. Might as well do it this week as next."

She rose, facing him. "Jake?"

"Yes." He ached for her to touch him with her hands, the way she caressed him with her voice. She stood but a shoulder-width, mebbe less, from his chest. If she took a deep breath her breasts might actually graze the fabric of his shirt, if he judged it right and breathed in at the exact same moment.

"Thank you for saving me from that horrid snake," she murmured. "I should not have given you the rough edge of my tongue for being late. I was rude."

The deep regret in her voice plumb puzzled him.

He grunted and put a hand on her fine-boned shoulder. It was like touching a bird, one squeeze and the bones would crush beneath his fingers. "I was just mighty thankful you didn't faint clean away."

She tipped her chin. "I've never fainted in my life."

She sounded so cross, he believed her. His gaze dropped to the lush lips that spoke with such cute feminine indignation and felt his own curve in a smile.

Her mouth parted with a small gasp and she leaned in a fraction.

His bollocks tightened in anticipation of her body against his. His fingers clenched instinctively to pull her close.

He jerked his hand away. "Go to bed." His voice sounded harsh. He couldn't help it, he needed to get away from her, before he did something they'd both regret. "You need to be up early."

She swung away with a small cry of disappointment. Or was it the laugh of a temptress?

He stayed where he was, watching her step through

the door and into his bedroom. His control hung by a fragile thread. If he caught one more glimpse of those high perky breasts through that filmy fabric, he'd be done for. God. He was going mad.

The kitchen smelled sweet with syrup and just a little smoky when Tess entered the next morning.

Jake at the griddle waved his spatula. "Please, sit. My turn to cook."

Dave looked up from his plate with a shy smile. "Good morning, ma'am."

Matt reined in a smile that had almost run away from him. He glowered an acknowledgement.

"Good morning, everyone," she said. "Am I late?"

"You're right on time." Jake dropped a plate with a pancake and bacon in front of her. "Help yourself to syrup."

She didn't need encouragement. She poured the dark brown liquid over the golden fried batter and tucked in. The combination of salty bacon and sweet syrupy pancake filled her mouth. "Delicious."

Jake brought his own plate over and hooked his chair beneath him with one booted ankle. "Coffee?" he asked waving at the pot in the center of the table. She noticed that he cut his food with the edge of his fork instead of his knife and already had a mouthful. She liked to see a man enjoy his food.

"When do we leave?" Not that it really mattered. She had little to pack. But she did want to get there before dark.

The kitchen door slammed back. Raven strode in. Sweat streaked the dust on his face. "Trouble. Steers down in Split Pine Canyon."

"Dammit." Jake leaped to his feet. "How many?" He reached for his hat.

"Twenty. Thirty. Too many for me. A couple already in the water."

"Ah, hell." Jake looked at Tess.

"What is the matter?" she asked.

"Some cattle have wandered into a gorge. Last time

they did that, half of them drowned trying to make it across the river instead of turnin' around and comin' back the way they went in."

"Can we come, Uncle Jake?" Matt cried out. "You said we could come on the next roundup."

Jake looked torn. "It's not a roundup. And we ain't gonna go."

Matt glared at him. "You promised." His gaze turned to Tess. His upper lip curled. 'It's 'cause of her, ain't it? You're gonna let your steers drown because she wants to go to the city."

"A promise is a promise," Jake said. "And I promised to take Tess into town today."

"I'll take the boys," Raven said. "We can fix the fence." While his expression remained impassive, his eyes showed concern.

Without thinking, Tess said, "I can go to San Antonio tomorrow." Then wished she'd bitten out her tongue when Jake looked appalled and shook his head.

"I can't leave you alone," Jake said. "And the country is too rough for the buggy."

"Can't you ride?" Dave asked.

"Yes," Tess said. "Yes, I can."

"Not in a dress," Dave said. "The thorns'll rip it to shreds. That's what Mama always hated..." His voice died at the glare from his brother.

"I sure hate to lose that many good steer this early in the season," Jake said. "Are you sure you don't mind?"

"No." Tess smiled, suddenly glad not to be leaving, despite the little clock ticking in her brain. Tomorrow was the fifteenth of July and any day now Albert might leave. But this was important to Jake and she wanted to be part of it, to do something useful. "I don't mind at all."

"Matt, fetch a clean pair of pants," Jake said.

"Why? I put these on clean yesterday."

"Now," Jake said, his drawl more like barked orders. "And a shirt. Bring them back here. And get a wiggle on."

The boy shot off.

Raven went to a cupboard and pulled out a sack, then piled the supplies on the table. Bread, dried pork, other things Tess didn't recognize.

"Dave," Jake said, "go fill the canteens at the pump. Tess, when Matt comes back tell him to leave the clothes and come and help me saddle up."

In just a few words, Jake had turned the casual breakfast into a well-ordered expedition.

"What can I do?" Tess asked.

Jake raised his brows, waited for Dave loaded with canteens to struggle out of the backdoor, then grinned at her. "You can change into Matt's pants and shirt, then come on out to the barn. We'll see if we got a horse that will suit you."

When Jake glanced up from tightening the girth on the grey, he almost swallowed his tongue. It was all he could do not to whistle. Tess in a gown, day or night, was one sweet sight, but in Matt's hip-hugging pants and white linen shirt, she was a man's wet dream. This day had just turned into a nightmare.

He aimed for what he hoped was a casual nod.

Dave giggled. "You sure do look funny in Matt's clothes."

Matt shot red-faced out of a nearby stall. "Tell her to take 'em off."

Oh yeah. Jake'd sure like to tell her to do that. "I asked her to wear them. It's practical for out on the range. That is, if we're gonna go rescue those steer, instead of standin' around here all day yappin'."

Matt opened his mouth, then clearly thought better of what was on his tongue, because he dove back into the stall he'd just exited. Moments later, he backed out his and Dave's piebald ponies. Uncle Raven took the other mare and led Jake's chestnut outside. He gave Tess a nod of approval as he passed.

She bit her lip.

"Don't take any notice of that boy," Jake muttered. "He's taken a dislike to women since his father died and his mother went back East."

She nodded. "I guessed it must be something like that." She approached the grey from its front quarter so as not to spook it and ran a hand down its nose, letting the horse get her scent before she moved to its side to mount.

The woman knew horses at any rate.

She frowned and touched the saddle, traced the complex pattern on the skirts with a fingertip. Her expressive green eyes widened. Her lips parted on a hiss of breath.

"Somethin' wrong?" Jake asked.

She shot him a quick glance from beneath her lashes. "Uh...no. I was admiring the work on this saddle. Did you buy it near here?"

She was lying. Again. Hell, he hated a lying woman. Reminded him too much of the boys' mother. "San Antonio." He watched her lips press together as if to seal in the excitement shining in her eyes.

It was none of his business.

He dropped the old hat he kept for working the barn on her head. The thick hair coiled on her crown kept it above her ears. "Come on, I'll give you a boost." She said she could ride. Now he'd see if she was lying about that, too.

She settled into the saddle and he adjusted the stirrups. With her long coltish legs, she needed them longer than Matt did.

"How's that?" he asked.

She pushed up in the stirrups and sat back down. "Good." She ran a hand down the gelding's withers. "Good boy."

He walked the grey out into the yard and handed her the reins, then mounted up. Uncle Raven and the boys had already moved out leaving him and Tess eating their dust.

They broke into a trot. She did that funny up and down thing the English did, her sweet round bottom popping out of the saddle in the most suggestive way until he imagined himself lying beneath her, those strong thighs lifting her along his length... He dug his spurs in Buck's flanks and broke into a canter. She caught up with him.

Yeah. How about that? She rode as well as any of them.

They settled into a steady rhythm. Fast enough to eat up the miles, steady enough not to wind the horses.

Tess gestured to the boys up ahead. "So why aren't those boys with their mother?"

"She remarried. It didn't work out too good, so she sent them out to me. Matt's hurtin' bad because she don't want him around right now. Their father was my younger brother, stepbrother. Went for a soldier and got hisself killed in the war. Now the ranch is all mine. Another reason their mother is mad."

"Oh," she said.

That was it? Oh. After he'd given his life's history except the real bad part? He never talked about family as a rule. So why now? And why her?

They rode on for another mile or two in silence. It was as if she were digesting what he'd said like a snake digests a bird.

"Are there more snakes out here?" she asked.

He almost fell off his horse. Could she read his mind? He held back a grin. "Cottonmouth, rattler. All deadly."

She edged her horse a little closer to his. "Are they likely to attack?"

He resisted the temptation to tease, but didn't want her more skittish than she was already. She'd only be a distraction. More of a distraction. "Only if you disturb 'em, put a hand on one, stumble over it."

"Oh, I see." She sounded a mite less tense.

"Course they can be unpredictable. You can't be sure they won't take a mind that you'd make a tasty meal."

She shot him a glance from beneath his hat that said she didn't believe him.

"Then there's coyotes and mountain lion, they sometimes attack cattle and the odd traveler," he said.

This time her eyes glittered like emeralds. "Why are you trying to frighten me?"

"Just tryin' to make you aware of the dangers."
Trying to make sure she didn't want to stay? In case he couldn't say no?

"You will take me to San Antonio tomorrow?"

Apparently it had worked. "Yes."

Her gaze swept the horizon. "Are we still on your farm...ranch?"

He shook his head. "This is free range. All the ranchers hereabouts use it."

She pointed to a distant grazing herd of longhorns. "Then how do you know which cows are yours?"

"Cattle. We brand 'em. My brand is the Circle Q."

"The same sign as over your gate." She said it as if she'd made a novel discovery. He had made the right choice. She was a town girl. Just like the boys' mother. After the novelty wore off, she'd hate it here.

"How much farther?" She shifted in the saddle. Another sign of her delicate constitution. Shit. He had to stop thinking about her bottom.

"Couple miles more, I reckon." He squinted against the sun. "See that outcrop of rock there in the distance. That's where we're headed."

They rode the rest of the way in silence.

The unexpected slash of rocky gorge, took Tess' breath away. After all the flat land, who would have imagined this beautiful wild and rocky place that seemed to appear from nowhere? Water rushed not far below them. Either side of the steep drop-off, fence posts leaned at crazy angles. Between them, protruding from ground churned by the hoofprints of many animals, other posts stuck up like broken teeth.

"Something must have spooked 'em and they busted through," Jake said, circling his horse around the broken ground. "C'mon. Uncle Raven and the boys must have gone down to the river."

Behind him, Tess leaned back to check her mount's awkward progress down the shale that sloped away at an alarming angle. The noise of the water drowned out the noise of their hooves.

Rounding a giant boulder, she saw Raven and the two lads facing a head of about twenty-five steer, brown, white and beige with wicked looking horns. The three riders had them penned against a sand-colored up-thrust of rock that looked as if it might have been sliced by a giant knife.

Two other animals struggled in the rapid flowing water, their cries pathetic.

Jake, his face grim, twisted around in his saddle to yell at her over the noise of the water. "Take over for Uncle Raven. We'll see if we can get those two onto the bank."

Tess nodded and eased the gelding around him. The little horse stumbled on the loose footing. Tess' heart leaped to her mouth, but she held firm in the saddle.

"Steady, boy," Tess murmured. "Easy now." The horse's ears flicked back at the sound of her voice and stepped forward as daintily as you please. "Good, boy," Tess crooned.

Jake shot her a glance that looked like surprise edged with a glint of admiration.

The moment she took up position beside Raven, he took off for Jake at the water's edge.

The two boys appeared anxious as they whistled and yelled each time a steer tried to make a break from the group. It was enough to keep the steers at bay. Tess grinned at the boys and picked up the rhythm, the horses pacing and circling, ever vigilant for the snorting, seething mass to surge. Up close, these beasts were huge, terrifying, brown eyes circled in white, saliva dripping from flared nostrils, and horns like bayonets. If they stampeded, she and the boys would be speared, or worse yet trampled, and the whole lot might drown.

Out of the corner of her eye, she watched Raven and Jake get a rope around the necks of the animals in the water. The way they looped the ropes in circles then tossed them was a work of art, not to mention an entrancing display of the power in Jake's muscular shoulders as he wrestled the roped animal to the bank.

Finally, both were out of the river and Jake and

Raven joined her and the boys in the slow painful process of herding them up and out of the gorge.

Sweat poured down her back, despite the shade in the depths of the ravine. Her shirt stuck to her skin, her bottom burned, but when she got to the top, she whooped and yelled along with the men. Elation filled her with a physical excitement the like of which she'd never encountered.

Once the beasts got sight of open range, they took off in a race for the horizon. Tess looked to Jake for instructions.

"Let 'em go. They'll stop to graze in a while as if nothing happened and we'll check that none are injured."

Tess nodded, weariness grinding right down to her bones.

The sun was already casting long shadows. She had no idea they had taken so long with the cattle. The day had disappeared in a flash. "It will be dark before we get home," she said.

Jake shook his head. "Can't leave yet. First we gotta mend the fence, then I need to figure out what spooked those steers. If it was a wolf or a cat, I gotta deal with it." His brow furrowed. "If them critters get a taste for tame prey, they don't never leave the herd alone. I either gotta chase it off for good or kill it."

Tess felt sorry for the creature. "How will we find our way back after dark?"

"We don't," Raven said, dismounting. "We camp. I'll light a fire while Jake and the boys mend the fence."

Jake touched the brim of his hat in acknowledgement. He flung his saddlebag at the old Indian's feet. "Use whatever you need. Boys, follow me." He turned his horse for the fence.

Matt and Dave followed him, their young faces grimy and weary, but still game.

Tess eased herself out of the saddle, keenly aware of the stiffness in her thighs and the chafing of her nether regions. It had been months since she'd been on horseback, and never had she spent so long in the

Michele Ann Young

saddle at one time. The thought of dipping her sore places in the cooling river below tempted her greatly.

Raven threw her a rope. "Here. Hobble your horse to graze. I'll fetch up water in a minute." He pulled the canteen from his horse.

Hobble? She stared at his horse and realized he had loosely tied its front feet together, so it couldn't run. She did the same to her mount. "I'll get the water."

He cast her a sideways glance. "You can walk?"

He must have noticed her awkward gait. "Easier than I can ride," she replied with a chuckle.

"You must go upstream, where the water runs slow. It's tricky. Better let me go."

She was sore, not an invalid. "I can manage."

He gazed at her from those fierce black eyes for a moment, then nodded. "You are a strong woman."

Ouch. He meant strong willed. Her greatest fault according to Mother. Well she wasn't going to change now, and since it was all she had, her will would have to see her through. She picked up all of the canteens and slung them over her shoulder.

She made her way past Jake and the boys working on the fence. Dave waggled his fingers, but Jake didn't look up. He knew she was there. She sensed his knowing in every fiber of her being, in the tension across his shoulders, the fixed gaze on his hands and the subtle angling of his body away from her so their eyes didn't have to meet.

His aversion could not be clearer.

To hell with him.

She trudged down the slope, slipping here and there on the loose rock. This bank was clearly a deathtrap for the unwary.

At the bottom, she headed upstream, clambering over rocks slick from spray, edging around boulders that teetered on the brink of the rushing stream, enjoying the respite from the sun. She could understand the cattle wanting to drink. Perhaps thirst had driven them into this dangerous place?

She rounded the bend, a sharp elbow of a turn, and

halted, mouth agape. It was a dead end. Water gushed from a fissure in a wall of rock into a placid pool. Here, the gorge narrowed to no more than a deep vee, with a pie slice of blue directly overhead and a patch of springy grass at the water's edge surrounded by bushes and trees. Perfectly secluded. The overwhelming need to feel clean turned the dust and sweat into a tight crust on her skin. She glanced around. Everyone else was busy with their chores. If she was quick...

She ducked into the bushes and stripped out of her borrowed clothes.

Working swiftly, Jake knotted the ropes to the standing post. "Here," he said to Dave. "Run these down to the post on the other side. Matt take the knife and cut the rope to length like I showed you last week, then join it to that other post. It'll have to do 'til we can get some more rails up here to rebuild the fence. I'm goin' to have a look farther along and see if I can see what sent 'em over the edge, then I'll come and see how you're doin'. Right?"

"Yes, boss," Dave said with a grin. He set off at a run, rope snaking behind him.

Matt hesitated. "That lady. Tess. She ain't so bad after all." He flushed red and dashed after his brother, head down and arms pumping.

Jake stared at the running boy, a knot forming in his gut. What the hell did he mean? Had Uncle Raven put some crazed notion in the lad's head? Jake wouldn't put it past the old buzzard to try some old Indian match-making trick.

Suddenly, he wished he'd kept his mouth shut back there at the crossroads, given the whole thing a chance. Who was he fooling? She'd made it perfectly clear she wanted to leave, to hit the nearest town. Hell, she would've been gone by now if not for those damned steers breaking down the fence. Just because she could ride a horse and had faced a herd of angry cattle as well as any of them didn't make her good wife material. Not when she didn't want to stay.

The same kind of woman had sent Bill to his death and left the boys deeply wounded. He couldn't allow the boys to suffer that kind of rejection again. He knew how bad it felt.

He gave his knots a hard tug, fixed one that looked loose and then followed the fence along the top of the cliff looking for signs of whatever had disturbed the herd. This wasn't the first time cattle had gone over the bluff, but never so many all at once. He inspected the ridge for tracks. Nothing. He peered over the sheer drop into the narrowest part of the fissure.

His mouth dried. He closed his eyes and opened them again to make sure he wasn't dreaming. There, where the water fell into inky depths, Tess lay in the shallows, her long hair a halo around her head and her body white and clearly visible through her thigh-length clinging shift.

Dear God. She looked like one of them mermaids. Her limbs were long and slender and beautifully curved, her belly flat like a young girl's and the curls at the juncture of her thighs a dark red triangle and all the more erotic because of their transparent veil. He let his gaze drift to her high tiny breasts and their rose-tinted peaks. He imagined the nipples tight and hard. They weren't the only things tight and hard. His erection was going to burst his belt buckle. He glanced over his shoulder, wanting to do the gentlemanly thing and walk away, not wanting anyone else to see her in all her glory.

Leisurely, she rolled onto her stomach, revealing rounded buttocks, the crevasse between a hypnotic draw. The dimples at the base of her spine begged his exploration. He groaned his frustration as a few splashy strokes brought her to the bank. She stood up, ankle deep, her hair cascading water down her elfin body.

She wrung the water from her hair, and pushed it back, her body arching like a bow. He knew poets had the words to describe women. The only one in his vocabulary was goddess. He wanted her. And the wanting drove so deep it hurt.

Lust grabbed him hard and wrung his withers. He

almost let go a yell of frustration as she slipped on her shirt, then sat to shimmy into Matt's pants. Jesus. What was he doing peeping at her like some perverted old man?

He turned his back and ran hell for leather to find the boys.

Tomorrow. He'd get her to San Antonio tomorrow, come hell or high water.

By the time Tess returned from her bath, Raven had a fire lighted and three small tent-like constructions made from branches and horse blankets. He told Tess the tents were for her and the boys, he and Jake would sleep in the open. He cooked over the fire while they waited for Jake and the boys to return from checking the cattle. They also went down to the stream to wash up.

The mess of pork and beans Raven called supper was mouth wateringly wonderful. She recalled the picnics of her youth, family outings on Hampstead Heath, when the food always tasted better in the open air. She glanced across the fire at Jake who appeared lost in thought, as he had been for most of the meal.

Dave yawned and rolled on his side, one hand propping his head.

"Bed," Raven said.

"Not yet," Dave whined. "Ain't we goin' to sing around the fire?" He appealed to Jake. "It's our first camp out of the summer. We always have singin'.'"

"What do you sing?" Fascinated, Tess leaned back against her saddle.

"Cowboy songs," Matt said, nicely excluding her.

She kept her smile to herself. "I've never heard any cowboy songs."

"Boys," Jake said his voice full of gravel, "next time."

Little Dave's face dropped.

"A couple of songs won't hurt," Raven murmured.

"You know, I ain't got much of a voice," Jake said. Then he threw up his hands at the sight of the two glum faces. "One. But y'all have to join in."

The song talked of cowboys and their work, dogies and lassoes and a lot of other words that made no sense to Tess.

He was wrong about his voice though. It was a beautiful bass timbre that carried soft and low on the night air. It strummed at her woman's core, and at her heart. This man spoke to her in ways she couldn't fathom. After tomorrow she would never see him again. The ache in her chest intensified. She swallowed her tears. Tears were for weaklings. She had come out here to find Albert, to make him come home. Jake and his strange little family were never part of the plan.

The boys joined in the chorus and she hummed along. It was blissful—the stars above, the warm night air with a faint breath of wind to keep it from being oppressive.

As the notes died away, she thought of her own family, the songs they had sung in the workshop, the scent of the leather saddle at her back sharpening the memories.

"You sing," Dave said pointing at her.

She opened her mouth to refuse, but couldn't quite resist the longing in his voice.

One song in particular stuck in her head from her childhood, a time when she still cherished the ideals of youth. It surprised her how easily she started the first verse.

"Early one morning just as the sun was rising, I heard a maiden singing in the valley below. Oh don't deceive me, Oh never leave me, how could you use a poor maiden so."

Her voice wasn't pretty, it grated like sand on metal Mother always said, but she had always loved the sad romance of that ballad. A wry smile curled her lips. Romance was for other girls. And besides, she glanced at Jake across the fire, who avoided her gaze, it could be a painful affair.

The men sat quietly until she finished the chorus.

"Hey," said Dave. "That was great."

Raven clapped and Jake joined him. Matt just stared

at the fire, the firelight glinting off moisture in his eyes. Obviously the wrong choice of a song.

"Time for bed," Jake said firmly.

Grumbling, but apparently good-natured, the two boys disappeared into their makeshift shelters.

Tess gathered up the metal dishes. "Since Raven cooked, I'll wash. I'll take them down to the river."

"I'll come with you," Jake said.

That was the last thing she needed. She'd thought to get out of his disturbing presence, not be alone with him. "No need."

"Snakes," he said. "Water Moccasins."

"What," she almost shrieked, thinking of her bath.

He raised a brow.

"Perhaps we should leave the dishes until morning?" she said.

He shook his head. "The smell of food will bring other critters once the fire dies down, coyotes, and such."

"Oh my, this is certainly a dangerous place."

He gave her a hard stare. "That it is."

"Is it safe to walk down to the river at night?"

"Sure. If I go with you."

Defeated, she picked up the tin plates and mugs. They walked side by side down the slope. The silvery light gave the damp ground a dull glow.

He handed her over the slippery rocks she'd clambered this afternoon and they knelt side by side at the edge of the pool, her washing, him drying on the rag he'd brought along, the waterfall splashing into the still water like a black snake with reflective scales. She tried to pretend this was nothing unusual, the dark and the presence of a large warm man at her side, that it didn't shorten her breath or quicken her heartbeat.

"You did a good job today," he murmured close to her ear.

Her heart seemed to grow and swell in her chest. Compliments were few and far between in her life. "Thank you. I am glad we managed to save your cows."

"Cattle," he growled.

She laughed.

He rose to his feet and helped her to stand. They faced each other, practically toe to toe. "I'm sorry things couldn't work out between us," he said, gazing down into her face, his eyes catching the light, his expression shadowed.

Was it really regret in his voice, or simply guilt? It didn't matter. The die was cast. "It has been an interesting experience." She preferred to keep things light rather than reveal the painful sense that she'd lost something far more valuable than her money and her luggage.

In the dark, he seemed dreadfully close, the heat of his body, the scent of hard working man, sweat and musk and a trace of cigar. If she didn't know it was imagination, she would say his heartbeat kept time with hers. She was having trouble breathing, as if he somehow used up the air around them. The night closed around them as if they were alone in the world, free to do as they wished, no duty, no obligations, just two strangers who would never meet again.

Longing overcame reason. She stretched up, her fingers encountering long silky hair at his nape. He leaned forward, just enough for his lips to be in range of hers. She rose on tiptoes and kissed him, discovered the warm velvet feel of his mouth, tasted the faint tang of tobacco and coffee.

A goodbye kiss. The kiss one might give a brother, if it were not for the pounding of her heart, the pulse beat at her temple, and the rapid rise and fall of her chest.

His arm slid around her back, a firm warm hand cradled her skull. He angled his mouth, nibbled her bottom lip and she opened to him. His tongue slipped inside, his hips pressed against her belly, one thigh eased between her legs sending sparks of lust skittering down her veins like embers from a blazing fire.

She moaned and leaned against him, let her mind empty and her body sing its own song.

He broke the kiss. "I want you," he said, his voice thick and hoarse.

Dazed, breathless, burning with desire, she recognized the request for permission. Her body clamored for her to say yes. Her heart warned of the danger. If she gave herself, it would be with her soul. And tomorrow she was leaving. He didn't want her as a wife.

Never had she felt such passion for a man. She also had no doubt that if she said no, that would be the end of it. They would return to the campfire and their own separate beds.

And convincing Albert to come home wouldn't help with her lonely nights.

After tomorrow, she would return to her old life, dutiful daughter, sister and widow. Convenient. Practical. Passionless.

She'd regret it for the rest of her life.

"I want you, too," she said.

He inhaled a sharp hiss of breath, pulled her shirt from the waistband of her pants, skimmed her ribs with calloused fingers, cupped her breasts.

A groan rumbled up from his chest and he pulled her close for a kiss. While his tongue worked magic in her mouth, his hands explored her breasts, rolled her nipples between thumb and forefinger, weighed and measured and caressed in gentle circles. Weakness invaded her limbs, her insides melted.

The hammering of his heart against her palm tempted her own exploration. Her fingertips followed the contours of a rock hard chest, lean powerful shoulder, sculpted biceps. The man was as sleek as a lion, but the shirt seemed to keep her at a distance when she wanted to blend into him. She unfastened the shirt's top two buttons and slipped a hand inside the fabric. Silky skin roughened by a patch of hair in the center of his wide chest, met her touch. She curled her fingers in the springy curls and tugged.

"Mmmm," he murmured against her mouth. Then stepped back and whipped the shirt over his head, tossing it onto the grass at his feet.

She undid her buttons and let the billowing shirt slide to the ground. Would he shy away from her skinny, almost boyish body? Her husband had tolerated it on the few occasions he'd felt the urge to copulate. She shivered, suddenly cold despite the warm night air.

Desire softened the hard angles of his face as his gaze skimmed lingeringly down her length. "Lovely," he breathed. He shook his head. "Beautiful."

The reverence in his hushed resonant voice meant far more than mere words. Tears of joy and hope welled up to blur her vision. She dashed them away with the heel of her hand before his mouth came down hard on hers, demanding, giving, wanting and blissfully generous.

Her core clenched and unfurled in quickening beats, sending waves of heat to her breasts, tightening her nipples, sensitizing every inch of her flesh where it came in contact with him.

The warm hand on her back stroked, circled, caressed her ribs, her spine the curve of her bottom, then rose to the waistband of her borrowed pants. He slid one finger beneath the fabric, following the edge from her back to the front, tickling the sensitive spot on her hip, grazing her stomach with tantalizing slowness until it paused at the button.

She held her breath, then swallowed.

"Are you sure?" he murmured against her mouth, his voice rough as if his throat had tightened to the limit of its endurance.

"Yes," she whispered, wanting to say hurry, before she started to think, to analyze, to regain her senses.

As if he sensed her urgency, the buttons popped free in quick succession. He crouched to peel the pants over her hips, taking her drawers along with them. He pressed his lips to her mound. A shiver wracked her body. She grabbed for his shoulder. He turned his cheek against her belly and the stubble on his jaw grazed her delicate skin in a delicious mix of pain and pleasure. She tangled her fingers in his hair for balance as, one foot at a time, he freed her from boots and trousers until she stood naked in the moonlight, white as a ghost against the tan of his hands splayed on her hips. Spray from the falling water cooled her skin and puckered her nipples. Still kneeling at her feet, he gazed at her woman's curls, pressed a warm palm to the flat of her stomach, brushed his fingers over her breasts. Their gazes clashed. Even in this palest of light, she saw blue heat in the depths of his crystal gaze. She bowed her head, let her hair fall forward to cover her shoulders and the tingling peaks of her breasts

"Now you," she gasped, suddenly tense, uncomfortable, as shy as a virgin.

His hands felt light on her waist, and hot, as he reached his full height without a word. He pulled off his boots, the spurs a faint jangle, then stripped his pants away.

His manhood sprang free. Big, hard, unerringly nosing in the direction of her woman's centre.

Her mouth went dry. Fear? Lust? A little of both.

He glanced around with a small wry grimace, bent to spread their clothes on the patch of grass giving her a view of lean buttocks, firm flanks and a broad back. Pure masculine beauty. Hers for a night. She wanted to feel that strength inside her, taking her. Hard and fast. Now.

She sank on the makeshift bed, pulling him down with her, taking his mouth, nibbling his lips, tasting the hot cavity of his mouth with her tongue. He didn't hesitate. His hands were all over her, touching as if they could taste.

She parted her thighs and he slid a finger insider her cleft. Pleasure weighted her eyelids and limbs. "Yes," she cried.

Was he dreaming? Like some schoolboy with his dick in his hand in the small hours of the night? Would he awake alone as usual? The moisture slicking his fingers, the sound of her mewling breaths in his ear, told him this was real and it was heaven on earth.

He stroked her inner flesh with his finger. Her passage was tight, almost virginal, and as hot and wet as a wanton. All contradiction, this fragile yet tough woman. Perhaps he was wrong to think she couldn't survive out here? He couldn't think, not with her writhing beneath his hands, her skin sliding over his. He pressed deeper, harder. She circled her hips, taking more pleasure for herself. Her demand drove him wild with want.

He found the beaded nub of her pleasure center with his thumb, teased and circled and rubbed. Her scream of pleasure hardened his balls to rock, but when her fingers slid along the crack of his ass and stroked behind his balls, his brain felt ready to explode.

Oh God, he was going to come before he got inside.

Grabbing for every shred of control in his power, he eased his finger from her soft wet heat and rubbed the head of his sex in her wonderful moisture. Slowly, aware of her narrowness, afraid he might cause her pain, he pushed into her entrance and held still, to get her used to his girth before he gave her the full length.

Her sigh created a storm of pleasure in his veins. She tilted her hips, opening to him, encouraging him deeper. "Oh God, Tess," he groaned. "Take it slow." He palmed her breast, felt it pebble, bent to lave it with his tongue, drew it into his mouth and suckled.

Her screams of encouragement ripped through the night. Pride swelled his shaft unbearably, the need to dominate, to pound, to climax, the instinct to spill his life force inside her shuddered his frame. Wait. She had to go first.

He eased deeper, feeling the squeeze of her inner muscles on his demanding sex, then pulled back, cold air hitting hot skin a delicious torture of the need to drive home. She lifted her legs around his hips, her feet dragging him closer. He let go and drove deep, pounding, thrust after thrust, giving hard and feeling her take and take and take more and deeper.

Tess thought she might die of pleasure. This was the lovemaking she'd missed out on. This urgent give and take, the deep penetration, the waves of pleasure so huge they blinded and shivered and pounded her senses until they were one being, one heartbeat, one flow of blood. She hovered on the brink of something wonderful and frightening.

"Come for me, Tess," he grated on a harsh shivery out rush of air in her ear. "Now, Tess." He sounded tortured.

It was there, just out of reach.

"Let go, Tess."

She shattered, screaming her pleasure, proclaiming her joy, her possession of this glorious man. Tremors shook her from stem to stern. She clung to his shoulders, felt her nails bite his skin.

He groaned, pulled out of her as if in pain, and then spilled his seed on her belly. Chest heaving, lips pressed to her cheek, he held himself over her, grabbing his neckerchief to wipe her skin. He collapsed on his side, nuzzling the point of her shoulder. He drew in a shaky breath. "That was close."

She snuggled against his chest and he put one arm around her shoulders. Never had she felt so happy, so sated, so content. She pushed away the sadness that there was no chance of a child. A memento like that would be her undoing.

Their heartbeats and breathing slowly returned to normal. The liquid heat in Jake's veins cooled. The thunder of his heart returned to manageable levels.

He rolled on his back, pulling her tight against his side, supporting her length on one arm to lift her clear of the hard ground. The warm night air cocooned them, but he pulled Matt's shirt across her shoulders in case she felt chilled.

An unexpected sense of exhilaration burst like rockets in his head.

What the hell? Yes, it had been a long time, but never had the primal urge to mate, to brand a woman as his, been so strong a life force.

His chest felt full of something he dimly recognized, but had suppressed for too many years to make its intrusion anything but painful. The same kind of crippling pain he'd felt when his efforts to please his father had been met by sneering slurs.

Compared to this sudden invasion of raw emotion, duty and responsibility seemed like pale shadows. He clung to them. They'd served him well these past years, allowed him to meet his obligation to his nephews without involvement. If their mother took them back, he'd be secure in the knowledge he'd done his best. Yet somehow this passionate, strong, ornery scrap of a female had stirred things up inside him so bad, he desperately wanted to take the risk and ask her to stay.

She was no beauty in the accepted sense, she was far too skinny. But strength of character shone from her green eyes. She didn't simper and bat her eyelashes, she faced the world full on and forthright, and didn't shrink from hard work. And her passion. Just thinking about her demanding responses made him quicken and harden.

In the sliver of sky above his head the stars seemed to wink with mocking scorn. 'You knew,' they seemed to say in bright tinny voices.

Yes. He'd known. The truth hurt, made him feel like a coward. He acknowledged it anyway. The moment he'd seen her dozing on that rock, he'd wanted her more than anything he'd wanted in a very long time. Instinctively, he'd protected himself the only way he knew. He'd rejected her.

Had he made a terrible mistake by not giving her a chance? Was it too late? He'd never know if he didn't ask. He steeled himself and cupped her angular jaw, his fingers tangling in her mass of tumbled hair.

She raised her face for his kiss and passion swept good intentions away.

Tess loved the feel of his velvet mouth against hers, the sound of his sharp intake of breath when she nibbled his bottom lip seeking entrance.

The kiss deepened until she felt dizzy with wanting, rather like the sensation of too much champagne at someone else's wedding. Knowing this would be their only night together made her want him all the more, while her heart ached for the loss.

To her disappointment, he broke the kiss and nestled her head beneath his chin on his chest.

Poor pathetic Tess, always hankering for what she couldn't have.

"You did a good job today," he said. The words pleasantly vibrated against her ear, as if they were man and wife, tucked up in bed discussing the day's events.

"Thank you," she murmured. "I loved the way you and Raven twirled those ropes. How you pulled those poor steers out of the water."

His fingers brushed the curls back from her face. "Hey. You called them steers. I think you're gettin' the hang of it."

She couldn't stop her sigh for what might have been, but disguised it with a laugh. "So I did."

He inhaled through his nose as if to say something important. The silence crackled with a strange sort of tension. She felt his stomach muscles tighten beneath her hand.

"You could stay a few more days," he drawled.

Tess realized she'd been holding her breath. She let it out slowly, hopefully. "Why?"

"I guess I didn't give you a fair chance," he said.

Not her longed-for answer. With a wave of her hand, she encompassed their entwined limbs. "If it's about... this, you don't need to worry. I wanted it as much as you."

The slight shift of his legs beneath hers spoke volumes about his discomfort, but didn't clarify his meaning.

"Perhaps you should stay a few weeks," he murmured. "Just to see how things...go on?" His voice sounded strained, as if he wanted to say more.

"You want to see if I'm going to have your child." The words came out flat and hard.

He didn't answer. It wasn't a question.

"And then what?" she asked. "Would you marry me?"

"Of course." He sounded relieved, as if she'd offered him some sort of escape. "It would be my responsibility."

He was a man who took his responsibilities seriously. Even in the two days she'd known him, she
understood that. She ought to appreciate his thoughtful-
ness, but the thought of his child in her womb was so
utterly wonderful, his stark practicality pierced a soft
place in her heart and it wept tears of blood.

"And that is the reason you think I should stay?" she
managed to say calmly.

"The boys seem to like you. You cook real good. You
ride as well as the rest of us."

These were the same kind of reasons she'd married
Pete. When she'd signed the contract with *A Bride for
All*, the convenience issue hadn't mattered. Now, from
this man, she needed so much more. She wanted to be
loved for herself, who she was, not for reasons of
economy.

Her heart sank in a headlong rush down a deep hole.
She hit the bottom, shaken and bruised and angry.
"Please, Jake," she said with as much sweetness as she
could muster. "Don't disturb yourself on that score. You
did your best to make sure there would be no unwanted
child."

He stilled, froze, even his heart seemed to stop
beating against her cheek. If she hurt him, she didn't
care right now. She had her own pain to deal with. She
pushed herself up, away, gathering her clothes, only
dashing the mist from her eyes, when she was sure he
couldn't see.

"We'll go to San Antonio first thing in the morning
as planned," she said.

He moved away, thrusting legs into pants, stamping
on boots. "What's so all fired interestin' about San
Antonio? You got someone waitin' there? A man?"

"As a matter of fact, I am hoping to meet up with
someone there."

"Is this man the reason you came to America?" He
asked it casually. Too casually.

She had no reason to hide the truth. "Yes. I was
robbed in New York, almost the moment I set foot on

land. The *Bride for All* offer provided the opportunity to get out here."

"How were you goin' to explain this man to me...if we'd married?"

Good God, he sounded...angry, and if it wasn't impossible, she might think him jealous. Her short laugh sounded rather more bitter than she intended. "I did wonder about that."

She followed his long strides across the boulders and out of the gorge.

They had broken camp the next morning before the sun was no more than a grey promise in the east. Tess had the feeling they were fleeing the scene of a crime, that Jake wanted nothing more than to forget what had happened down by the river.

He growled when Matt complained about having to wait to get home to have breakfast. He snarled when Dave failed to tighten his cinches properly. The only person unaffected by Jake's black mood was Raven. He had ridden out and left them to it the moment he arose.

And now she and Jake were driving down the main street of San Antonio, after hours of a silence so taut it vibrated. The buildings were low and whitewashed, their interiors looked dark, cool and inviting.

Jake pulled up in front of a door beneath a sign: *A Bride for All*, with smaller writing beneath: *Let us help you find yours.*

"I'll go in and tell Tom Wilkins to cancel the contract," Jake said. "At least I can get some of my money back."

Her throat felt as dry as the dust on the road. And besides, how could she speak when tears of regret lay so close to the surface. So she grabbed her satchel and climbed down before he offered to help.

Jake hitched the horse to the post. He jerked his thumb over his shoulder. "Hotel's across the street."

Her throat fuller than ever, she nodded again. Her vision blurred. Dammit she wouldn't cry. She would not let him see how much he was hurting her. She knew all about men and their needs. So he'd used her. She'd used him, too. Enjoyed it.

She swallowed hard and forced herself to speak crisply. "Goodbye, Jake. Thank you for the drive. Wish Raven farewell for me please." Raven hadn't been at the Circle Q when they got back. She'd been worried about leaving the boys alone, but Jake had told her Raven was close, that he hated goodbyes. Dave had announced he hated them too and had hurtled off to the bunkhouse, followed by the dragging steps of his older brother.

Jake didn't look her in the eye. His hat pulled low on his forehead, his thumbs in his belt, he stared at the dirt. "Goodbye, Tess."

That was it, then. No more to be said.

She swung away, took a swift look up and down the street for traffic, then crossed the road and entered the hotel.

"What can I do for you ma'am," the clerk behind the counter asked.

"Is there a saddle maker in town?"

"At the north end."

"I am looking for a man who does fine decoration."

The man scratched his nose with the end of his pen. "I wouldn't know, ma'am. Do you want a room for the night or not." He glanced at her satchel suspiciously. "Is that all the luggage you got?"

Tess bit her lip. That was a complication she hadn't thought of. That and her lack of money. The whole reason for agreeing to be a mail order bride had been because she'd been robbed of everything she owned. She still didn't have money. And she wasn't about to ask Jake. He'd probably see it as payment for services rendered and give it to her. Anger at the sudden pain in her heart reddened her vision and brought a hard lump into her throat. She forced her words around it. "Actually," she said, "I'm looking for work."

The clerk's pale face flushed. "You cheeky little bitch. Get out of here, before I call the sheriff. Didn't you see the sign?" He pointed to the inscription on a varnished board above his head. "Or can't you read?"

"Yes, I can read," she snapped. "It says no soliciting."

"And that's what it means. This is a respectable establishment. Be off with you before I call the sheriff to put you in the hoosegow."

Heat flooded her cheeks as she realized what he thought. She turned about face with a flounce of her skirts and marched out.

Jake's buggy was gone.

She glanced up and down the sleepy street, saw a couple of Mexicans dozing in the sun outside the saloon, a couple of horses waiting patiently outside the general store, and that was it. It was siesta time, according to Jake. Things wouldn't get busy again until the sun went down.

Oh, Albert, please be here. If he wasn't, she might well find herself back in the *Bride for All* office looking for another husband. But she really didn't think she could. Not after her encounter with Jake. She'd always compare any man she met to him. And that wouldn't be fair or endurable.

She straightened her shoulders and set off up the street. After coming all this way to find him, Albert just had to be here.

At the north end of town, Fred Tuttle's Saddle Shop was no different than the other adobe buildings. Tess peered into a window full of decorated saddles, each one with Albert's trademark AW worked into the design, exactly like the one Jake owned. As she pushed the door open, a bell tinkled above her head. She stepped into the blessed cool and let the door swing shut.

A dark-eyed woman of Spanish extraction with a black shawl over a pristine white blouse hurried from somewhere at the back of the shop. A full black skirt decorated with exquisite embroidery swirled around her ankles. She halted when she saw Tess, her expression turning doubtful, her black eyes huge. "Can I help you, señora?" Her soft accent was charming.

Tess smiled. "I'm looking for my brother, Albert White. He made the saddles in your window."

The woman's expression shuttered. "There is no Albert here."

Tess stared at her. Why would the woman lie? Was Albert in some sort of trouble? "My name is Tess. Albert is my brother. He wrote to me from San Antonio. I know he made those saddles."

The woman shook her head, hands clasped at her breasts. "I'm sorry, señora. It is a mistake, I think."

She made a shooing motion with her arms.

Tess pushed passed her.

"Señora," the woman cried, "you cannot go there."

Tess didn't stop. She passed through a storeroom and out the back door, where the dazzle of the white painted walls almost blinded her and the heat of the day hit her like a wall. On the other side of the courtyard was an open door to a workshop and stable. The woman trotted after her. Tess ran through the door, blinking in the sudden dark.

"Tess," said a familiar beloved voice. "What in hell's name are you doing here?"

She flung herself at her brother. "Oh, Albert. Thank God I found you."

"Well, well," said a voice from behind. "How about that? Good thing I didn't marry you after all."

Jake. His bright blue eyes hot and angry and full of hurt. Damn him. What right did he have to be hurt?

The little Spanish lady hurtled through the door. "I am sorry, Alphonzo. I could not stop her."

Albert's sun-tanned face split in a grin beneath his straggly brown moustache. "Ain't no one can stop our Tess, I'm afraid." Heavens, he sounded like an American, and he'd only been here four years.

He looked at Jake. "But I'm not quite sure where you fit into the picture, mister."

Jake stared at Tess. "Nor am I. Or rather, I believe she used me to get to you." He made it sound ugly. Very ugly. And she didn't want him telling Albert exactly what they'd done.

"Albert, you have to come home," Tess pleaded. "Mother has married again. Her new husband doesn't want the business. They plan to sell it and move to the country. If you don't come soon, there will be nothing left."

"Did you come all this way to tell me that?"

She stared at him. "It's my home."

Jake was staring from one to the other. He looked sicker than a colicky horse. He jabbed his hat on his head and turned to leave.

"Just a moment, Redmond," Albert said. "Just how do you happen to know my sister?"

Jake pivoted. "Your sister?"

Albert narrowed his eyes. "Who did you think she was?"

Jake shook his head. "Your wife? Maybe your woman? She was so damned keen to find you."

The little Spanish lady sidled up to Albert and put her arm through his. "Alphonzo *es mio*."

"You are married?" Tess asked.

"Very much," Albert said, planting a kiss on the woman's dusky cheek. "And I'm not going back to London. I like it here. These cowboys,"—he gestured to Jake, who was staring at Tess so hard, her stomach clenched—"love my work, and they pay for it. Not like in London where all they do is expect something for nothing."

"But what about the business? It needs you. I need you. I can't go and live with Mother in the country. There's nothing for me to do." She blinked back what felt horribly like tears. She was making a fool of herself.

And Jake was watching her do it.

Albert gave her a bit of a cheeky grin, laced with a smidgeon of pride. "Sorry to knock the wind out of your sails, Tess, but I'm managing quite all right without my older sister's help. I'm thinking about going into politics. I can't do that in England. I don't have the right kind of education. Out here, they don't care which school a man went to."

She sank down on a stool. She shook her head. "Mother doesn't need my help," she gave a helpless little laugh. "And neither do you it seems. Oh dear. Now what shall I do?" Suddenly, she felt like an idiot. She'd spent all her savings thinking she was doing it to help her brother and he was managing perfectly well without her.

No one in the family needed her anymore. They were all happily married. And the only man she'd ever wanted had rejected her at first sight.

Jake, who she wished would leave, stepped out of the shadows. She shot him a glare. "Don't you have feed to buy? What are you doing here, anyway?"

He took a step closer. "I saw your interest in that saddle. Your urgent need to get to San Antonio and knowin' he was from England helped me put two and two together." He squeezed his eyes shut for a moment. "I think I made five."

Albert cracked a laugh, then frowned. "You still didn't say how you know each other."

"Mail order bride," Jake said.

"What?" Albert yelled. He leaped up and grabbed Tess' arm. "Why would you do such a harebrained thing? I thought Dalton left you comfortably off. Don't tell me you sank it all in the business."

Tess shook her head. "I invested some of it in the Funds and used the rest to travel here. But I was robbed in New York, had no means of proving who I was, so I signed a contract as a bride. I've always wanted a family, it seemed like the perfect opportunity." She shook her head. "Only he didn't want me."

Jake couldn't stand the pinched look on Tess' face. Clearly she'd been thrown off balance. He desperately wanted to haul her close and tell her everything would be all right, that she would come home with him and they would make a perfect life together. He took a deep breath...and held his peace.

Tess got slowly to her feet. "Well, I suppose there's nothing for it, but to go back to London, if you wouldn't mind lending me the price of a ticket."

"You are welcome to stay with me and Maria," Albert said.

A flash of hope jolted through Jake. He hated the

idea of never seeing her again. Hated it like hell. Perhaps, once she learned the truth, she might get used to the idea and then he could woo her the way she deserved.

She shook her head. "I think I need to go home. Make sure Mother gets a good price for the business and doesn't pay too much for her new house. You know how hopeless she can be with money."

The hope in Jake's chest blew away like dust.

Albert frowned. "Do you think Ma's new husband will listen to you, Tess? What you need is your own man and your own life. I never did understand why you married an old stick like Dalton."

The misery in Tess' eyes drove a stake through Jake's heart. He took a step forward, saw her freeze rigid as if his very presence chilled her. He halted.

She straightened her shoulders and gave a little toss of her head. "You know there isn't a man in the world who'd make me an offer. Not without a bribe. I did it because it helped the family."

Albert tossed her an amused glance, which to Jake seemed rather cruel given she was on the edge of tears.

"Just like you would have married this cowboy, huh, Tess?" Albert said. "For the family?"

She stole a glance at Jake and quickly looked away. "Yes," she whispered. Her face turned bright red.

She was lying. Jake felt heat spread out from his chest. Damn it, she wanted to marry him for himself. He knew it in his bones. His Indian blood that told him things in a way white men never knew or understood. But did *she* fully understand what she would get herself into with him?

"I'm part Cherokee," he said.

She looked blank.

"Indian."

She now looked puzzled. "You mean Raven really is your uncle?"

"Not my uncle. My grandfather. I just got used to callin' him uncle when I was a boy." Before he knew.

"Folks round here ain't keen on mixing their blood

72

with Indian blood," Albert said.

Jake shot him a glare, but said nothing. How could he deny the truth?

Tess' eyes widened. "Oh," she said. "I see." She stared down at the ground.

Blood rushed in Jake's ears, his heart thundered painfully. He wanted to turn away, to avoid the pain of seeing her disgust, but kept his gaze fixed on her face.

He sure wished he hadn't spoken up, but honor demanded he tell the truth. Especially with her, this woman who had stolen his heart when he wasn't looking. Right now she held it in the palm of her delicate hands. At any moment, she could squeeze it as dry as the desert.

"I have Irish blood," she said. "How do you feel about that?"

Jake felt thoroughly confused and must have looked it because she gave that raspy little laugh that sent him mindless with lust...and love.

"People in England aren't keen on the Irish," she said. "And with my red hair, they always knew right away."

Albert nodded. "It's true."

Tess frowned him into silence. "But," she went on, "I think if you love someone, it doesn't matter what runs in your blood." She smiled at him shyly. "Does it?"

It took a moment for the words to sink in. Was she saying she loved him? The look on her face, all soft, sweet, shy, her eyes a little moist, said she was, but inside his gut twisted. He didn't feel sure. His father had despised him for his tainted blood, favored his younger stepbrother no matter how hard Jake worked to please him.

She must have sensed his doubt, because she glided to stand right in front of him, hands on hips and stared up with a gaze that seemed to see right through to his soul.

"I love you, Jake."

He felt as if a dam had broken in his chest. Moisture choked his throat, burned behind his nose, blurring his eyes. Somehow, he forced words through the flood, around it. "God, Tess, I...Goddammit." He swallowed. She looked so hell-bent anxious, he wanted to kill himself. "Stay with me, Tess. Marry me. I love you, Tess."

Albert gave a whoop. His tiny wife jumped up and down.

But Jake only had eyes for Tess. Tiny, delicate, uniquely beautiful Tess, who was stronger and braver than ever he could be without her.

"Yes, Jake. I will marry you."

He picked her up and swung her around in a circle, his heart delighting at her happy shriek. "We need a preacher. I want daughters just like you."

"And I want sons. Matt and Dave will teach them to be Texas gentlemen."

"You'll keep the lads, then?" It had been his biggest worry in this whole marriage thing.

She gently held his cheeks in her hands, gazed into his eyes. "Of course we will keep the boys. And Uncle Raven."

He stared into her honest truthful eyes and shook his head in wonder. "Tess, you truly are an angel." He raised his voice, shouted, wanted the world to know he'd found his woman. "Let's find a preacher."

She cupped his face and raised her lips to claim his mouth, soft and gentle and demanding his attention.

His woman. And he was her man.

Truly, there was a bride for every man—and she would be his bride for all time.

GRAY WOLF'S BRIDE

Kimberly Ivey

Gonzales, Texas
May 1885

Gray Wolf McKinnon's heart slammed in his chest as he stared at the photograph on page seven of the new *A Bride for All* mail order catalog he'd picked up that morning. It couldn't be—yet it was. *Evangeline Braddock Payne.* He sprang from the writing desk with such vigor, the chair he'd been sitting in toppled to the floor. He read the words beneath the photograph. *Twenty-eight year old widow with young child seeks matrimony with kind gentleman. Excellent cook and seamstress of strong constitution, wishes to relocate as soon as possible. Courtship unnecessary.*

He flung the catalog across the room and stalked the floor of his cabin. Evangeline was a widow. While it should have pleased him Garrick Payne was dead, somehow it didn't hold any satisfaction—not that he truly cared whether she'd married another man. Any tenderness he'd felt for her died ten years ago on the night they'd tried to murder him.

Opening the door, he braced himself against its frame and drew in a deep, steadying breath of night air. What an interesting turn of events. The Reverend Garrick Payne dead and Evangeline free to marry. To marry *him*.

No! Shoving away from the door, his steps propelled him across the porch that spanned the length of the house. What the hell was he thinking? She'd betrayed him, her lies nearly costing his life. He shoved a hand through his thick, shoulder-length hair and let out a ragged breath. Evangeline hadn't cared for him. He'd only been a dalliance, a novelty to pass the lonely summer on her father's ranch.

He strode into the cabin, kicking the door shut behind him. He glanced at the catalog on the floor, then to the writing desk. His body shook with rage as a plot coalesced in his mind. Snatching up the book, he thumbed through until he found her photograph again. Crossing over to the desk, he righted the chair and took a seat, then placed the book before him. This was insane. No, *he* was insane.

"Do it," the voice said.

He adjusted the lamp's wick, illuminating the room. What would he gain by such a deed? *Revenge.*

Opening the desk drawer, he took out the inkwell, pen and a sheet of paper.

He blew out a breath, cracked his knuckles, then picked up the pen.

Dear Mrs. Payne, he wrote with flourish, *My name is Mr. Adam Smith of Gonzales, Texas. I read your advertisement in A Bride for All mail order catalog and would like to begin a correspondence with you. I have never married, am of sound body and mind and the owner of a comfortable log cabin situated on a one-hundred sixty-acre ranch in south central Texas. I am in need of a wife and helpmate and would welcome you and your child immediately. Please advise concerning transportation expenses.*

As he laid the pen aside and blew on the ink lightly to hasten the drying, his gaze fell upon her photograph. A disturbing thought crossed his mind. What if she'd already answered another man's correspondence? A chill shook him at the thought.

He signed the letter and sealed the envelope, knowing he must act swiftly. He could not let her get away again.

Luling, Texas
June 1885

Evangeline Braddock Payne Smith hugged her nine-year-old son, Mac, close as the train rolled through the outskirts of town. She'd traveled from Savannah to Houston, where she'd taken the Pierce rail line west. Today she would meet Adam Smith, the man she'd married one week ago by proxy after a correspondence of less than one month. Although she'd hated to marry in haste, there was no time to squander. The anonymous letters had become more frequent this past month and she feared their author might strike at any time. Now she and Mac would be secure with their new identity in another state. At least she prayed her past wouldn't catch up with her.

The first threatening note had arrived five weeks ago. She'd immediately placed an advertisement in the *A Bride for All* mail order catalog, hoping to flee Georgia as soon as possible. A Texas rancher had responded.

Someone knew the details of her late husband's death and she feared they'd stop at nothing to expose the truth. Before leaving Savannah, she'd burned the letters and donated her late husband's estate to charity—all furnishings intact. Her only remaining possessions were two trunks—one of keepsakes, and the other containing her and Mac's clothes, scheduled to arrive at her new home in ten days.

She lifted an embroidered handkerchief and blotted her cheeks and forehead, fretful Mr. Smith should meet her for the first time in such an untidy state. She fought to contain wispy ringlets of damp hair that slipped from the once neatly coiled bun at the nape of her neck. She licked her parched lips, tasting salt. Perspiration saturated the bodice of her new blue dress. Mac was in no better condition from the long train ride. She glanced over at her son who busily picked at a festered insect bite on his arm.

"Mac, please stop," she whispered. "It's impolite before the other ladies on the train."

"But I itch, Mama." He scratched his head. "I think I have fleas."

She sighed. They both needed a sound scrubbing. What would her new husband think of them, given their disheveled state?

She closed her eyes and imagined her first day in her new home, enjoying a luxurious soak in the footed bathtub Mr. Smith wrote he'd installed as a wedding present. She'd purchased a new bottle of rose-scented bath salts for the occasion. On second thought, perhaps she might use them tonight at the hotel. She supposed Mr. Smith—or Adam, as she should think of him—might wish to consummate their union tonight.

A shiver crawled up her spine at the thought of intimacy with a man—a stranger at that. She drew a deep steadying breath. She hadn't suited her late husband's peculiar tastes, and was thankful he'd not visited her bed the last four years of their marriage. Somehow she would manage to move beyond those dreadful experiences with Garrick Payne and fulfill her wifely duties with her new husband.

She was hardly naïve at twenty-eight. She'd known precisely two men in her life—her first love, Gray Wolf MacKinnon, or 'Wolf' as he was known, and her late husband, the Reverend Garrick Payne. A shudder rippled through her at the memories of Garrick's abuse, but she quickly dashed the demons away, reminding herself that all men weren't cruel like her first husband. She prayed Mr. Smith was as kind as he appeared to be from his letters, and that he'd not take her coldly, without care for her comfort.

Memories resurfaced, reminding her of the passion she'd once enjoyed in Gray Wolf's arms—evidenced by the beautiful child at her side. Perhaps she might find that passion again. If she couldn't be with the only man she'd ever loved, then she'd accept her fate and settle for marriage with a man who would provide well for her and young Mac.

Mac jerked upright at the sound of the whistle. With a hiss of steam, the train slowed to a jolting stop. Evangeline's heart fluttered in her chest knowing her life was about to forever change. She thought she'd prepared herself for this moment. Now she had second thoughts.

"Mama, are we there yet?" Mac's dark eyes darted about the car as a few passengers whooped with excitement. "Is this our stop?"

"Yes, I believe so, Mac." She stared out the filmy window at the bustling depot. "Remember, there is still a full day's ride to Mr. Smith's ranch south of Gonzales. He wrote he would bring a wagon."

Mac rubbed a spot on the dirty window pane with his fist and peered out. "Do you see him, Mama? My new pa?"

Evangeline stroked her son's soft, shiny hair. At nine years of age, Mac resembled his real father more than ever. A shame he would never know him. She had no idea where Wolf was or how to find him even if she wished.

She glanced out the window and a twinge of sadness squeezed her heart. She had fallen in love with Wolf the summer he worked as a hand on her father's ranch. She loved him still and always would, although time had lessened the wound in her heart.

Reluctantly, she pushed aside the memories and hugged her son close again. It was of no use to dwell on the past. Besides, Mac was excited at the prospect of having a new father and the move to Texas.

She shook away the painful memories and turned her attention to her son. The past only brought pain. She must stop looking backward and embrace the bright new future ahead.

"I do not know if your new father is here, Mac. I have never seen a photograph of Mr. Smith. I was instructed to meet him at the hotel. Hopefully, we might have a chance to freshen up first."

"You look real pretty in that new blue dress, Mama. It matches your eyes. Mr. Smith's gonna be happy he picked you."

Smiling at Mac, Evangeline reached beneath the seat and grasped the handle of the bag that held a few clothes. Taking her son's hand in hers, they wove through the exiting crowd, a mass of unwashed bodies that had sweltered aboard the train for hours. Mac jerked free of her grip and she turned in time to catch a flash of embarrassment in his eyes. Not quite a child, he wasn't a man either. She indicated with a motion of her head for him to follow.

Her heart beat wildly as the porter took her valise and assisted her from the train. Texas soil was underfoot for the first time in ten years. Her knees almost buckled, but she clutched Mac's shoulder, steadying herself. *This was home. Such a foreign notion now.*

She blinked back tears once again. She must be strong for Mac's sake and not cry for the life she'd once known. Steeling herself against the heat, she fanned herself with her hand. She'd forgotten how unforgiving Texas weather was in summer.

Mac surprised her by looping an arm in hers like a true gentleman and they stepped onto the wooden walkway and moved away from the blowing red dust and soot.

Mac lugged the heavy valise as they walked through the train station.

"Since it appears no one is waiting for us here, we shall check at the hotel," she told Mac as they exited and burst into bright sunlight again. She spied the two story hotel several buildings away. "Mr. Smith has reserved two rooms for us tonight, one for you and one for Mr. Smith and me."

"Why two rooms, Mama? Can't I stay with you and my new Pa tonight?"

Evangeline cleared her throat. She supposed it was time someone explained the delicate matter of male and female relations to Mac. Perhaps Mr. Smith—*or rather, Adam*, her new husband should be the one to instruct the boy.

Her breath caught in her throat as a new revelation struck. She'd written Mr. Smith that she'd married her first husband seven years ago. What if he learned her child was nine? He'd know he hadn't been fathered by Garrick Payne. Her heartbeat pounded out a deafening tempo in her ears. How could she have overlooked such an important detail? She paused on the walkway as her mind went into a whirl. Mac eyed her curiously.

"Mama, are you all right?"

No, she was not. She felt ill, her stomach roiling about like a pot of greasy broth. Her father had disowned her when he discovered her pregnancy and forced her to go to a home for girls in Georgia. Savannah society had also scorned her when Garrick Payne announced she was to be his bride. As the mother of an illegitimate child, she was tainted in most people's eyes. Would Mr. Smith feel that way, too, if he learned the truth?

She lifted a hand and smoothed back an unruly lock of hair from Mac's sweet face. He was innocent. Although he knew Garrick wasn't his real father, she'd tried to shield him from the townspeople's stares and harsh talk. Should the truth become light, she would do everything in her power to protect him now. She prayed her new husband would understand.

As they strolled along the sunny boardwalk, people passed on horseback or in carriages, churning up the road's red dust. A man and woman nodded politely as they moved past.

"You didn't answer my question, Mama." Mac turned to walk backward alongside her. "Why will we have separate rooms?"

Evangeline sighed. "Mac, turn around and walk correctly. You're going to trip or bump into someone."

"Naw." He smiled. "I'm gettin' real good at this backward walking. I've got eyes in the back of my head I tell you. Besides, I want to know why I can't stay with you and Mr. Smith? Won't he like me? I'll take a bath if that'll help."

She paused and bit back a smile. "Of course he will like you, but you must have your own quarters because you are becoming a man. You cannot sleep in the same room with your parents."

"Mama, I think I see him!" Mac looked in the direction from which they'd come.

Evangeline turned and pulled her bonnet to shield her eyes from the strong rays of the midday sun. "How can you tell?" She searched through a crowd of people who hurried along the street. "We have never even seen a photograph of Mr. Smith."

"It's that man." He pointed. "The tall cowboy in the black hat and long coat."

Evangeline squinted, trying to make out the dark figure in a long duster moving stealthily toward them. He appeared menacing, his face dark and hidden beneath the brim of his black hat, his spurs churning up dust in the street. He looked more like an outlaw than a cowboy, and a chill skittered up her spine. She'd read about unsavory sorts in western cities these days. *Oh, my! He was fast approaching.*

She concluded he must be a bandit set to pounce upon a woman and child alone in a strange town. Lifting her full skirt with one hand, she grasped her son's hand in the other and hurried toward the safety of the hotel. One glance over her shoulder and she realized he was on their heels. She picked up the pace.

"Come with me, Mac, and don't encourage him."

"But, Mama, the luggage is heavy."

She paused to take it from him, then continued on.

"Hey, he's waving at me."

Evangeline never broke her stride. "It matters not. We do not know that man. Now hurry." How unseemly. They had been in Luling but a few minutes and some ruffian had the audacity to approach them on the street.

She'd almost reached the hotel steps when a strong, gloved hand snagged her arm from behind. Evangeline whirled around. A scream caught in her throat. She looked up at the dark figure casting a formidable shadow over them.

"Evangeline."

The deep rich voice slid over her warmed skin, reminding her of someone she once knew. His face was undeterminable, shadowed by the brim of his hat. He was dressed similar to one of her father's hands—a long leather duster, thick gloves and boots. Still, his presence, his very touch on her arm sent a tremor of fear through her. Before she could ask his name, he removed his hat revealing his identity. Her knees buckled. Oh, dear God! What was *he* doing here?

A strong hand reached out to steady her.

"Hello, Evangeline," he said again in that deep, sensual voice that sent ripples of scorching heat washing over her flushed skin. "You look as though you've seen a ghost."

She swallowed hard. It became difficult to breathe. His black eyes were cold and no emotion registered on his deeply tanned face.

"Or perhaps I should say good afternoon, *Mrs. Smith*?"

He released her and she swayed unsteadily. *What were the odds that Gray Wolf MacKinnon would find her?* "How did you know my married name?" she asked, barely above a whisper.

"Because I am Mr. Smith, Evangeline—your loving husband of little more than one week."

He caught her before she hit the ground.

Wolf carried an unconscious Evangeline to his hotel room and laid her on the bed. The desk clerk, a short prissy man named Perry with a pencil-thin black moustache, lingered at the door, staring as if he feared Wolf might harm her. Wolf turned and glared at the man.

"That will be all. Leave me to tend my bride."

The man waited, a sour look of disapproval on his face. The same look of disgust as last evening when he'd arrived and registered at the hotel. "No Indians" the man had said, scowling until Wolf produced a bill of sale for goods bearing his legal name of Smith, silencing the bigoted man.

"You've been asked to leave."

In a huff, the man closed the door behind him. Wolf turned Evangeline on her side and began unbuttoning the back of her dress.

"Bring a wet cloth," he told the boy. "There's a pitcher of water and fresh towels on the wash stand."

He didn't see it coming. The child jumped onto his back and swung from his neck like a wild cat.

"You leave my mama alone! Take your filthy hands off her, you hear!"

Wolf peeled the boy off and dropped him to the floor like a sack of potatoes. "Your mother can't breathe and she's overheated. Calm down or I'll put you across my knee."

The red-faced child picked himself off the floor and dusted off his pants. Wolf had dropped him hard on his rump and he figured he'd bruised more than the youngster's pride.

"I just don't want you lookin' at her undressed and all. She's a real lady, you know."

Wolf eyed the kid up and down. *Brave little cuss.* He rather admired the child for protecting his mother.

"I won't look at her, kid," he lied, suppressing a smile. The hell he wouldn't. They were legally married now and he'd do a lot more than look if the notion struck.

He finished working open the annoying row of tiny pearl buttons on the dress, then tugged open the laces on her corset. *Damned contraption.* Why did women feel the need to truss themselves in this ungodly heat? Within moments of his loosening the binding garment, she gasped for air like a banked fish. He turned her onto her back and her eyes fluttered open, a look of confusion on her beet-red face.

The boy rushed to her side. "Mama, are you all right? Can you breathe now?"

She sputtered, then coughed. "What happened?"

"You fainted," Wolf said. "Your corset was too tight."

She glanced at the child, then fixed her gaze on Wolf. "Where is my husband? Where is Mr. Smith?"

"You're looking at him, sweetheart."

A shadow of alarm crossed her face. "No. I married Adam Smith. That's not your name."

"It has been my name for the past nine years, Evangeline. At least on paper. I legally changed it."

The boy piped up. "You sure don't look nothin' like I imagined."

Wolf eyed the kid. That made two of them. Evangeline had stated in her letters the child was quite young, but this boy appeared to be older—at least eight or nine by his estimation. He stared at the boy for the longest time, studying the planes and angles of his face, his coal black eyes, the high-set cheekbones. His hair was the same shade of dark blonde as his mother's, but thick and straight as a post, not wavy. His skin color was the shade of coffee diluted with a lot of cream. If Wolf didn't know better, he'd swear the child was of mixed blood heritage.

Then a thought occurred to him, and it took him in a direction he wasn't certain he wanted to go.

"You don't look like a Smith," the boy said, interrupting his thoughts. "Is that your alias? Are you an outlaw, mister?"

Wolf chuckled, amused at how the boy's eyes lit up at the prospect of meeting an outlaw. Every boy's dream. "No. It's not an alias and I'm not an outlaw, son. My real name is Gray Wolf MacKinnon, but I legally changed my name to Adam Smith a few years ago so I might acquire land."

"Gray Wolf? You're an injun?"

"Mac!" came Evangeline's admonishment.

The boy shrugged. "I just want to know."

Wolf hesitated. He'd changed his name on paper, but it altered nothing. People only saw his Indian-ness.

"Don't scold the boy, Evangeline. He's curious." He turned back to the child. "Yes, son. I'm what they call a half breed. My mother was Chiricahua Apache, but she died long before I had any memory of her. My pa, James MacKinnon, was a miner and fur trapper who raised me."

Wolf tossed a room key to the child. "Mac is your name, is it?" He looked at Evangeline. *Interesting name. Short for MacKinnon, perhaps?* Pieces of this odd puzzle began to fall into place and he didn't much like the conclusion. "That's for your room next door, Mac. Run along and allow your mother time to rest." As if he had any intention of allowing her to rest. Once the boy was out of earshot, they'd have a serious discussion.

Wolf pitched a coin to him. "First, go down to the hotel lobby and buy a candy stick from the jar on the desk. New peppermints and licorice arrived this morning. Afterward, return to your room and bathe. We'll call on you when it's time for supper at the restaurant. Just don't eat too much candy."

The boy jostled the shiny penny from palm to palm. "Mama, is it all right if I have candy?"

Evangeline sat up and pushed the golden hair that had come unbound away from her face. The sleeves of the dress slid from her shoulders, revealing delicate porcelain skin and a hint of cleavage. Wolf swallowed hard, unable to tear his eyes from her. His sex stirred to life as blood rushed to his groin. She was still as beautiful and youthful as he remembered. Looking at her, he'd almost forgotten her eyes were the same shade of blue as a Texas sky in summer, her skin the color of fresh cream. How many nights had he caressed her body, tasted her soft, sweet skin?

"Yes, Mac, it's all right for you to have one piece of candy. Please do as Wolf...I mean, as Mr. Smith asked."

After the boy left, Wolf locked the door.

He turned to find Evangeline standing near the bed, clutching the loosened bodice to her bosom. "Where is my luggage?"

He leaned casually against the door and eyed her from head to toe. She was a mess from her trip, but a pleasing mess to look at. Her silken hair had come unbound and cascaded over one bare shoulder. Her cheeks were tinged bright pink, her lips dark as rubies. He allowed himself a moment's fantasy—kissing her and divesting her of her dress—which did nothing to quell his desire. Still, he dared not touch her with this much anger and resentment clouding his heart.

"Planning on going somewhere, my dear wife?"

"You lied to me to trick me into returning to Texas—into marrying you."

He shrugged. "And you lied to me, too, so I'd say we're about even on that account."

She withdrew a handkerchief from inside her dress sleeve and blotted the perspiration on her forehead. "I do not know what you are suggesting. How have I lied? *You* deliberately withheld your true identity."

"The boy. He's mine isn't he?" he asked point blank.

She flinched and looked away, but said nothing.

"What year was he born, Evangeline?"

She picked at her skirt's folds. "That's none of your concern."

"Oh, but it is. Your letters stated the child was quite young. You married Payne seven years ago, did you not?"

She visibly shuddered as he moved closer.

"The boy is older, Evangeline. He's at least nine, if not close."

Her eyes lifted to his. "Mac is tall for his age."

"*Mac*," he repeated. "That's short for MacKinnon, isn't it?"

She didn't answer, reinforcing his suspicions. A sickening wave washed over him. Quickly, he counted the months from the time she'd left the Braddock ranch until the date of her marriage to Garrick Payne. No, there was no way the child was Payne's. He couldn't be. The boy he'd dismissed from the room was much older than six or seven.

He stood before her and she cringed as if she feared he might strike her. *What the hell?* His eyes searched hers. He had never harmed a woman, and despite his anger, he didn't intend to now. "You were pregnant with Mac when you left Texas ten years ago, weren't you?"

She lowered her gaze, but said nothing.

"Weren't you?" His voice boomed in the tiny room.

Her shoulders slumped and her eyes lifted to his. In them he saw the truth before she admitted it.

"Yes."

He reeled away from her, feeling as if he'd been punched in the gut. He'd suspected it weeks ago when he'd learned the boy's name was Mac. He drew a deep breath and clenched his jaw, willing himself to calm down. The child was his son! Pain tore at his heart at the revelation. How could she have kept this from him all these years? His body trembled with anger as he looked at her. "And you didn't have the decency to tell me?"

Words tumbled out in a rush of breath: "Papa threatened to kill you if I ever spoke to you again. He sent me to the girl's home in Georgia—to Reverend Garrick Payne's School for Girls. It turned out to be a blessing in some ways, a nightmare in others. Mac's resemblance to you at birth was indisputable, the dark skin and eyes, his Indian features. Everyone at the ranch would have known you were his father."

He scarcely heard her words. His hands curled and uncurled into fists. He wanted to punch something. No, he wanted to shake the woman standing before him, shake her until every tooth in her pretty blonde head rattled. She'd denied him his own flesh and blood for a decade, years that could never be reclaimed. Was she even aware what violence her father had perpetrated upon him because of her lies? He doubted so. He blew out a deep, pent up breath and forced himself to calm down before his anger took control and he said something regrettable.

"I would have protected our child!" he thundered out.

Her eyes were wild, frightened. "I couldn't take that chance, Wolf."

"Even if it was a chance *I* was willing to take?" he replied through gritted teeth.

Uncomfortable silence stretched between them for several moments as he absorbed her words. She had fled Texas to protect him? Is that what she expected him to believe?

He tore open his shirt, popping buttons from their threads. She stared, horrified, her mouth open as he exposed the wide scar on his throat.

Her hand lifted as if to touch it. She quickly withdrew. "W-what...happened?"

"Your father gave this to me. He and half a dozen of his hands beat the living shit out of me, then sliced open my throat and left me to die. Only I didn't die. I had at least one friend on that ranch—John Patterson. It's because of him I'm alive now."

Deep choking sobs erupted from her. She turned her face away, but he grasped her by the arm and forced her to look at him. "The time for crocodile tears is long past, Evangeline. I want the truth. Why did you tell your father I forced myself upon you?"

A look of horror spread across her face. "I never told him such a thing! Oh, Wolf. Is that what he said?"

"You knew what they were going to do to me that night, didn't you. Why didn't you warn me?"

Her lip trembled as tear-filled eyes lifted to his. "I had no idea. I promised Papa I would never see you again."

"Liar!"

She clung to his arms, her eyes filled with tears. "Please believe me! I had no idea what they'd done. I begged Papa not to harm you. He agreed to spare your life if I would leave Texas and go to the girl's home to have the baby. He said I could never contact you again, that if I ever returned to you he would kill you *and* our child."

Wolf jerked free from her clutches to pace back and forth. Was she telling the truth? He paused before her.

Her face was sincere enough, but... "He said you accused me of raping you."

"I never said such a thing."

His stomach roiled as he recalled that night. "They beat me until my face was unrecognizable, until my ribs were broken. They threatened to castrate me. Fortunately, they didn't."

Evangeline slumped to the bed. He stared down at her tiny shoulders which shook with each sob.

"Mac doesn't know I'm his father, does he?"

"No."

He thought of the years he'd missed with the boy, time that could never be recaptured. Although he was inclined to believe she hadn't been involved in her father's sinister plot to murder him, how could he ever forgive her transgression of denying him his own flesh and blood? Didn't she know he'd have taken them away from the Braddock ranch—away from Texas? He would have protected her and their child with his own life. Her father never had to know of their affair.

He took a seat beside her. "How did Elijah Braddock learn of your pregnancy if you didn't tell him?"

She sniffled, daubed the handkerchief to her eyes. "One of the housemaids told him. She knew I'd missed my monthly."

When Wolf had found her advertisement in the mail order bride catalog six weeks ago, he'd reveled in the idea of exacting revenge—of tricking her into marriage and making her pay the rest of her life for the pain she'd caused. Now he had serious regrets about what he'd done. What if she was telling the truth about her father? If so, *he'd* been terribly wrong. And he'd wronged an innocent woman. The very idea shook him to the core.

"Do you want an annulment?" he asked.

She turned her face to look at him. Tears shimmered in her blue eyes, but she said nothing.

His body shook with both rage and shame. He'd tricked her into marrying him! He dragged a hand through his hair, his body trembling. There was only one thing to do—the right thing.

"If you want out of the marriage, Evangeline, I'll give you money today to board a train back to Georgia. There you may obtain an annulment. But the boy stays here with me."

A look of horror spread across her face. "I would never leave without Mac."

He rose to tower over her. "And you'll not take him from me again either."

Gathering her skirts, she stood to face him. "But he's my son!"

"He's mine, too, and I'll never let him go again. You're free to leave if you so choose, but my son stays."

Dinner at the restaurant that evening was a near silent affair. Evangeline sat across the table from him, picking at her meal. Mac possessed the appetite of three burly men and ordered a second helping of fried chicken and buttermilk biscuits. After dessert, Wolf dismissed the boy to his room to speak privately with Evangeline.

"You've barely eaten," he commented as he set his napkin on the table. "The apple pie was delicious."

She turned her face away. "I've no appetite tonight."

He studied her delicate profile, a short, pert nose, small chin, long brown lashes. She'd gathered her shiny blonde hair atop her head, pinned the curls with sparkling, jeweled pins. Delicate wisps framed her oval face. The pale orange dress she'd donned accentuated the natural blush in her cheeks, creating a most stunning sight. She was the most beautiful woman in the room and he hadn't missed the open stares she'd elicited from both men and women as they'd walked from the hotel.

"Shall I order another coffee for us?"

She bowed her head, folded her hands in her lap. "Do as you wish, Wolf. I do not care for anything."

He didn't care for anything either. His stomach had been bound in knots since the moment he'd laid eyes on her outside the train depot. Did she hate him now? Or was she merely angry? He half-wished she'd look at him so he might see the truth in her eyes.

"What are you thinking, Evangeline?"

She looked at him, her blue eyes as cold as a winter sky. She opened her mouth as if to speak, but hesitated.

"Go on," he prompted.

"I never thought I'd see you again."

That made two of them. When he'd found her advertisement, a myriad of emotions had overcome him. Anger, rage, betrayal. He'd wanted to hurt her, cause her as much pain as he'd endured all these years without her. But when he'd reached out and taken her by the arm and gazed into her eyes for the first time in nearly ten years, he realized he'd never stopped loving her. How was it possible to feel so much anger toward a person, and yet love them at the same time?

"You haven't changed much," she continued. "Only a small thread of gray in your dark hair. The years have been kind to you, Wolf."

His face warmed at her tender expression. Damn, was he blushing? He swallowed the hard knot that formed in his throat, feeling as flustered as a schoolboy. "The years have been most gracious to you, too."

She dropped her gaze to the napkin in her lap. "My father is deceased now," she said quietly. "He passed away two years ago."

Wolf already knew Elijah Braddock had died, not that it made any difference. Did she expect him to offer condolences for a man who'd tried to murder him? He sipped his coffee and held back a caustic remark.

Evangeline's eyes misted with tears. "I am so sorry for what he did to you. Please believe I knew nothing of that night." She lowered her voice and glanced about as if to make certain no one was eavesdropping. "I never told him you forced yourself on me. That much I promise you on my life

He set his glass down. "Still, you admitted we were lovers."

She placed her napkin aside and fiddled with her utensils, aligning them neatly beside the plate. "He already knew. He'd witnessed us together."

Wolf let out a pent up breath. That would explain the man's peculiar behavior toward him in the days leading up to the attack. "That doesn't excuse you from not telling me of your pregnancy."

"No, I suppose it doesn't, but the last night we were together I lost my nerve. You spoke about leaving Texas to buy a ranch in New Mexico. I saw how your eyes lit up when you spoke of striking out on your own. I didn't want to interfere with your dreams."

Anger rolled through him like a ball of fire. *His* dreams? His dreams were never about owning a damned ranch in New Mexico! His fondest desire was to marry *her*, to take her away from the bigotry in Texas so they might enjoy a life together! He sprang from the table. Good God! Is that how she'd felt? His stomach churned. "We should return to the hotel."

She rose slowly. "You're angry." It wasn't a question.

He signaled for the check, then turned back to look at her. How could she have misread his intentions all those years ago? Had she thought their lovemaking meant nothing more to him than a quick release? She was no dalliance. He'd never given his heart so freely to a woman. He wasn't in the habit of deflowering virgins, either.

The waiter brought the check and he paid the man. Looping his arm through hers, they strode out of the restaurant. In silence they hurried along the walk.

"Might you slow your step?" she asked.

He had no intention of slowing.

She struggled to keep up with him. "Why are you angry, Wolf? What have I done to upset you?"

He paused on the walkway, yanked his arm free from hers. He caught her by the shoulders, squeezed them gently.

"Did you truly think I didn't care about you? That I only used your innocence to satisfy my urges?"

She shuddered in his grasp. "Please, lower your voice," she said barely above a whisper. "Such a public display is most unseemly."

He glanced about. Several people had gathered nearby to watch. Damn them all! Let them look for all he cared.

"It was you,"—his voice broke, tears burned his eyes—"you I wanted Evangeline, not some damned ranch in New Mexico, not some elusive dream."

In the hotel room, Evangeline prepared for bed. Wolf spent a sleepless night in the chair by the door, listening to her soft weeping. Sometime during the night, he awoke to her fitful cries. She thrashed in the bed, sending the blankets to the floor. He covered her with a quilt again and stood watch beside her.

At one point, he fantasized of sliding beneath the covers, awakening her with a gentle kiss. Would she welcome his touch again or push him away? His sex grew and lengthened, painfully so, and it took all the willpower he possessed not to act on his desires. To do so would influence her decision to stay in the marriage, and the last thing he wanted was to force her into an arrangement she didn't truly want.

He and Mac spent most of the next day securing food staples and supplies for the trip home to Gonzales. They packed coffee, flour, cornmeal, sugar, salt and a basket of fresh tortillas from a local vendor into the wagon, along with handwoven woolen blankets and two new iron skillets. He also purchased rope, a roll of baling wire and two sacks of cracked corn for his hens.

By late afternoon Evangeline had still not informed him of her decision. She'd gone shopping that morning and didn't meet them at the restaurant for the noon meal. He supposed it was best they keep their distance. At least he would be spared the pitying look on her face, now that he'd divulged the innermost secrets of his heart.

He returned to their room, intending to bathe and change into fresh clothes for dinner, but it gave him great pleasure to watch the shocked expression on Evangeline's face as he stripped off his shirt and undid the first two buttons of his trousers. A slow blush crept over her cheeks and throat. Still, she didn't look away. After the erotic dream he'd had last night, his need for release ran high, but as angry and confused as he was he dared not touch her.

"I'd suggest you freshen up, too." He poured water into the basin. "It's been an unseasonably warm day again."

She clutched the collar on her dress as her flushed cheeks paled. "Wolf...we cannot do this. We simply cannot."

He stared. Did she think he'd returned to consummate their marriage? If so, why did she appear frightened of the prospect of intimacy? Was it the revolting scar on his throat, the reminder of her father's brutality? Or had she made the decision to leave?

He bent and splashed water on his face, then reached for the towel. Keeping his best poker face, he tested her. "You know as well as I do that our marriage vows aren't sealed until I've bedded you. Besides, Mac is in his room, enjoying a new dime novel. We have a few hours to kill."

"Yesterday you asked if I wanted an annulment."

Was she seriously considering such? He lay the towel aside and turned to face her. "You never answered, so I assumed you did not."

"I cannot easily obtain an annulment if we have had relations."

Damn her. She *was* considering it! He shrugged indifferently so as to give nothing away. "You can always divorce me later," he suggested, unable to keep from breaking into a smile. "That will not preclude our becoming intimate."

He perused her boldly as he recalled last night's dream. The pulse beat wildly at her throat. The bodice of her pretty pink dress rose and fell with each shallow breath. He was moments away from pulling her into his arms, kissing that frightened little girl look from her face, and carrying her to bed.

"How can you ask me to stay in this marriage when it is based on lies?"

"You're one to talk of lies," he shot back. "You kept the truth of my son from me for ten years."

"I had no choice. I've told you before, my father threatened to kill you. He threatened Mac's life if I ever returned. I left Texas not knowing what they'd done to you." She reached out to touch him, then dropped her hand at her side.

Gritting his teeth, he unbuttoned his trousers. "So, dear wife, what do you suggest we do for the next two hours? Play cards? Discuss the weather?"

She swallowed hard. "Perhaps we might nap."

He laughed. "Nap? As I recall, you once enjoyed my pleasuring. We wiled away many hours by the creek. Do you remember, Evangeline?"

She clutched the high collar on her dress. "That was many years ago."

He chuckled. "You would still enjoy my attentions, I assure you."

He dropped his trousers, revealing his arousal and she turned away. He grasped her by the arm and gave her a sobering yank toward him. Her gaze locked with his. "Nothing has changed between you and me except we're now legally married." He released her, then kicked out of his trousers and reached for a fresh pair that lay folded across the valet. "What's wrong, Evangeline? Was sex with me more titillating when forbidden, when you were forced to sneak around with the savage and steal moments in the barn or under the moonlight at the creek?"

"You know that's untrue. I never thought of you as a...*savage*." She whispered the word.

In hopes of provoking her, he added, "Sometimes I think I was merely a toy, a way for you to pass your boredom on that lonely isolated ranch." He pulled on his pants. "After all, I was a 'breed.' I could brag to no one of my conquest with Elijah Braddock's pretty white daughter, lest I wished to be hanged. Was that it? Did

96

you consider me a safe outlet that summer for your sexual experimentations?"

She gasped. "Wolf! How can you say such a horrible thing?"

He was in her face. "Because if you'd given a damn about me you would have told me of the child growing in your belly!" He reeled away trembling, hating himself for his rage. But he couldn't control himself, couldn't stop the angry words that followed. "Perhaps you still pine for your late husband, Garrick Payne? Was the old fellow a better lover than I? Did he care for you more than I?"

Her chin went up a notch. "Garrick cared for no one but himself. And to answer your question, I feel nothing for Garrick's memory except hatred. I'm glad he's dead. He deserved worse than death—far worse if there is such a thing."

Wolf lifted a brow. She'd never mentioned much about her late husband in her letters, except that he'd been an older man—somewhat distant and unaffectionate. Before he'd believed it due to their age difference, but now he wasn't certain. "Such unkind words for your late husband, a man of the cloth no less."

"Garrick might have been a minister, but he was a despicable bastard first and foremost."

"Rather like I am in your opinion?"

Her gaze poured over him and he watched the anger in her eyes change to desire. Was this his imagination? No. A soft blush crept over her cheeks as her gaze slipped over his semi-nude body. She brushed the back of her hand across her brow as if his nearness made her uncomfortable.

Trembling, not so much from rage but from desire, he quickly finished dressing, then left her alone to bathe. Evangeline could stay with him and Mac or board a train back to Georgia. He wouldn't force her to stay in the marriage. Nor would he touch her unless she came willingly to his bed.

Once Wolf closed the door, Evangeline loosened the bodice on the dress and dipped a sponge into the basin of fresh water, drawing it over her burning cheeks and chin. *Oh, my!* She'd forgotten how the man's mere presence affected her. She washed her face, then looked into the mirror. Would Wolf ever forgive her for what her father had done to him?

He'd made it clear she couldn't get out of the marriage without surrendering Mac, but did she want out? After all, he'd changed his name to Adam Smith. He was a respectable landholder in south central Texas and his ranch was fairly isolated, situated a few miles south of Gonzales. The person who'd sent the threatening notes in Savannah would never find her now. Perhaps it was best she stay in the marriage, at least for Mac's sake.

She eased the front of her dress off her shoulders and bathed her heat-flushed throat and chest. She didn't blame Wolf for his anger toward her. However, she hoped in time he might find it in his heart to forgive past hurts. She hadn't married Garrick Payne for love. Her father paid him to marry her. She also hadn't participated in her father's underhanded dealings.

Fire ignited in the pit of her belly as she recalled the evidence of Wolf's desire when he'd undressed. It had been so long since she'd been touched with tenderness and she wondered what it would be like to take him inside her body again.

Gazing into the oval, beveled mirror on the washstand, she drew the front of the dress down, pretended it was Wolf undressing her. She closed her eyes and caressed her shoulders, wishing she could make him understand how much she'd loved him.

Her breath caught in her throat as the startling realization washed over her.

She *still* loved him.

The ache for his touch grew nearly unbearable. Reaching behind her, she unbuttoned her dress and stepped from the garment, allowing it to puddle at her feet. Then she untied her petticoats. One, two, three, they fell into a heap atop her dress. She stepped from the pile of garments and laid each piece neatly across the bed, smoothing out the wrinkles. Then she unlaced her corset. After she'd fainted yesterday, Wolf had forbidden her to wear one, but she couldn't have left the hotel this morning without proper underclothes. Wrenching free of the confining garment, she reached up to caress her breasts through the fabric of the thin, cotton chemise. She felt naughty, decadent for touching herself, but it had been so long since she'd been loved.

"You are still as beautiful as I recall, Evangeline."

She whirled about, having not heard him enter. Heavens! Had he caught her? "You might have knocked," she snapped, reaching for a towel to cover her bosom.

"I did knock but you were...*occupied*." He grinned, that silly boyish grin that always made her heart turn over. "Entertaining lusty thoughts of me?"

She steeled herself from the onslaught of his magnetism as desire for him warred within. She hadn't wanted a man's touch in years, but this was Wolf, the man she still loved with all her heart. She craved him even now with a hunger beyond reason, despite the fact they'd both hurt one another. "Why have you returned so soon?"

"I came to apologize for my harsh remarks. Besides,"—he reached for his scarf—"I forgot this." He whisked it around his neck and knotted it in front, concealing the ugly scar.

He moved closer and a shiver of delight danced up her spine at his nearness. While she tried to avoid looking at the blue bandanna around his neck, oddly she was drawn to it. She longed to untie it, press her lips against his scar and kiss away the pain he must have felt. She wanted to undress him slowly, melt against his bronzed skin and slip her arms around his neck, take him inside her body and feel the hot fire raining down on her as they moved together in a rhythm as old as time. There would be nothing but pleasure in this handsome man's arms, beautiful indescribable pleasure.

"Shall I help you dress for dinner?" His smooth voice slid over her like a warm summer wind. "Or have you not finished your bath?"

Evangeline shivered. If she wanted to keep Mac, she must stay with Wolf and honor her wedding vows. Not that it would be so terrible enjoying his bed again.

"N-no. I've finished my bath," she answered. Trembling, she boldly drew the chemise open.

He flinched as if her brazen behavior stunned him. Then his lips slowly curled into a lazy, sensual smile. She stood before him in nothing but her blue satin drawers and stockings, her body thrumming in anticipation. His hot gaze slid over her and her breasts warmed and ached for his touch.

"I see you've had a change of heart." He moved so close she could feel the heat emanating from his body. "You're trembling." He reached up to give her bare shoulders a gentle squeeze. His hands were warm, his palms rough. "Are you certain this is what you desire?"

She swallowed hard. "Yes."

No.

She was never more uncertain of anything in her life. She was terrified of giving her heart to him again. What if Wolf never put aside his mistrust and forgave her? Could their marriage survive such a divide? It must, for Mac's sake, and she must try to let him know how much she still loved him. She reached for the scarf at his neck and plucked at the knot.

His hands came up to still hers. "Don't."

"Please, Wolf." She unbuttoned his shirt, stared at the scar, then her eyes traveled over his chest as she revealed him to her gaze. The shell and turquoise necklace that had belonged to his Apache mother lay in stark contrast against his dark skin. She smoothed her palms over his chest, sliding them downward to his pants. She untucked his shirt, eased the sleeves from his bronzed, muscular shoulders and cast it aside. Her eyes followed the soft dusting of black hair that formed a line from his navel and disappeared below the waistband of his pants. Her eyes lifted to his and she raised up on tiptoe and parted her lips slightly to encourage a kiss.

"You're still so lovely." His mouth hovered within an inch of hers.

She closed her eyes and waited for him to kiss her, to take her into his arms. Her legs grew soft like jelly, her heart pounding so hard in her chest she was almost certain he could hear it.

"Does this mean you've made a decision?"

She swallowed hard as she gazed into his coal-black eyes. The untended ache between her thighs grew. Her breasts ached to be caressed. Of course she intended to stay in the marriage.

"Y-yes,"—a shiver of desire rippled through her—"I will stay with you."

Questioning eyes held hers for a moment. "Only because of Mac?"

She hesitated. Mac was one reason, but not all.

"You must be certain this is what you want, Evangeline."

Words wouldn't form in her mouth. His sensual presence overtook her, the stubborn set of his jaw, his dark, smoldering eyes—the raw sensuality he exuded. Never had she been so ambivalent. If they made love, their marriage vows were sealed. If they didn't, she would lose him yet again—possibly even Mac.

Before she could answer, he hauled her against him. His mouth slammed hard across hers in fierce possession. His tongue thrust past her lips, tangling and mating with hers in an erotic dance. He kissed her hard and deep as if he couldn't get enough, pressing his male hardness against her hip. She felt all of him, even through the thick canvas pants which separated them.

He lifted her and carried her to the bed.

Evangeline closed her eyes as his mouth sought out her breasts. Her breath caught as his hand eased between her thighs to caress her through the fabric. Her fingers threaded into his hair and she arched against his palm, signaling her need.

But it was over before it began.

With a groan, Wolf reeled away. She touched her fingertips to her lips, bereft of his touch. A fine sheen of sweat glossed his face and body. His eyes flashed as his chest rose and fell with every heavy breath he took. Why had he stopped?

"What happened here," he paused to catch his breath, "cannot happen again Evangeline. Not until you are absolutely certain you're ready to be my wife in every sense of the word. You are free to get an annulment if that is what you wish, but I'll not rush your decision." He snatched up his shirt and whisked it on. "I'll also not touch you until I am convinced of your sincerity."

Tears stung her eyes. She opened her mouth to speak, to tell him she *did* want to remain with him as his wife—she truly did—but he was headed toward the door.

"Change into your traveling clothes." He set his hat on his head. "We leave Luling this afternoon."

A storm rolled in before dusk and Wolf was barely able to make camp before it hit full force. He hobbled the mules under the thick cover of live oak so they wouldn't become spooked and run, then took cover in the cramped wagon with Evangeline and Mac as the lightning and thunder raged. They shared a jar of spiced peaches for supper, along with fresh venison jerky and a few *gorditas*—thick corn tortillas he'd purchased from the street vendor in Luling. Afterward, Mac read a few verses from the Bible while Evangeline crocheted.

Later that night, as he lay in his bedroll beneath the wagon, a canvas tarp to protect him from the continuing drizzle, he cursed his decision to leave and set out for Gonzales. If they had stayed in the hotel, he might have been warm and dry tonight. Instead, his new bride and their child lay sleeping in the wagon above while he wallowed miserably in the mud below like a hog.

He rolled onto his side and drew the woolen blanket up to ward off the damp chill. If the rain eased up in the night and the road was passable by morning, they might be able to make decent time. If not...no, he would not think of the alternative—being forced to remain in camp a day or two. Instead, he turned his thoughts to his last moments with Evangeline in the hotel room and drifted off to sleep.

"Hey, mister. You awake?"

Wolf opened one bleary eye and peered at Mac who was crouched at a wagon wheel, staring. The youngster was backlit by a halo of brilliant pink light. It was morning already? Wolf jerked upright and banged the top of his head on the wagon, then cursed three shades of scarlet as he collapsed onto his rain-soaked bed roll. *Smart move, MacKinnon.*

"Bet that must've hurt," Mac said.

Wolf shot him a look. "If you want breakfast, son, I'd suggest you poke about for some dry wood." The boy took off toward the woods.

Momentarily he saw Evangeline taking careful steps toward the wagon, her blue skirts lifted high enough o reveal the white lace hem of her pink drawers, a wisp of petticoat and an enticing glimpse of creamy bare ankle above brown kidskin boots. He swallowed hard. It was going to be hell trying to get through another day without touching her.

She bent to look at him, her long blonde hair free of its usual tightly coiled bun. A few buttons were undone on the front of her dress, revealing a deep crease of cleavage.

"The canvas sprung a leak last night during the storm and half the flour is ruined. I think the sugar is salvageable."

Wolf rubbed the knot forming on his head as he tried to quell the lump simultaneously rising in his britches. He tried not to stare at her ankles, at the delicate lace trimming of her undergarments, but failed miserably.

"Since the sun is shining this morning, do you think we might get a late start today? I'd like to hang our bedding out to dry."

Wolf rolled out from beneath the wagon and got to his feet. "Sounds like a reasonable request." Besides, he was hungry and chilled from a night of exposure and his head pounded like he'd been in a saloon brawl. Fresh buttered biscuits with a slice of fried salt pork and strong hot coffee were in order. "Hang this to dry while you're at it," he said, stripping off his shirt. He tugged off one boot, then the other.

Her gaze slid over his chest, the unmistakable look of desire in her eyes as he unbuttoned his pants. At least he thought it was desire. Was she remembering their last moments in the hotel?

"I need dry clothing. Mine is in the black trunk in the back of the wagon. Think you can fetch it?"

She averted her gaze when he dropped his pants. He didn't wear drawers—never had—and he didn't intend to start now simply because he was married. He kicked out of his britches and handed them to her. No, it wasn't wishful thinking. The sultry look in her eyes told him she wanted him.

Her eyes darted to the woods, then back to him. "I would appreciate your exercising some measure of propriety around Mac, Wolf. He's not accustomed to nudity." Her lips thinned into a pout as she whisked off her shawl and tied it around his hips.

"What the hell are you doing?"

"You will cover yourself until I return with your clothes."

Wolf looked down at himself—at the ridiculous green and red paisley shawl wrapped around him. "Evangeline, I'd be more concerned if Mac saw his father traipsing through the woods wearing his mother's shawl than if he saw me naked."

"He doesn't know you're his father."

His gaze held hers. "A matter I intend to remedy today."

Alarm spread across her face. "You wouldn't."

"The boy must know the truth."

"But he just met you two days ago! At least give him time to settle into his new home and become accustomed to you before springing such a surprise on him. This isn't a good time."

"If we wait, there will never be a good time. Nine years have already been lost."

Tears shone in her eyes. "Then you will make me a liar in my son's eyes."

For a fleeting moment he felt sorry for her. Then he reminded himself she'd helped herself into this situation and it was the consequence of her actions. She'd had plenty of time in the past twenty-four hours to prepare the boy for the news. Mac needed to know the truth and the sooner the better.

She followed him to the chuck box at the back of the wagon and laid a delicate palm on his arm.

"Wolf, I'll tell him when the time is right."

He looked at her hand, so pale against his dark skin. There had always been differences between them, but he'd never realized how much so before now. They had both come from different worlds. That hadn't changed. Even now they couldn't agree on the proper course to take with their child. "I will tell the boy after breakfast," he said.

She sighed. "Do you hate me so much that you would jeopardize my relationship with my son?"

He didn't hate her, but too much time had been wasted on lies. Mac deserved to know the truth. He adjusted the damned ridiculous shawl that kept slipping from his hips. Impatient, he yanked it off and tossed it aside.

Evangeline picked it up and shook it out, then attempted to tie it on again.

"Stop." He danced out of her reach. "I'm not wearing your shawl!"

She made a face. "Mac is a child. Please put it on. He should not see you in such a state."

Gritting his teeth, he allowed her to tie the shawl around him again. "You'd better get used to nudity, Evangeline. The Guadalupe river runs near my property and if I know Mac, he'll be joining me for a skinny dip from time to time." He wiggled a brow at her. "So will you once I've rid you of the inhibitions you apparently acquired in Savannah. I don't recall you ever being this stiff and straight-laced."

Her blue eyes flashed. "Mac will wear proper bathing attire. So will I should I choose to swim."

Wolf snorted. "If I leave any more of his raising up to you, woman, you'll turn him into a lily boy. Now go and fetch my clothes."

At that she stormed back to the wagon.

Wolf opened the chuck box and gathered a coffee tin and the pot. On the way, he lifted the shovel from the hook on the side of the wagon, then dug a shallow firepit in the mud a few yards away.

Mac returned with an armload of wood.

"Hey, that's my mama's shawl." Mac grinned and dropped the wood. "Why are you wearing my mama's clothes, mister?"

Wolf grimaced. "My clothes were soaked from last night's rain. Now stop looking at me like I'm a freak in a traveling carnival and arrange those logs in the pit." He turned and whistled toward the wagon, but Evangeline didn't answer. What was taking so long?

The boy stared at the shallow dug out. "I don't know how to start a fire. Can you can show me how, mister?"

"Only if you'll stop calling me mister."

Wolf blew out an exasperated breath. Garrick Payne had neglected his fatherly duties. A boy Mac's age should know how to build a fire. At nine he should be able to clean a gun, swing an axe, and hunt and skin game. He doubted Mac knew how to do any of those things. Apparently Evangeline's first husband never taught the boy anything except how to be a clingy mama's boy.

Wolf arranged a few logs in the pit and added strips of kindling beneath.

"There's a box of matches in the chuck box." He rose to his feet. "Use them sparingly. Light the kindling first. Once the fire catches, shield the flame from the wind. Understand?"

"I think so."

"Good." He patted the boy on the back. "You can do it. Stay with it now, and don't set the woods on fire."

Mac smiled at him. "I won't. I promise."

Although it was time Mac learned to do things on his own, Wolf still had much to teach the child. Once they were home, he'd be expected to pull his weight at the ranch. Evangeline as well. She'd grown up privileged with servants to tend her every need. He supposed her life with the Reverend Payne in Savannah hadn't been much different. The only assistance Wolf had at the ranch was his best friend, John Patterson.

He headed to the wagon. Where was the confounded woman? Sidetracked with her nose in one of those ladies magazines?

"Hey mister..."

Wolf wheeled around.

"Sorry, I forgot not to call you that. Where are you goin'?"

"To get my clothes, son."

"You'd better have a darn good excuse for taking so long, woman," Wolf growled as he climbed up and threw back the canvas flap on the wagon. Evangeline sat stone still next to his black trunk, her back turned to him. "What's going on?"

She turned and her tear-filled eyes lifted to his. "Here are your clothes." She set a folded stack before him.

"What's wrong, Evangeline?"

She dabbed at the corner of her eye with a handkerchief. "What must I do to convey how sorry I am for everything that happened?"

He wasn't sure if there was anything she could do. His bitterness over the lost years with his son ran deep. Hatred for her dead father also remained fresh. Perhaps in time he might forgive her where his son was concerned, but today was too soon.

"Do you want my forgiveness? Do you want me to forget you left Texas without so much as a word to me knowing my child was in your belly? Do you expect me to forget what your father did to me?"

"No. I do not expect you to forget, but I had hoped we might begin anew."

He swallowed hard as he studied her shadowed face. What was she talking about? "Anew?"

"I fear you don't believe the things I've told you."

Oh, he believed her. Elijah Braddock was a hard man and Wolf had no doubt he'd threatened both his and Mac's life. Still, the truth did nothing to quell the hurt.

Her eyes lifted and she met his gaze. "Papa forced me to go to the girl's home in Georgia. He eventually paid Garrick Payne to marry me."

Wolf blew out a breath, not wanting to hear any more. "Hand me my clothes."

She complied. "It's the truth, Wolf. He swore he'd kill you if I ever returned, if I ever contacted you again. The girl's home was Mac's and my only hope of survival."

He shook the wrinkles from his shirt, then flung it aside, anger spewing forth again. "I would have taken you and our child far away where no one could harm us. I would have married you, would have cared for you and Mac!"

"Things were different ten years ago. There was nowhere for us to go. After what happened in Palo Duro canyon the year before with the Comanche, no town would have accepted our union, considering you're half Indian and I'm white. No minister would have married us."

"Enough of this talk."

She implored him with her eyes. "You know what I say is true, Wolf. You were forced to change your name to acquire land. Have you forgotten that fact?"

No, he hadn't forgotten the bigotry he'd encountered all his life.

She drew closer to him on her knees. "Please, Wolf, I can't bear to see hatred in your eyes. I would rather you not look at me at all, than have you look at me with such contempt."

His heart softened. He almost reached out and touched her beautiful face, but refrained. "I do not look at you with contempt, Evangeline."

"But you do! How long before our son realizes you despise me?"

He blew out a breath of disgust. "For God's sake, I don't despise you."

She sniffled. "Yes, you do. You wish I'd go away."

"I never said such a thing."

Her lower lip quivered. "Perhaps not, but two days ago you were prepared to put me on a train back to Georgia, ready to give me an annulment."

True, but only after he'd realized the wrong he'd perpetrated against her. "Only if that's what *you* wished."

She shook her head. "It is certainly not what *I* wish. And after what happened between us yesterday at the hotel, I do not think it is what you wish either."

Then he touched her, lifted a few strands of her hair and twirled them around his fingertip. "It does not matter what I want. What do *you* want, Evangeline?"

"I wish to be your wife. In every sense of the word," she said, quoting him from the previous day.

He watched as she reached up and finished unbuttoning the bodice of her dress and drew it open. "Please do not make me beg you to touch me, to make love to me."

He swallowed hard and stared at her breasts, both surprised and pleased she hadn't donned a chemise or corset. She rose up on her knees and shimmied out of the garment.

Quickly, he dropped the canvas flap behind him. Darkness filled the cramped space.

"What if Mac comes looking for us?" He unknotted the shawl and drew it from his hips.

Cautiously, she struck a match and lit a small candle. Her eyes lifted to his and he heard her breath catch, saw her swallow hard as her eyes caressed him. "I am certain Mac will be no bother. Yesterday I explained you and I need our privacy. He'll not interrupt when we are alone."

After setting the candle aside, Evangeline turned her face away and lay back on the feather tick, clad only in pink, lace-trimmed drawers. She was beautiful, gloriously so, her waist-length golden hair spread out on the pillow, her firm breasts full and luscious, the tips erect and waiting to be tasted.

Wolf knelt and moved closer to fan out her long silky hair among the pillows. He wanted her, wanted the physical pleasure her body could give, yet this would change nothing between them. Ten years of hell, lies, and betrayal still burned hot between them.

She gazed up at him with soft, misty eyes. A part of him wanted to forgive the hurt, but the wound in his heart was too fresh. Perhaps someday, but for now he would take what she offered and hope it would be enough to sustain him.

He drew the pink, satin drawers down her legs, over her ankles and feet, pausing to feast his eyes on her nude form. So lovely and perfect. He brushed his knuckles against her cheek and she trembled.

"You are uncertain?"

"Not at all," she replied.

Still he wasn't convinced. He sensed her apprehensiveness, saw it in the rapidly beating pulse along the side of her throat. Did he expect too much from her too soon? How could he come to their marriage bed with this much anger and resentment clouding his heart? He started to ease away, but she reached for him, lay a delicate hand on his arm, stilling him.

"Don't go."

His eyes searched hers. "Do not toy with me, Evangeline."

"I'm not. Please," she whispered, "stay with me."

"This isn't a game."

"No, it isn't."

Her hands reached behind his neck and she pulled his mouth down to hers. Her lips were soft, warm, and she moaned low in her throat, opening her mouth to receive him. She returned his kisses hungrily.

Unable to control his raging desire, he tore his mouth away, eased down her body and kissed the side of her throat. He nipped at the tender skin, tasted her sweet flesh and she cried out. Her hands threaded into his hair and urged him lower. He suckled at her breast, rolling the pebbled nipple over his tongue like a sun-ripened berry. She arched beneath him, her hands cradling his head. She smelled fresh, of soft rain and talcum powder and he went back and forth between her luscious breasts, unable to get enough of the taste of her.

He plucked her rosy nipples into stiff peaks, loving the soft mewling sounds she made in her throat as he pleasured her. His hand moved lower and she moaned her approval, arching upward as he reached between her thighs to test her readiness for him. He listened to her sharp intake of breath as his fingertips skimmed over the delicate petals of her dewy sex. Finding her slick, he paused to brush his thumb in a circular motion over her pleasure center. His gaze locked with hers as he slid one finger into her core, followed by another. She appeared ready enough, but her body tensed.

"Shall I stop?"

The look in her eyes softened as she relaxed around his fingers. "No."

"Good," he whispered, still confused by her reaction to his intimate touch. She sucked in a breath as he pressed deeper, then she began to undulate her hips to his own sweet, slow rhythm. He increased the tempo and she rode his hand, bucking against him as if trying to get closer to him. He smiled, pleased he could still elicit such a response from her.

He rose up over her, quickly insinuating his legs between hers. His manhood was thick, erect, aching for release. It had been a long time since he'd been with a woman and he feared he wouldn't last. She gazed up into his eyes and an emotion he couldn't discern crossed her face as he pressed into her. She stiffened as he settled his entire length within, then she began to move her hips to the slow rhythm he set. Whispering a curse, he stilled, squeezed his eyes shut and savored the feel of her hot sheathe as it contracted around his him.

"Don't move," he whispered, then opened his eyes to look at her. "I'll take my release if you do."

She smoothed her warm palms over his shoulders. "It's all right, Wolf."

He gave a half laugh. "No, it is *not* all right. You haven't received any pleasure yet."

Drawing in a deep, steadying breath, he willed his body to slow down. He withdrew almost completely, thrust slow and deep into her silken wetness, pleasuring her with long deliberate strokes. Her legs snaked around his waist, her ankles locking behind his hips, holding him captive. He watched her eyes flutter shut, felt her muscles constrict around him as his own body hurtled toward release. A sob escaped her lips as he exploded in a soul-wrenching climax.

A moment later, he moved off her and lay beside her, his heart pounding. The only sound in the wagon was their harsh breathing. It felt almost like old times, their lovemaking as passionate as it had once been. A few minutes later she sat up and brushed the hair from her face, then drew a blanket over herself.

He stroked his fingertips lazily up and down her arm. "Why do you cover yourself?"

She shrugged. "I don't know. I suppose it seemed the proper thing to do."

He watched her gather her clothing and under-garments. She had changed from the uninhibited young woman he'd fallen in love with years ago. What had happened to quell her passion?

"We're married. There is no need to be ashamed."

She nodded. "You're right."

He continued to stroke her arm. "You are still as beautiful and fiery as that young filly I once knew."

She lowered her eyes. "I'm not. My waist is thicker, my breasts not as firm as when I was young." Absently, she shook out a petticoat. "Perhaps we should dress."

"What's your rush?" He lifted the garment from her hand and tossed it aside.

Her gaze caught his. "Mac is alone. He needs me."

"Mac is old enough to look out for himself for an hour or so, Evangeline. You must stop coddling him."

A noise of protest passed her lips. "I do *not* coddle him."

"The hell you don't. You're always at his side overseeing his every move." He snorted. "I'm surprised the boy can use the privy without you holding his hand."

She gaped at him, her eyes turning to narrow slits. "How dare you."

Wolf gritted his teeth, instantly regretting his words. Perhaps he'd been too harsh, but she *was* overly protective of the boy. "I apologize for that remark. You are a caring mother." He sat up and brushed the hair away from the nape of her neck and kissed her there. "Do not be angry with me."

She inclined her face to his and their lips brushed. "Oh, Wolf, let's not argue." She reached up and traced the scar on his throat with her fingertips before leaning forward to press her lips to it.

"I cannot imagine the pain you must have suffered," she whispered against his skin.

No, she could not possibly know how he'd suffered. Wolf choked back tears as his throat constricted. "Do not think about it now. He pressed her down to the feather tick again, drew her nipple into his mouth, and plucked it into a stiff peak. Reaching down, he parted the soft blonde curls and teased the little pearl of her femininity with his fingertip. She panted.

"I want you again, Evangeline."

"I want you again, too."

Moving over her again, he nudged her thigh with his growing erection. "Let me make it better this time."

There were no more words between them. Wolf possessed her body with a fierceness that shocked him. Hot skin melted against skin as they clawed toward mutual release. His dark hands moved over her pale body, rediscovering every silken inch of her. Still, it wasn't enough.

Wanting to watch her, he rolled onto his back and lifted her over him. She slid down the steely length of him, rode him, her glorious golden hair spilling across her full breasts, her head thrown back in wanton ecstasy. He grasped her hips to still her when he came, then opened his eyes to watch her beautiful face by candlelight as she drifted down from passion's storm.

When Wolf left the wagon half an hour later, his body temporarily sated, heaviness still weighed on his heart. She'd wanted him to claim her as his wife, but this interlude—no matter how passionate—changed nothing other than to officially seal their marriage vows. Now she couldn't leave him without obtaining a divorce. He prayed she wouldn't choose to do so.

"Come see the fire!" Mac cried when Wolf approached. "I did it! I really did it!"

Wolf surveyed the fire. "You sure did, Mac. Now let's see if we can wrangle up some biscuits."

"My ma makes the best biscuits," Mac offered. "Hey, why were you gone so long? Isn't my mother gonna make us breakfast?"

Wolf cleared his throat. He figured Evangeline wasn't in much shape at the moment to be doing chores. "Your mother is resting. Why don't we surprise her and make breakfast ourselves?"

The lad nodded. "She'd like that."

Wolf brought the bowls, flour, salt and a tin of canned milk. Mac stirred the ingredients together and mixed the sticky dough with floured fingers while Wolf poked about in the chuck box for his favorite Dutch oven. He showed Mac how to set the three-legged pot into the glowing coals, then scoop a few on top of the lid to create an oven effect. Afterward, he set a grate atop the fire and put a pot of coffee on.

Evangeline emerged from the wagon, her cheeks tinged bright pink, a faint bruise on the side of her throat, evidence of his impassioned kisses.

Wolf grew hard again as he recalled their love-making only a few minutes before. He fantasized about taking her to the river and having her again tonight.

"I see you two have already started breakfast." Avoiding Wolf's eyes, she ruffled Mac's hair, giving him a loving squeeze. "Did you build the fire by yourself, sweetheart?"

Mac smiled up at her. "Naw, mister...I mean, *Pa* showed me how to do it."

Her eyes caught Wolf's. "Pa?"

Wolf shifted from his spot on the ground. "Mac, your mother and I need to talk to you about something."

Evangeline shook her head at him and mouthed the word, *no*.

Mac slipped from his mother's embrace and picked up a stick to poke at the fire. "I think the flames are dying. Let me poke at it."

"It's not dying," Wolf said. "Now put the stick down and listen."

Mac tossed the stick in the dirt and took a seat beside Wolf.

He turned to the boy. "You know that your mother and I were married by proxy—but that we are man and wife."

He nodded. "That's why I didn't go to the wagon when you didn't come back. I figured you two were doing married things."

Wolf cut his eyes at Evangeline whose face had turned crimson. Wolf bit back a grin.

"Your mother tells me you're aware that Reverend Payne wasn't your real father."

Mac lowered his eyes. "I know."

"Stop this now," Evangeline interrupted. "Mac, please leave us alone to discuss a matter."

Mac rose.

Wolf came off the ground and squared off with her. "No, Evangeline. The boy must know. Mac, stay where you are."

"You don't understand," she whispered. "Garrick was cruel."

Wolf looked over at the boy whose head was bowed. "What the hell did Payne tell him?" Taking her by the arm, he pulled her out of earshot of the boy.

"He told Mac he was born a bastard, that I was a prostitute and that he had saved me from iniquity by marrying me and giving Mac a name."

"And you allowed such talk?"

"I didn't allow anything. Garrick did as he pleased. He beat me if I dared question him. He locked Mac and me in our rooms for days if we disobeyed."

"The boy will be scarred by the abuse."

Tears glistened in her eyes. "I know. That's why I try to be exceptionally kind to him. He's been through too much. Now do you see why I protect him as I do?"

"And you?" He suddenly recalled that first day in Luling when Mac tried to prevent him from undressing Evangeline. "Is that why Mac has been so protective of you? Did he witness Payne abusing you, too?"

She tried to pull away, but he reeled her back to him. "Answer me."

She shook her head. "Only once. The other times he was whisked away by our maid."

"What about in your intimate relations with the man?"

She shuddered. "I do not wish to speak of it."

"Don't deny what happened earlier, Evangeline. When we were together in the wagon, you flinched. I felt your body tense when I first entered you. At first I thought you were repulsed by me, by my scar, that you regretted your request for me to join you in bed. Then you relaxed and eventually enjoyed my pleasuring."

"Garrick's technique left much to be desired."

"He took you violently?"

"He took me without care for my comfort."

"He raped you." It wasn't a question.

She blinked. "A man cannot rape his wife."

"The hell he can't. If a man forces himself on a woman, he is violating her whether they are married or not."

She looked away. "The laws do not view it that way."

Slipping a finger beneath her chin, he turned her face to his. "Why didn't you tell me before that Mac endured such cruelty...that you were abused as well?"

"There was no time. We left the hotel so quickly yesterday I hadn't a chance to speak to you."

"You could have explained the situation in your letters."

Her eyes widened. "Oh, dear heavens, I could not put such detestable words in a letter! Someone might have read them!"

Wolf looked over at the child, then back at her. She had a defensible point. "Payne didn't harm Mac in any other way, did he? Beat him?"

Her face paled and she appeared as though she might be ill.

His stomach turned. "Oh, God, Evangeline did he abuse Mac physically?"

She shook her head. "No, I...I always managed to protect Mac from his outbursts. Garrick took his anger out on me. I was the one he beat when Mac misbehaved." Tears sprang into her eyes. "He tried to hurt Mac once, but I arrived in time to stop him."

He brushed a strand of hair from her face and tucked it behind her ear. "If the bastard weren't dead, I'd kill him right now for what he did to both of you."

She flinched.

"What is it?"

"Nothing."

Damn! She was still keeping something from him. "No more lies, Evangeline. No secrets between us. If our marriage is to survive, there can be no further deceptions between us."

Placing a finger beneath her chin, he turned her face up to his. "You always appear anxious out of Max's sight. Has something else happened I should know about?"

She swallowed hard. "A few weeks ago, I received an anonymous note. From a man, I assume. He said he knew the truth about what I'd done and one day I would pay for it. He didn't elaborate."

Wolf led her from earshot of Max. "What was he talking about?"

She kept her voice low. "I'm not certain, but I presume it's about Garrick's death."

He took her by the shoulders. "Does Mac know of these letters?"

She shook her head. "No. I've shielded him from worry, but there were two more before I left Savannah."

"Where are the letters?"

"I burned them before I left for Texas."

"You didn't alert the authorities?"

"I couldn't, Wolf." Her eyes fixed on his. "There's something I've never told another soul, something only Mac and I know, with the exception of the person who sent the notes. It's about how my late husband *truly* died."

Wolf's gut churned. "And how *did* your husband die?"

She looked away. "Garrick's death report states a head injury from a fall."

Reaching up, he turned her face back to his. What was she hiding? "The fall wasn't accidental, was it?"

A commotion with Mac drew their attention away. The boy was having difficulty lifting one of the pots from the fire.

"I cannot speak of it right now." She hurried to assist Mac.

Wolf blew out a breath of exasperation. Why did she avoid his questions? His thoughts turned a dangerous direction as he watched her hug the child. Her love for Mac was strong. Still, he realized why she coddled him now. Had she killed Payne to protect Mac? It wouldn't be inconceivable for a mother to fight to the death to protect her child, particularly if the man pushed her to the edge of sanity. Had Payne beat the boy, or God forbid, worse? He didn't have a good feeling about this. Tonight after Mac was asleep he'd get to the bottom of this matter once and for all.

Thunderheads began to build on the horizon by

noon. Evangeline managed to get the still damp bedding she'd been line-drying into the wagon before a brief downpour. Wolf decided not to break camp, but to stay put until the heavy storms passed and the roads were passable again.

After a meal of cold tortillas with softened butter and fruit preserves, he sent Mac to bed early. He figured they had at least a good hour or two before another squall arrived, enough time for a relaxing dip in the cool waters of the nearby creek.

"I don't feel safe." Evangeline hugged his partially submerged body tightly as thunder rumbled in the distance. "Perhaps we should return to the wagon before the storm hits. Mac might awaken and become afraid."

Wolf reached around and removed her arms from his waist, then lifted her chin with his fingertip and bent to silence her with a gentle kiss on the lips. "The boy is fine, Evangeline. I told you to stop worrying."

She shivered. "Do you think we're in danger?"

He wiggled a brow at her and pressed his growing arousal against her belly. "*You* most definitely are, Mrs. Smith."

At the flash of lightning overhead, she cried out. He lifted her into his arms and Evangeline slipped her arms around his neck.

"We should go." Her breath was as soft as a caress against his cheek.

Since he'd apparently misjudged the advance of another quick moving storm, he agreed they *should* take cover. But he didn't want to return to camp, not when he still had so many questions. Her palm lifted to his cheek and he turned to look at her. Soft, desire-filled eyes met his.

"Make love to me again."

Evangeline moaned softly as his tongue probed her mouth. She opened wider to receive him, her hands sliding into his hair even as the lightning flashed around them. He thrust deep into her mouth, imitating with his tongue what he wanted to do to her body. She arched into him, whimpering her need as her hand reached down and curled tightly around the most intimate part of him. He staggered deeper into the brush with her in his arms, her hand still gripping him. Distracted, his body humming frantically and aching for hers, he narrowly missed walking into a tree. He took cover beneath the canopy of a dense grove of live oak.

So urgent was his need to claim her again, there were no preliminaries once they hit the ground. He took her swiftly at exactly the moment snaking fingers of lightning flashed across the sky. Her eyes closed and she surrendered herself to him as forceful gusts of dry, hot wind buffeted them, scouring their naked bodies with leaves and grass and dirt. Thunder crashed and boomed around them, rattling both heaven and earth. Tall sycamores and spindly oaks bent and swayed, their dry limbs creaking and groaning eerily in the darkness. So lost in passion, he was scarcely aware a light rain had begun to fall.

Evangeline matched him with a need as urgent as his own. Cold raindrops pelted his backside and thunder growled long and ominous as they made love. Her body contracted around his at the exact time of his release. He stilled and clutched her hips tightly as he spilled his seed deep inside her.

Afterward, they lay together in the mud, clinging to one another's rain-slick bodies in the darkness as the storm subsided and until lightning was but an intermittent flicker far off in the southern sky. He was muddy from head to toe and all points in between. So was she. She shivered in his embrace.

"I think we need another bath." He propped himself on an elbow and looked at her. She smiled, a soft, sated look on her face. He caressed her breast, smoothed his palm over her flat belly and imagined what she'd looked like with Mac growing within. So many years had been lost and they'd both endured much pain. Their marriage might have been founded on shaky ground, the result of his desire for revenge, yet she'd chosen to stay with him in spite of his trickery. Now they shared the possibility of having created new life. If they were to make the marriage work, the time for secrets was over.

"Can you talk freely now that Mac isn't near?"

"I didn't kill Garrick, if that's what you're wondering."

"I didn't accuse you."

"I saw the doubt in your eyes earlier when we were talking. You don't trust me."

"And you don't trust me. Otherwise, you would have told me the truth."

She sat up and pushed the damp hair from her face. "I *have* told you the truth. Garrick *did* die from a head injury and he *was* in a fall, Wolf, but it wasn't by my hand, or by Mac's."

"You're protecting someone else."

She shook her head and sighed. "I simply cannot speak of it now." She gasped, placed a hand on his forearm. "Did you hear that?"

He lay still and listened to the rippling waters of the nearby creek. Was this her attempt to change the subject? "What did you hear?"

"It sounded like the snap of a twig beneath someone's foot."

He sat up and listened a moment, again hearing nothing. "Perhaps you heard a deer."

She rubbed her hands briskly over her arms. "I don't feel safe here. Our clothes are still at the river bank where we left them. We must get cleaned up and hurry back to the wagon."

Still, she avoided the subject. Why?

Rising to his feet, he offered his hand. Her tiny palm slid over his and he lifted her. She was beautiful standing there in the moonlight, nude, muddy, her wet hair clinging to her head and hanging in ringlets. He took her by the shoulders and kissed her hard.

"I'd almost forgotten what a lusty man you are." She laughed softly when he released her. "I'd also forgotten the uninhibited passions you raise in me."

"You have a body made for lovemaking, Evangeline. I knew it the moment I laid eyes on you—the night of your eighteenth birthday at the ranch."

"I remember." A hint of sadness tinged her voice.

"I watched you dance with other men, wishing I could have been your partner. I dared not approach you before any of them. They would have hanged me if I even touched your hand."

"It was you I wanted to dance with that night, Wolf."

He led her down the now muddy trail toward the water. The night sky had cleared after the storm, the moon pinned like a pearl on a swatch of black velvet. He watched as Evangeline scooped handfuls of water and splashed them over her chest and throat. As if she were suddenly shy, she turned her back to him, ducked into the water and rose up, her lush curves glistening as water cascaded from her body in the hazy half-light from the moon. He moved in behind her, slid his arms around her and reached up to caress her breasts. Her nipples were tight beads.

"Cold?" Drawing close, he pressed his cheek against hers.

"A bit." She leaned back against him. "This night has been so perfect, Wolf. I don't want it to end yet."

He didn't want the night to end either. "In many ways it reminds me of our last night together all those years ago."

She turned in his embrace, her arms sliding around his neck to pull his mouth down to hers. She took his mouth hungrily, hotly, her hand reaching down to caress him as her tongue plundered his mouth. He'd already taken her twice that morning and once tonight. He wasn't certain he had the stamina for another round.

"Whoa, there, Mrs. Smith." Drawing back, he broke the kiss. "Shouldn't we save a little something for when we arrive home?"

She laughed, then slipped from his embrace and gathered their clothing. "I'm only Mrs. Smith on paper. In my heart I'm Gray Wolf's bride."

After dressing, they strolled back to camp, his arm looped in hers. Regrettably, there wasn't enough room in the wagon for the three of them.

"You stay with Mac," he told her, assisting her up. "I'll sleep in the tent tonight. See you in the morning."

As he watched her lift the flap and disappear, a familiar ache tugged at his heart. It had always been this way when he'd watched her go.

She still hadn't given him all the details of Garrick Payne's death, but he hoped in time she would open up and trust him. He pitched his tent and bedded down near his family.

Two days after leaving Luling, they arrived in Gonzales.

The log cabin on Wolf's property was small, but cozy. Though it had been built more than forty years before, the structure was in remarkably sound shape. A roofed porch wrapped around the house. The floors were puncheon, the windows lacking glass, but shuttered. Since Mac had taken ill with pneumonia last year, she would ask Wolf to remedy this situation before winter arrived.

Wolf left her to explore the cabin while he and Mac went to check on John Patterson, his hired man. She recalled what Wolf told her, that John had rescued him on the road after her father's brutal attack. She was grateful to the man who'd saved his life and hoped to one day offer her sincerest thanks.

She inspected every inch of the quaint structure. A narrow staircase in the corner near the fireplace led to a small attic loft for Mac's sleeping quarters, or for an intimate hideaway for her and Wolf. A tiny, square dining table sat in the middle of the room—barely enough room for the three of them. The bedroom, parlor, kitchen and bathtub were all in one room. She wondered if Wolf might add on to the back of the structure for a second bedroom.

They hadn't made love again since the night of the storm and she looked forward to their first night at the cabin. Finally, she might be able to use her new rose-scented bath salts.

Warmed by the thought of a romantic evening, she drew open all the shutters in the house, allowing a cool breeze to enter. She ran her palms over the new stove he'd purchased for her, eager to begin her duties as the mistress of the household. She'd ordered a cookbook from the Montgomery Ward's catalog and expected her trunks from Savannah to arrive within a few days. They contained a few things she'd crafted, but never used, such as a lace tablecloth and several doilies, two quilts and assorted tea towels and hot mittens. She looked about the rustic room. Although lacking indoor plumbing and much different than her spacious town home in Savannah, she could put her feminine touches here and there and make it a place Wolf and Mac would be proud of.

After setting her shawl and gloves aside, she untied her bonnet and laid it atop the pile. Still feeling flushed from the heat, she unbuttoned the collar of her blouse and the cuffs, donned a tea-towel for an apron and commenced sweeping.

On her father's ranch, she'd had servants for housework. Garrick also kept domestic help. Still, when he was away, she'd worked alongside them, cooking and cleaning. She taught them the art of crochet and needlepoint and taught their children to play simple tunes on the piano. The fine ladies of Savannah would have scorned her more had they known she socialized with the hired help, but in the process, she'd befriended Nell, possibly the most propitious move in her life.

She shuddered as she remembered her last days with Garrick. He'd become irrational and violent, striking her for merely standing in his path. Nell sacrificed everything to aid her and Mac that afternoon, and she would never forget the woman. She shook away the memories. Garrick was dead now, hopefully rotting in hell if there was any justice in the afterlife.

She turned her attention to the future, not the past, and opened her new cookbook. Bread. Yes, she'd bake a loaf of bread and perhaps a pie to celebrate their first day home. Then she'd ask Wolf to invite his friend, John Patterson, to join them one day this week for a meal.

The next few days passed easily and she and Mac settled in. Soon, it felt as if she belonged there, as if she'd always been the mistress of the house. Wolf had asked no more about Garrick's death and for that she was thankful.

They made love every night, but quietly so as not to disturb Mac who'd taken the loft. She silently hoped that the following summer might bring new life into their home.

A few days later alone in the cabin hanging curtains, she felt Wolf's presence before she turned around.

"You're back." She stepped down from the chair and laid the tack hammer aside. She hadn't expected him home so soon and was glad she'd drawn the bathwater earlier. "Shall I heat the kettles to warm your bath?"

He closed the door behind him and dropped the bolt, the desire in his eyes unmistakable. "I'd rather heat *your* kettle, woman."

She bit back a smile, her heart pounding out a near deafening tempo in her ears. Was her excitement due to the fact he'd surprised her in the middle of the day? Or was it from the anticipation of the lovemaking to come?

"No bath for me." He grinned like a possum in a sweet potato patch. "I'll wash in the basin."

"Where is Mac?" she inquired.

He hesitated, then hung his hat on a peg by the door. "John took him to town to the cattle auction. They'll be back tomorrow or the next day."

She almost swooned. "Oh, dear heaven, Wolf! You should have asked!"

He frowned. "Don't worry. John will look after him."

She gripped the chair's back to steady herself. "What do you know about this John fellow?"

"He's the most honorable man I know, Evangeline. Believe me, I wouldn't have sent my son with him if I thought otherwise."

She swallowed hard, the hysteria slowly calming. Wolf was right. He'd never put Mac in harm's way. Then she realized he'd sent their son with John so they might have privacy. He began unbuttoning his shirtsleeves.

"I thought you might appreciate my exclusive company tonight" He stripped off his shirt and strode to the washstand. "What do you think of the house, Evangeline?" He kept his back to her as he splashed water over his face and throat. "Now that you've had a chance to survey every nook and cranny, will it do until I can add another room?" He dropped his trousers and kicked out of them. "By the way, have you seen my carved handled pocket knife?"

Evangeline perused his bare back, bronzed and muscular, narrowing down to lean, tight buttocks. It became hard to breathe as she studied his physique. Knife? Had he said something about a knife? She unbuttoned the next few buttons on her blouse. "N-no, I've not seen your knife."

"Must've lost it." He turned around, his manhood thick and jutting in the air. He smiled. "What's wrong, woman? Cat got your tongue?"

She composed herself as desire washed over her in waves. "I...I hung curtains today." She gestured to one of the windows. "On our next trip into town I'll purchase more fabric, if that is acceptable."

He glanced at the window, then returned to bathing. "They brighten the place up. I like them. You should know I plan to add an indoor privy soon—just like the fine homes in town. And next spring I'm going to build a hen house on the east side of the barn and fill it with a hundred Leghorns. The added egg and poultry business will help pull us through any lean times or droughts."

He snatched the towel and turned around to dry his face and throat. His face was somber.

"Evangeline, I sent Mac with John so that we might continue our discussion from the other night."

Oh, no! He wanted to talk about Garrick again.

Crossing the room, he stood before her and placed his hands on her shoulders. "We've been officially

126

married for two weeks. There can be no more secrets between us as husband and wife. I need to know the truth about what happened to your first husband."

Her knees buckled, but he quickly righted her.

"Payne didn't fall down those stairs on his own, did he?"

She shook her head.

"Who pushed him?"

The room grew darker and it became difficult to breathe. She fanned herself with her hand as her cheeks began to burn.

"You caught him with Mac didn't you?"

A sob escaped. "Oh, Wolf!" She tore away from him and slumped into the chair as the world around her careened off course. "Yes!" She bit to still her trembling lips as her stomach twisted into a knot at the sickening memory.

"And in a rage you killed him?"

"No! I didn't kill Garrick."

"I would understand if you did. I would kill the bastard, too, if I'd caught him molesting my child."

She could hold back no longer. Resolve crumbled and she burst into tears. "I am so sorry, Wolf."

Then he was at her side, lifting her from the chair. He pulled her into his arms and she sagged against his solid form, clinging to him as if to extract strength. She needed him, needed his steadfastness right now, yet there remained between them suspicion and bitterness. He claimed to not understand the sacrifice she'd made to protect their unborn child so many years ago. Would he ever?

It had been a terrible year following Garrick's death. She'd endured the accusing stares of the town folk, the whispered rumors that somehow she'd contributed to her husband's demise. Before she'd left Georgia for Texas, the anonymous letters had frightened her so much that she and Mac ceased appearing in public. The secret remained, however, lying dormant, waiting for the right moment to reawaken and ruin their lives forever. Someone out there knew the truth. Now Wolf would know, too.

"Tell me everything," he prompted as his gentle fingertips stroked up and down her arms.

"I can't."

"You must."

She drew in a steadying breath as she composed her thoughts. "Very well. One evening I walked into the study and caught Garrick with his pants open. Mac was crying. Fortunately, things hadn't gone very far." She shuddered and put her face into her hands.

"The son of a bitch."

"Garrick was enraged I'd discovered his dirty secret, the real reason he kept an orphanage on the back property. I threatened to tell his congregation of his perversions. He came after me and beat me nearly unconscious. I don't remember much, except before I fainted Mac pounded on the other side of the door, screaming for Garrick to open it. Then I heard Mac call for Nell, our housekeeper. She used the spare key I'd given her to open the door. Garrick pulled a pistol from the drawer and aimed at me. Nell intercepted. She slammed Garrick's head with an iron. The blow killed him."

"Was Mac an eyewitness to Garrick's death?"

Evangeline nodded, realizing her body was trembling so hard her teeth were chattering. "Mac told me later what happened. In her rage, Nell dragged Garrick's body out of the room and shoved it down the stairs."

"Why didn't you tell the authorities?"

"Nell saved my life, Wolf. To tell the authorities would have meant certain death for her. Do you know what they would have done to a black woman who'd killed a white man? She wouldn't have received a trial, no matter that I claimed she came to my defense. Savannah society viewed Garrick as a saint. He made his ministry larger than life so he'd be above reproach should his dark deeds become light. He told his congregation he'd found me in a brothel, cleaned me up and gave my illegitimate child a name. People believed him, only tolerating me because I was Reverend Payne's wife. They praised him for his orphanage work, for founding a girl's home for unwed mothers...for turning *my* depraved life around. If I dared try to speak out against him, he'd have beat me severely. He was brutal and twisted, Wolf, the most evil human being I've ever known."

"Does Mac ever talk of what happened to him?"

She bit down on her lip. "No, but sometimes at night he cries in his sleep. I believe it's then he remembers."

"You do know if the truth is discovered, you can be held as an accessory to Payne's murder?"

"No one will ever know, Wolf. Nell passed away two months ago from a weak heart, bless her soul. Only you, Mac and I know the truth—with perhaps the exception of the author of those anonymous threat letters."

"What about Payne's body? Could they exhume his remains and reexamine the injuries? An examination of the skull might prove *exactly* how he died."

Her heartbeat sped up. "Wolf, you're frightening me."

"Surely you've thought of it."

"No. I never considered such."

"A look at his skull might reveal what type of instrument damaged it. I would think a ten or fifteen pound sad iron did a great deal of damage, more so than a mere tumble down the stairs."

"It was a closed casket service. I never saw Garrick's body. I was told by the undertaker's assistant that his injuries were so extensive that he wasn't suitable for public viewing."

"Who else besides you, Mac, and your housekeeper could have known the truth behind Garrick's *accident?*"

"No one. Not another soul witnessed anything but Mac and me."

Wolf shuttered the windows, then lit a lantern and hung it on the hook beside the bed. Although he believed her story, he still worried for her and Mac's safety. Apparently someone else knew the details.

He sighed, dragging a weary hand down his face. This was why Evangeline was so protective of Mac. His stomach turned at the thought of Garrick Payne abusing his son. He looked at Evangeline. Tears streaked her pale face. He brushed them away with his fingertips.

"We'll talk no more of this tonight. You and Mac have endured enough, and since no more letters have arrived I feel you're safe in Gonzales. Perhaps the person who wrote them has lost track of you now that your last name is Smith. Besides, you're here with me and I'll never let anything bad happen to either of you."

In the buttery glow of lamplight, he undressed her, assessed her with his eyes and fingertips. Dark blonde hair framed her delicate face and shimmered with highlights he could only compare to spun glass. He laid her on the bed, sat beside her and fanned the silken strands over her shoulders. Splaying one palm across her flat tummy, he imagined what she would look like heavy with his child and his heart swelled with joy as a new image rose up in his mind—Evangeline cradling a tiny new life they'd created. He bent to kiss her belly reverently.

"Evangeline," he said quietly, keeping his ear to her stomach. "I hope soon to hear our baby moving inside you."

"I'm pleased you want another child, Wolf. I do hope I conceive soon."

He lifted his head and looked at her. "I want children more than anything." He leaned over and cupped her cheek in his palm as he bent to brush his lips lightly across hers. "I want us to fill this cabin with a dozen."

He lowered his mouth to her breast and suckled tenderly. She whimpered, arching into him. Her fingers locked behind his neck and she held him firm.

"You enjoy this, do you?" He lifted his eyes to gaze at her flushed face. Her eyes were soft and misted with desire.

"It's quite pleasurable."

"I love giving you pleasure." Sliding up her body, he nibbled the silky flesh on the side of her throat, then dragged his tongue back down between her breasts, causing her to shiver.

Evangeline reached up and touched his cheek, then trailed a lazy finger along his jaw line and downward over his Adam's apple. She lingered on the scar at his throat.

"Why are you looking at me like that, Wolf?"

He shrugged. "I still have difficulty believing this is real, that we're married and have a son."

She sat up and inched closer to him, her hands cradling his face. "If I could change the past I would. I've searched my heart a million times and know that if I had yesterday to do all over again, I might have done many things differently."

He saw the sincerity in her eyes, heard it in her voice. Still, guilt gnawed at him. "I shouldn't have believed your father's lies. Once I'd recovered from his attack, I should have searched for you. I should have believed in the love we shared. Then none of this would have happened. Garrick Payne would never have harmed you or Mac."

Tears sprang into her eyes. "It's of no use to look to the past. We have one another and Mac and a bright new future ahead of us. That's all that matters now."

He caressed her face, thumbed away a warm tear that inched down her face. "If I'd known Payne had abused you, I'd have been gentler in my eager approach our first time together as husband and wife."

She smiled softly. "I enjoy your *eager approach* just as it is."

"The thought of him hurting you makes me murderous."

She lowered her eyes. "He didn't make many demands of me."

Wolf didn't want to imagine what she'd been forced to do, but tonight, if it were in his power, he would make her forget.

She swallowed hard. "It might surprise you to know that Garrick visited my bed precisely three times during our seven-year marriage."

Wolf lifted a brow.

"It's true. The few times he came to me, he slipped in quietly in total darkness. The first time was brutal—one month after we were married. Unannounced, he came in the night and took me forcibly. Thankfully his subsequent visits never lasted long. At first I believed he avoided me because I'd born an illegitimate child, that he felt I was tainted. Years later I learned exactly why he didn't come to my bed. He rather enjoyed the company of young men...boys if they were available, as evidenced by the vile act he tried to commit on Mac."

Now it made sense why she'd flinched when he'd taken her that first time in the wagon. He squeezed his eyes shut a moment and swallowed down bitter bile that rose in his throat. If only he'd known the abuses she'd suffered, he'd have been gentler.

As if she sensed his discomfort over the subject, she propped herself on one elbow beside him and smoothed her palm over his shoulder. "I received no pleasure from Garrick, Wolf. Although he took his release with me those occasions, I'm certain he was abhorred by the fact he'd lain with a woman. He wouldn't look at me for several days afterward."

He drew her hand to his lips to kiss it. "You don't have to tell me."

"But I do. During those empty years I held onto the memories you and I shared, the passionate moments we spent alone, the way you kissed me, the way you caressed my body and made love to me. That was what helped me get through the lonely nights."

"If you were lonely, why didn't you take a lover?"

She sighed. "I didn't want a lover. Certainly I had opportunities for male companionship, but I wanted *you,* and if I couldn't have you, I wanted no other man." She smiled, her fingertip circling his dark nipple. "What about you? Have *you* taken a lover in my absence?"

Ignoring her question, he rose over her and moved between her thighs. He'd known many women, before he met Evangeline and during her ten years away, but he'd never loved any of them.

"Wolf, you didn't answer my question."

He positioned himself as he gazed down into her eyes. "You are the only woman I've ever loved, Evangeline. Therefore, you are the only *lover* I've ever known."

He silenced her with a swift thrust.

A knock on the door jolted Evangeline from sleep. Pale beams of yellow light filtered through the cracks of the window shutters signaling morning. Wolf rose from the bed and reached for his trousers.

He opened one of the windows. "Mac and John are back early." He pulled on a shirt. Evangeline gathered her clothing.

"Give us a moment," Wolf called toward the door.

Once they were dressed, he unbolted the latch and swung the door wide open. Mac skidded across the floor with a terrapin in his grip.

"Ma! Look what John did. He caught me a turtle on our way back from town. Can I keep him in a box? Please? I got a name all picked out—Horatio. Don't you think he looks like a Horatio?"

Evangeline turned her face away, not because she disliked turtles, but out of embarrassment. In her haste to dress she'd failed to draw the quilt over the rumpled bedclothes. She was certain John had noticed.

"Y-yes, of course, Mac." She dared a sidelong glance at the creature. "He's awfully big to keep in the house, though."

"Looks like we're having turtle soup tonight," Wolf joked. "Guess I'll have to sharpen my fork and knife for the occasion."

Mac hollered. "No way! You can't eat Horatio. He's my pet." The child clomped to the door in a pair of oversized boots. "I'm gonna build him a box right now where he'll be safe from your dinner fork, Pa. Then I'll try to find him a friend so he won't be lonely."

Once Mac raced outside, she proffered her hand to Wolf's hired man, John. Since her arrival he'd stayed in his own quarters behind the barn, keeping to himself.

He looked vaguely familiar and she recalled Wolf saying he'd once worked for her father. "Thank you for taking such good care of Mac, Mr. Patterson. He appears to have enjoyed his trip to town."

"Call me John, ma'am." He lightly clasped her hand.

John looked older than Wolf, but not by many years. His hair was like sun-bleached straw, dry and pale in stark contrast against his dark, leathery skin. He was a handsome, rugged-looking man with clear blue eyes and deep wrinkles at the corners of his eyes.

"I believe you worked for my father, Elijah Braddock?" she inquired.

He nodded. "That I did, ma'am...one summer about ten years ago. Same as Wolf here."

Wolf stood silently and she knew he was remembering the night her father and his ranch hands attacked him. She wanted to thank John for saving Wolf's life, yet she sensed Wolf didn't want her to bring up the topic.

John cleared his throat. "Ma'am, I picked up a slab of salt pork in town. Would you like me to bring potatoes up from the root cellar for your supper?"

She hadn't thought that far ahead, but she supposed she should begin planning their evening meal after breakfast. "Yes, thank you. The salt pork will be nice. I found dried hominy in a crock on the counter yesterday and some fresh green onions and peppers in the garden. We'll have a spicy stew tonight. Oh, and John, you'll dine with us."

There had been no sign of Mac for hours, not since he'd set out that morning to look for a friend for Horatio.

Evangeline paced the floor of the cabin as long as she could while John and Wolf left at dusk to search for the child again. The stew she'd cooked for their supper had grown cold in the pot and she'd thrown the hours-old corn fritters to the dogs. She told herself Mac was simply lost, that he'd wandered too far in his search for a turtle and he'd find his way home before dark. At least that's what she wanted to believe. For all she knew Mac had been bitten by a rattlesnake, or had fallen into the swift moving waters of the nearby creek and drowned.

Night was coming fast, closing in around the hills. Mac was terrified of the dark. Unable to stand the silence of the lonely cabin any longer, she donned a thick shawl, pulled on heavy boots, then lit a lantern and went to check the barn again. Wolf had searched it, had pulled almost every timber and hay bale out of place until it looked as if it had been hit by a cyclone. Still, perhaps he'd overlooked a clue.

She pulled open the creaking double doors and slipped inside. Eerie shadows grew long on the walls as she crept through. The night wind whispered between the cracks in the roof. A small, white owl perched high in the rafters hooted, and she shook off a chill that skittered up her spine.

"Mac? It's Mama. Are you here?"

Silence answered. He'd done this once before—hidden for two days after Garrick's death. He'd been ashamed and confused, although she couldn't imagine what could have happened to cause a repeat behavior. "Please come out if you're in here." Pleading, she bit down on her lip to keep from bawling. "You've done nothing wrong, sweetheart."

Still no response. She slumped into an empty stall as tears overtook her. What if they never found him or worse—found him dead. Something was wrong. She felt it deep in her soul. Mac hadn't wandered away, nor had an accident befallen him.

Someone had taken him, someone with a grudge against her.

The author of the threatening notes.

Wolf pulled hard on the black's reins as he rode into the night. He and John had split up two miles back. John's orders were to return to the house and check on Evangeline, then follow the south trail and meet him at the fork where the San Marcos and Guadalupe rivers merged. Mac hadn't wandered away and become lost.

Nor had he fallen into the rushing river and drowned. He knew it, felt it in his gut.

The horse pulled up short, screamed and reared. Wolf fought for control, talking softly to his mount. The horse had never behaved this way, not even during the fiercest storms. Then he felt the burning in his side, reached down and felt the warm wetness with his fingertips and realized he'd been shot.

He heard another pop, felt the searing hot pain rip through his right thigh. The horse bucked him off and he hit the hard ground face down. His mount galloped away into the night and Wolf rolled onto his back, drew his pistol. It was too dark to see his assailant. He dragged himself into the brush for concealment. Another shot grazed his upper arm and the gun slipped from his hand.

A booted foot kicked it from reach.

He looked up to see a dark form standing over him.

"Well if it isn't Gray Wolf McKinnon—or perhaps I should say *Adam Smith*. Allow me to introduce myself. The name is Garrick Payne. I believe you know my wife, Evangeline, quite well."

Garrick Payne? The man was dead. Was this some sort of sick joke? On second thought, perhaps the man wasn't dead after all. In fact, it all became clear now— the threatening notes to Evangeline before she left Savannah. Had Payne faked his own death, been stalking her all along? Had he taken their son? Fear sliced through him.

"What the hell have you done with my boy?"

The man laughed. "I always suspected the dark-skinned little bastard was sired by a breed. He looks exactly like you."

Payne's boot struck Wolf on the side of the head and pain splintered through his skull. His stomach roiled.

Payne squatted, pressed the cold barrel of his gun to Wolf's temple. "With you out of the way, Evangeline will be my wife again. Everything she owns—your home and land—will be mine." He leaned closer. "I cannot wait to see the look on her face when she learns I'm alive and you're dead. I'm certain she'll need special comforting."

Wolf started to roll onto his back, but heard the click of the gun's hammer and froze.

Payne chuckled. "Now, now. I will take very good care of Evangeline and the boy. Actually, I am quite fond of young Mac...quite fond."

If Wolf could have gotten to his feet, he'd have ripped the son-of-a-bitch's head off his shoulders and shoved it up his ass. "You touch my wife or my child and I'll kill you, Payne. By God, I'll tear every limb from your perverted body and feed them to my hogs."

"Don't worry yourself, McKinnon. You'll be long gone by the time I reach your ranch and your dear little family."

"Where's my son?" Wolf fought the darkness that threatened to swallow him, no longer hearing the man's words.

The door to the barn creaked open. Evangeline sprang to her feet, held her breath. She expected to see Wolf or John—or even Mac silhouetted in blue moonlight. Instead, it was *Garrick*. It couldn't be. Oh, dear God, it couldn't be! Garrick was dead!

He stepped closer. "Hello, Evangeline."

"Garrick." His name tumbled out in a rush of breath as her knees buckled. Her mind went into a dizzying whirl. "You're dead."

He laughed. "No. You only wish I were." He drew his gloves from his hands and tossed them aside. "And when I finish with you tonight, darling, you'll wish *you* were dead, too."

Pieces of the puzzle clicked into place. His closed-casket funeral. The hasty departure of the undertaker from Savannah before the funeral. Now she knew the man hadn't left town on urgent family business. Garrick must have killed the undertaker, put his body in the casket and switched places.

Her hand flew to her mouth to quell a sob slowly rising in her throat. Garrick had survived the blow Nell delivered to his forehead as well as the fall down the stairs. Now he'd returned to silence her for threatening to expose his dark deeds. Then another thought slowly coalesced in her mind. Mac. He'd taken Mac.

"Where is my son? What have you done with Mac?"

He shook his head as he uncuffed his shirtsleeves. "Always doting over that boy, aren't you. Do not worry. I've not harmed him."

Her eyes searched the darkened corners of the barn, looking for anything she might use as a weapon. Hoping to buy time, she added, "My husband will return shortly. You'd better leave before he arrives."

Garrick laughed. "Your husband won't be returning tonight or any other night for that matter. I shot him on the road tonight."

It was a lie! In her rage, she grabbed a hay fork and jabbed at him. He ducked. "Get off my property, Garrick!" She stabbed at him again. "Wolf will kill you when he learns you've come here!"

Garrick grabbed the handle, wrenching it away from her. He tossed it aside, then backhanded her, sending her stumbling backward against the wall. "Did you not hear me correctly, you stupid little bitch? I shot your husband and left him to die."

He stormed toward her, seized her shoulders and shook her violently. "You cost me everything in Savannah—my ministry, my orphanage. Because of you I had to fake my death so you wouldn't ruin me. Now, one year later, I still have nothing. So I've come to collect what belongs to me—including my dear little wife."

"But you were buried...your estate settled. I thought you were dead. We all did. I waited an appropriate mourning time before deciding to remarry. You cannot come back and make demands on me. I am Gray Wolf's wife, now."

"You mean Gray Wolf's widow." He smiled coldly. "With your husband dead, you're free to marry again. As your new husband named *Mr. Jackson*, I'll take control of the property. I will prosper again, Evangeline, and this time you're going to help me!"

At that moment it would have been so easy to give in to defeat and accept that Garrick had killed Wolf, but she couldn't. She must fight to keep control of her emotions. He squeezed her shoulders so tightly she feared he'd crush them.

"You wrote the letters didn't you, Garrick?" She tried not to sound nervous.

"And they frightened you all the way to Texas and into the arms of another man." He shook her violently. "I took you in when no other man would have you. I fed and clothed and schooled your illegitimate child. And what did you do? Donate my house to charity and return to that Indian lover of yours! No, you owe me, Evangeline."

"I owe you nothing. My father paid you to marry me. I didn't want to, but what choice did I have? He wouldn't allow me to return home." She shrugged free of his bruising grip. "I told no one your filthy deeds— even after your supposed death. I thought with your demise that would be the end of your dark secret, that Mac could heal and we'd both be free again."

"Lying bitch! You kept silent because you didn't want to be implicated in my murder!"

"I did nothing to you. Mac did nothing."

"You protected your housemaid. Your silence implicates you in a murder plot against me to obtain my money."

Oh, the bastard had some nerve suggesting such a thing! True, Nell had struck him and pushed him down the stairs, but she'd only been defending Evangeline. She'd certainly not prospered off his death as he'd left her with many unpaid debts. No, this despicable piece of filth had faked his own death to avoid being exposed as a child molester. He was a murderer also now if her instincts were on target. "I didn't want Mac scandalized after what you tried to do to him. That's one of the reasons I remained silent—not to protect myself in any manner."

"As if anyone would have believed you—a whore and her bastard child. Or would they have believed that darkie maid of yours? Who would they have believed, Evangeline, you or me?"

"Your words no longer hurt or shame me, Garrick. I am not a whore and Mac was never a bastard. True, he might have been born out of wedlock, but he was conceived in love. Now where is my husband? What have you done to Wolf and Mac?"

"The boy is perfectly fine, but I'm afraid your dear husband is dead, Evangeline."

In an instant, her world crashed. Wolf couldn't be dead! He couldn't! "You're a liar!" she screamed, beating her fists into his chest.

He reeled back. "Am I? Then tell me if any of these items look familiar." Reaching inside his coat pocket, he withdrew Wolf's pistol.

"You stole the gun!"

Then he pulled out the necklace, the one made of turquoise beads and white shells. Wolf wore it at all times—the only keepsake he had of his mother. He never would have surrendered it.

She lunged at him, delivering a blow to his groin with her knee. He went down with a string of curses as she shot from the barn. He was close on her heels as she sailed toward the house. Wolf kept a loaded rifle propped behind the door and she prayed she could reach it in time. She also hoped he'd left an extra box of ammunition handy, because she was going to blow so many holes in Garrick Payne that no undertaker would ever be able to count all of them.

Garrick tackled her, knocking her to the ground.

"It's time I teach you a lesson you'll never forget."

He dragged her by one leg across the yard to the barn. Sharp stones bruised her body. She bucked and thrashed, her skirt and petticoats bunching up around her face where she could no longer see. At the very least he was going to beat her, but she knew he wouldn't kill her because he needed her alive if he wanted to gain control of Wolf's ranch. As much as she wanted to fight him, she knew his strength. She'd been beaten many times by him and managed to survive each one. She would survive whatever he did to her now

He flung her into a stall. On her hands and knees, she lifted her head and looked up at him. Before, she'd always feared his wrath, viewing him as a powerful and violent force from whom she dared not try to escape. Now she saw him as he truly was—a weak and desperate man who enjoyed bullying women and children into submission. He was nothing in that instant—not the powerful, indomitable Reverend Garrick Payne of Savannah. He was a mouse of a man with a deep perversity that rotted his soul from the inside out.

She attempted to stand, to face her tormentor, but he kicked her legs out from beneath her. She fell upon the clean straw, her shins smarting from the blow. Gritting her teeth, she held back tears, not wanting to give him the satisfaction of seeing her cry.

"When I get through, you'll damned well know you belong to me." A feral gleam lit his eyes as he produced a riding crop. "Remove your clothes, you little tramp. It's been a long time since I've been forced to discipline you."

"Don't you mean abuse me, Garrick?"

He leaned over and slapped her face. "Take the goddamned clothes off or I'll slice them from your body!"

"Go to hell! You'll have to kill me before I let you beat me."

Garrick laughed. "Is that so? Would you prefer I whip your son, instead?" He stormed off to a neighboring stall and yanked a canvas tarp off a small heap, revealing Mac. Grabbing the child by his shirt collar, he yanked the boy to his feet and roughly dragged him back to her. Mac swayed unsteadily on his feet, his eyes half closed.

"Mac!" What was wrong with him? Garrick pushed him down onto the hay and raised the riding crop again.

Evangeline's heart leapt in her chest. She flung herself over Mac's form, crying out as the first blow stung through the fabric of her dress.

She dared to lift her head. "Let him go, Garrick!" she

pleaded. "Do as you wish to me, but don't harm my son!"

He grabbed her by the hair and dragged her into another stall. She watched as he returned and yanked Mac to his feet and shoved the sleepy-eyed youngster away. "Get the hell out of the barn and don't come back unless I call for you!"

"I won't let you beat her!" Mac cried, staggering toward the man. "You leave her alone, you stupid asshole!" Garrick backhanded the boy, sending him sprawling on the hay.

"Mac!" Evangeline pushed past, but Garrick yanked her back by one arm and shoved her into the stall again. He drew a knife from his boot.

"I'll slit the little bastard's throat if he interferes!"

"Mac, run! Run to the house and lock the door."

With much difficulty, Mac staggered to his feet and took off running toward the open barn door.

Garrick turned her around and shoved her down on her hands and knees. He reached down and tore open the back of her dress. She stiffened, awaiting the slap of the whip, praying Mac might have time to escape or hide. Then her fingers curled around something cold and metallic in the straw. Wolf's missing knife. Her heartbeat thundered wildly in her chest. She concealed it in the folds of her skirt.

"This land and the house on it will be mine, Evangeline." Garrick raged on as she opened the knife. "With Gray Wolf MacKinnon dead, you are free to remarry. I will assume another man's identity—Mr. Jackson as I've been using this past year—and you will keep silent of this. You owe me for all you have taken from me."

Her body trembling, Evangeline turned slowly, her eyes lifting to meet his. "And what about what you've taken from me, Garrick, or from Mac, an innocent child? I didn't hit you in the head with the iron. Nor did I shove you down the stairs. Nell was only protecting us. No, Garrick. I owe you nothing, and even if Wolf is dead as you claim, I'll not marry you. I'll not allow you to spend one moment on my land, in my house or in my bed, abusing me or my son ever again. I will expose you for the sick, indecent bastard you really are and you will be hanged for Wolf's murder."

With every ounce of strength she possessed she stood, keeping the knife hidden within the folds of her skirt. Her legs trembled and her heart pounded out a near deafening tempo in her ears. His expression was fierce, his face drawn, teeth clenched. "You are finished, Garrick Payne!" she shouted and thrust forth the knife.

The crack of a rifle split the silence of the barn. Evangeline screamed, tossed the knife aside and fell back on the hay at the deafening blast, then lay perfectly still. Garrick's lifeless body fell on top of her.

She lay numb beneath Garrick's dead weight. Silence settled over the barn. After a moment, she squirmed and wriggled from beneath him, then scrambled to her feet expecting to see her savior in the open doorway. No one was there. Something warm and wet in her hair caught her attention and she panicked. At first she feared she'd been shot, too. Then she realized it was Garrick's blood and not hers. Trembling hard, she took a few wobbly steps, her knees barely supporting her. She had to find Mac, to make certain he was all right. She dared a glance back at Garrick who lay face down on the bloody hay. Most of the top of his head was gone. Her stomach turned at the sight and she leaned over and vomited. From outside, John called her.

"I'm in the barn!" She wiped her mouth with the back of her hand.

John appeared in the doorway, lantern in hand. He froze when he saw her. "Godamighty!" He hurried to her. "Your head's bleeding." He tilted her head toward the lantern light to look at it. "Are you injured anywhere else?"

"It's Garrick's blood." Numbly, she stood shaking all over, staring at John's Adam's apple while he examined her head. The back of her dress was open, her bare shoulders exposed. But after all she'd been through she was too numb to care about modesty. Then John looked beyond her to Garrick's body and swore softly under his breath. He whisked off his vest and draped it around her shoulders.

"You saved my life, John."

John shook his head. "No, ma'am, I didn't shoot him. That husband of yours managed to get off that shot even as he stood in the barn door, swaying and bleeding and about to collapse. I was just lucky enough to ride up in time and witness every bit of it."

Her heart soared with hope.

Wolf was alive!

Tears of joy flooded her eyes. "Garrick told me he was dead."

"He's not dead, but he's shot up pretty bad, ma'am. I'm going to need your help getting the bullets out of him—a sharp knife, some scissors and clean bandage material. You sure you're all right?" He stopped in front of her and lifted her face to his, then grimaced. "Your face is bruised."

"Garrick struck me, but I'll be fine." She clutched his arm as they made their way toward the house. "Tell me what happened to Wolf? How serious are his injuries? Where's Mac?"

"Mac is fine," he assured her as they hurried to the door. "The little rascal's shaken up, but otherwise he says he's okay. Said that Payne fellow made him drink something that made him sleepy." He assisted her up the steps.

"I'll get the water kettle on to boil, John."

"From what I've been able to get out of Wolf," John said as he opened the door, "Payne ambushed him on the road about two miles north of here. He put three bullets in Wolf and left him for dead. How he did it, I'll never know, but your man made his way home on foot."

Evangeline rushed past John to where Wolf lay on his back in the middle of the floor.

"I rode up and saw Mac runnin' toward his Pa with the shotgun, hollerin' that you were in the barn with Payne. Wolf fired once, staggered a few feet and collapsed He's lost a lot of blood. We need to get him onto the bed and get them bullets out or I expect he might not make it 'til morning."

It was no easy task lifting a man of Wolf's size, but between the three of them they managed to heft him onto the mattress. John was right. Wolf had three wounds—one in his left side, another in his right forearm and one in the upper thigh. Fortunately the bleeding had slowed, but she'd never seen Wolf so pale and lifeless. She feared the worst. There was no time to send for a doctor. With her and Mac's help, John assured her he could remove the bullets. After that, they could only hope for the best.

Evangeline wanted to comfort Mac after all he'd been through with Garrick, but John needed her immediate help with Wolf. While John collected a couple of knives from her kitchen, she undressed Wolf and bathed his bloodied body quickly, taking care to clean each wound carefully. Mac brought wood for the stove, then hurried off with a pail to draw water from the well.

When she'd finished cleaning Wolf, she covered his trembling body with a fresh quilt and lay her head gently on his chest to listen to his weak, erratic heartbeat. She wept silently. All of this had been her fault. If only she'd never placed an ad in the mail order bride catalog, Wolf wouldn't have found her and she wouldn't have led Garrick Payne to him.

"You *will* survive this," she whispered. "I promise. You're going to recover and we're going to be a family again."

"E-van-ge-line." Her broken name was a whisper on his dry lips. "Forgive me."

"Oh, Wolf!" She kissed his cheek, her tears splashing onto his face. "I should be begging *your* forgiveness. All of this is my fault."

"I'm going to die," he said weakly.

"No, you're not going to die. I won't let you!" she cried, furious that he would say such a thing. "You can't leave us now, Wolf. We have to raise Mac together."

He lifted a trembling hand. "I must talk to John. My

son, too."

Evidently John had overheard and rounded the bed. "Right here, MacKinnon."

"If I die, I want you to marry Evangeline," Wolf began slowly. "She needs a man who will be kind to her. My son needs a decent father."

John snorted. "Dad-blame it, Wolf. You're too mean to up and die on us. Besides, you got your boy to raise now. The good Lord ain't gonna take you yet." John lowered a flask of whiskey to Wolf's lips. "Take a good long swig, my friend. Time's a wastin' and this is goin' to hurt like hell."

Wolf turned his face away. "No, John, you must promise me—you'll marry her and take good care of my family. I must have peace."

Evangeline felt her face warm when John looked at her. As Wolf's best friend, she had no doubt John would marry her in the event Wolf didn't survive. But she couldn't think of marrying anyone else—not even a kind and decent man like John. No, there would never be another man for her. She would go to her grave Gray Wolf's widow.

"All right, buddy," John answered. "I give you my word I will look after the missus and your young'un in case you don't make it."

"My son? Where is he?"

Evangeline rose from the bed and crossed the room. No sooner than she'd reached the door, Mac returned with the water bucket. He'd been so brave throughout this ordeal. Still, the thought that Garrick might have beat or abused him again tore at her heart. The bastard lay cold and dead in her barn now, and still she felt like storming out there and killing him again for terrorizing her child.

"Come with me, Mac." He set the pail down and she guided him to the bed, but Wolf had fallen unconscious again. She took a seat beside her son, who stood, watching Wolf. With the exception of his straight dark blond hair, Mac resembled Wolf in every way. He was dark complexioned, with eyes as black as the midnight sky. He had the same stubborn-set jaw, the same dimple in his right cheek—the one Wolf always denied having. Mac would grow into a handsome man some day, no doubt breaking dozens of girl's hearts along the way.

She took Mac's small hand and placed it on Wolf''s. "This is your father, Mac." She fought back tears and and added, "Your real father. His name is Gray Wolf MacKinnon, not Adam Smith. That's only a name on paper."

Mac nibbled his lower lip. "I kinda figured he was my real pa."

"You did?"

Mac nodded. "Well, we look alike. My skin is dark like his and we have the same eyes. You also named me Mac." Mac looked up at her with big, sad eyes. "Is he gonna die?"

She shook her head, then rumpled his hair. "I don't know, sweetheart. He's very weak. We must pray for a miracle."

Mac toyed with a loose thread on the quilt. "So he really is my pa, huh?" He avoided her eyes.

"Yes."

"I'm glad, 'cause I like him...even if he did threaten to eat my turtle."

She smiled through her tears. Even John, who'd since pulled up a chair and was seated on the other side of the bed, had tears in his eyes.

John cleared his throat and stood. "Ma'am, I think the boy could use a bowl of warmed stew." He placed the knives on the bed. Evangeline realized it was an excuse to get Mac away from what would likely be a gruesome sight. She nodded.

"I'll get things ready here while you get the boy settled down. Perhaps you might also tear us some clean bandages while you're at it."

Evangeline did as John asked, then hurried back to assist. She found he'd already removed the bullets from Wolf's forearm and upper thigh and was now preparing to take out the one in his side. She marveled at his surgical knowledge and silently thanked God he'd been

147

there.

She washed the blood from Wolf's arm, then wrapped it carefully with a fresh bandage she'd cut from a new tea towel. John worked at digging out the bullet in his side. Wolf moaned as if in terrible pain, but he lay still. Every so often she glanced at Mac to make certain he was all right. He'd finished eating his stew, most of which he now wore down the front of his white shirt.

John dislodged the last bullet, but the hole, freshly re-opened bled copiously. She held a compress at the site, hoping to staunch the flow. Once the bleeding was under control, John quickly put in two sutures, then wiped his bloody hands on the towel before handing it to her.

"I've done all I can do, ma'am. The rest is up to the good Lord." Heading for the door, he motioned for Mac to follow him. "I'll take the boy to my cabin so you can have some time alone with your husband. Once he's asleep, I'll bury Payne's body in the woods. " He tipped his hat to her. "I'll come back and check on you in the morning, ma'am. If you need me sooner, just put a lantern on the porch and I'll come when I see the light."

She knew from the look on John's face and the tone of his voice he wasn't certain Wolf would survive the night. He was too kind a man and didn't have the heart to admit her husband was dying.

An eerie silence settled upon the house, except for the sounds of Wolf's heavily labored breaths and the occasional scratching of doves that had built nests in the porch eaves. She prayed Wolf wouldn't linger for days, suffering horrible pain or even gangrene and that if God sought to take him that his passing would come soon. Although they had only known true happiness for little more than a few weeks, Wolf had given the gift of himself in their son, Mac. She could go on, knowing that a part of him continued to live on in the world. She placed a palm over her tummy and prayed a new life already budded within.

Numbly, she rolled up the blood-soaked quilt that had covered him and set it in the corner for washing.

Then she bathed Wolf's ashen face, combed his thick, dark hair and covered him with a fresh blanket. If he died, she would have John bury him on the rocky hill beneath the stand of towering sycamores. She and Mac would visit his grave every day.

Pouring fresh water into the basin, she shed her blood-stained dress, then bent forward and rinsed Garrick's blood from her hair and Wolf's blood from her hands. She sponged the side of her bruised face and lips with a cloth dipped in cool, clean water before pinning her wet hair up tightly on her head. She turned around to look in the mirror at the red mark on her back, the one Garrick had made with the riding crop. Never again would he lift a hand against her and Mac—nor any other defenseless woman or child. He was truly dead now, and the hideous past buried.

After her bath she dressed in a gown, whisked a thin cotton shawl around her shoulders and took a chair beside the bed. She watched Wolf for the longest time, listened to his deep, labored breaths, his soft moans of pain. The man she loved was dying and there was nothing she could do to save him.

Waiting for him to go was the hardest part. She wasn't certain she could go on living without him. Even during those dark years when they'd been separated, his memory continued to burn brightly in her heart. The hope that they'd one day reunite and live happily ever after had kept her sane in spite of the abuse she'd endured at Garrick's hands.

She studied Wolf's face, committing every inch of it to memory, promising never to forget a single detail. Then she realized she didn't even have a photograph of him. She hugged herself tightly, the tears bursting forth. The pain of losing the only man she'd ever loved, the father of her child was unbearable. She wished it was his arms holding her like this again. She wished she would awaken and discover all of this had been a horrible nightmare.

She clenched her eyes shut and prayed for a miracle.

Evangeline awoke with a start at the sound of Wolf's voice. The room was almost pitch black, the oil in the lantern burned out. Pink rays of dawn streaked the eastern sky beyond the open window. Where were John and Mac? At first, she thought she was still dreaming when she saw Wolf's dark silhouette sitting on the side of the bed. She blinked. Was he alive? Perhaps in her grief she was hallucinating. She'd seen it happen to people many times before.

"Evangeline," he called into the darkness. "Where are you?"

"I'm here." She rose unsteadily to her feet. Her heart pounded so hard with excitement she thought it would burst. He was alive!

Wolf was alive!

"You must lie down." Quickly, she groped for matches in the darkness, then lit the wick on the bedside lantern. Tears of joy and relief blinded her as the room filled with light and she saw his face. She swiped at her tear filled eyes. "Don't try and get up, sweetheart. You've lost so much blood."

With her help, he lay back down slowly.

The moment his eyes met hers in the soft amber glow of lamplight, she crumbled. She couldn't help it. She'd not allowed herself to mourn for him, wanting to be strong in front of Mac, but once tears began flowing, she couldn't stop.

Slowly, he extended one hand to her. "Come and lie with me," he said quietly.

"I don't w-want to...h-hurt you," she sobbed.

"It would hurt me more if I could not hold you in my arms."

Gently, she took his hand and eased down beside him, trying not to bump his bandaged leg and side.

"Why are you crying? Don't you know the time for tears has ended?"

She didn't truly know why she was carrying on, except that she was overwhelmed with a floodtide of emotions. So much had happened in such a short time. The dark, ugly secret from her past had finally been set free. Garrick was dead and Wolf was alive. She sniffed hard and tried to compose herself, failing. Another round of sobs shook her. He drew her closer, letting her have a good, long cry.

"I've said things in anger that I deeply regret now," he said once she'd ceased crying. "Can you forgive me for all I've put you through?"

She was the one who should ask for forgiveness. She snuggled closer. Rising slightly, she kissed his stubbly cheek, knowing she would never take this man or her love for him for granted again. Somehow, she'd make up all the lost years to him. "I am the one who should be asking forgiveness," she whispered.

He sighed heavily and stared at the ceiling. "I know you've told me the truth about how your father forced you to leave Texas, about his threat to kill me and our child...how he sold you into marriage with Garrick Payne. But, I must confess what terrible thing I've done. When I found your advertisement in the mail order bride catalog, I wanted revenge for what your father and his ranch hands did to me. That night, just before your father put the knife to my throat, he told me something I have never forgotten. He said I wasn't good enough for you, that I needed to go find me a squaw if I wanted a woman. But when I laid eyes on you that day in Luling for the first time in years my heart melted. I realized I was still in love with you, that I'd never stopped. I was wrong to want revenge. Can you forgive my deception?"

Evangeline shut her eyes. "Oh, Wolf, the past is behind us now. Let's not dwell on it any longer."

"How is our son? Did Garrick hurt him?"

She caressed his cheek and jaw with her fingertips. "Garrick gave him a sleeping tonic, but other than that he appears well. I don't believe he harmed him."

"I still cannot believe the man faked his own death, changed his identity and stalked you all the way to Texas. After getting me out of the way, he intended to have you again—to take possession of my ranch."

"Garrick was always a greedy man. He thought of no one but himself, and didn't feel he must be accountable for his illicit deeds."

Wolf shut his eyes. "Thank God he didn't harm Mac. The boy has lived through enough." His hand lifted to her cheek. "The bastard bruised your face, didn't he?"

She covered his hand with hers. "Let's not talk about it anymore. The past is over."

He nodded. "Very well. Perhaps I should tell you of my dream—a more pleasant topic."

"Yes."

"Next summer a daughter will be born to us, Evangeline. I saw her—a beautiful little girl with straight dark hair like mine and blue eyes like yours."

"You had this dream while you were fevered?"

"Yes, but it is the truth. Her name will be Lily. I need to add a room to our cabin and build a cradle."

She sat up and mopped his brow with a damp cloth. Secretly the idea of having a daughter thrilled her, but it was too soon to think about. "Perhaps next summer *will* bring us a child, but you should rest now. There is plenty of time for talk about the future. Mac is safe and you're alive. We have so much to be thankful for. The past is truly behind us once and for all."

"Not quite. There's more business we must settle."

Evangeline eyed him curiously. What else could there be? She sucked in a breath, waited for him to answer.

"Evangeline..." He reached for her hand and cupped it gently in his. "We've been married two weeks. Last night I nearly died. Do you know that I haven't said 'I love you' yet?"

Her breath caught. No, she hadn't realized until now, but it dawned on her that she'd not said the words either. His words hit her hard. *Last night I almost died.*

"I love you." He squeezed her hand. "I've always loved you, even when we were apart all those years. I hope you know how much."

Laughter bubbled up as tears threatened. Yes, she knew. Deep in her heart and soul she'd always known. She leaned over and brushed a soft kiss to his lips. He moaned deep in his throat and his hand lifted, his fingers twining through her hair. Pins fell upon the blanket and he shook her hair free, drew it over one shoulder.

"Let me say it again." A smile tilted the corners of his mouth. "I love you, Evangeline MacKinnon, forever and always."

She choked back a sob. "And I love you, too, Gray Wolf MacKinnon. Forever and always."

THE CHANCES ARE BRIDE

Billie Warren Chai

Shiloh Springs, Texas
1872

Sheriff Josh Morrow heard his office door burst open, then slam shut, rattling the windows.

"She's here!" Deputy Roger Miller rushed down the hall toward the cells. "The mail order bride's here."

The sheriff stepped out of a small back room. "I heard you the first time." *Hell, half the county probably heard him.*

"Ya tole me to come git ya." Roger dogged his steps. "What ya goin' do, Sheriff?"

"Go meet her." Josh picked up his hat and exited the office. A moment later he heard the door slam and Roger fell into step beside him. "Run over to Reverend Huddleston and tell him and the missus to come to my office right away."

A tiny woman dressed in a blue traveling suit sat on a bench outside the depot. A ridiculous hat with a veil and green feather sat atop blonde curls. What had Barry Woods been thinking? She couldn't have been more than twenty, and how old was Woods? He had to have been at least forty.

"Excuse me, ma'am?" He removed his hat. "I'm Sheriff Josh Morrow, are you Miss Yeager?"

"Yes, I am." She looked up at him.

Damn, she was so young, so petite...and so pretty.

154

This wasn't going to be easy. He wished the stage was still there so he could put her back on it. It wasn't, and he couldn't.

"I'm afraid Mr. Woods is unavailable." He fudged. "Why don't you come to my office?" She didn't move. "You can wait inside, out of the sun."

"Will Mr. Woods know where to find me?" The veil hid her eyes, but not the uncertainty in her voice.

"Yes, ma'am." If he were in condition to find her. Which he wasn't.

"What about my bag?" She chewed a finger, despite her gloves.

"Roger'll watch your bag."

"All right." She stood and slid a small hand through the crook of his elbow.

She barely came to his shoulder. If Barry Woods wasn't dead already, Josh would've seriously considered killing him for bringing a sweet, innocent thing like her to an untamed frontier town like Shiloh Springs. He led her into his office and offered her a chair.

"Would you like some coffee or maybe some water, ma'am?"

"Water," she answered with a soft southern accent.

He picked up a coffee-stained cup and wiped it with his sleeve before filling it from a pitcher. He handed it to her.

"Thank you."

The front door opened and Reverend Huddleston and his wife entered. "Sheriff," Huddleston greeted him as his wife scrutinized Miss Yeager. The minister's wife found fault with any woman she met, especially if the woman was younger or prettier than she, which meant any woman under the age of forty or better looking than a horse. She clearly regarded herself the epitome of proper etiquette and Christian behavior and didn't mind expressing her opinion whenever she felt the need.

"Reverend, Mrs. Huddleston. This is Miss Yeager. She's a friend of Mr. Woods."

The young woman stood, extending her hand first to the minister.

"Nice to meet you, Miss Yeager," the minister said, barely touching her hand.

"Same here, sir," she replied.

Mrs. Huddleston stuck out her hand, reluctantly Josh thought, and then hastily retracted it after only slightly grazing the younger woman's hand. Damn, he hated this part of the job. But he was the sheriff and frequently it was his duty to do unpleasant things.

"Miss Yeager." He moved to face her. "There's no easy way to tell you this, but..." Her face paled. "Mr. Woods died unexpectedly three days ago." The cup clattered to the floor. "We buried him yesterday. No one was certain when you'd get here."

She started to crumple. He caught her, holding her limp body against his. The ensuing stirring of his body was unexpected. "Damn Barry Woods," he mumbled.

"Now, now, Sheriff. You shouldn't speak ill of the dead," Mrs. Huddleston tsked.

It galled him she never had a good thing to say about Woods when he was alive, or anyone else for that matter, but now that he was dead... A lot of good it did to have them present to help break the news. His horse would've been more help, if not more comfort. Ignoring them, he carried her to an empty cell and laid her on the bunk. Grabbing a towel, he wet it.

The front door opened and closed as the Huddlestons left. Good riddance, he thought.

He removed her hat and veil, then patted her pale skin with the towel. "Miss Yeager?" She remained unresponsive. Woods may have been a fool, but Josh had to admit he'd picked a pretty little thing.

Her lids fluttered, then opened—deep blue eyes mesmerized him. At that moment it seemed his heart forgot how to beat and his lungs hung in suspension as he fought for air.

It took extreme effort for Annabelle to open her eyes. Her gaze locked on the sheriff, kneeling in front of her. Was that concern she detected in his dark brown eyes? Then she remembered. She'd traveled to Shiloh

Springs to marry Barry Woods, a man she'd never met. The sheriff said Mr. Woods was dead. The room reeled when she jumped up.

"Take it easy, ma'am. You've had quite a shock."

Shock. Yes. Barry Woods' death was a shock, but while she regretted his death, how could she mourn him? Truth be told, she had no feelings one way or the other, although she was certain that in time they would have grown to love each other.

What was she going to do now? She had no money to return home. Besides, she had disgraced her family by running away to get married, so she couldn't go back to Georgia. Panic raced through her. A feeling of utter hopelessness began to sink in and she stifled the tears. Lord, she needed time to think.

"Here, drink this." The sheriff handed her a cup. "It'll calm your nerves."

She smelled the fiery fragrance of whiskey. She'd had spirits on occasion—during her monthlies when the cramps got unbearable. This pain wasn't physical, but with nowhere to turn, it was no less real.

She cradled the cup in both hands. "Thank you." The fiery liquid burned as it traveled to her stomach, landing with a thud. Warmth spread throughout her body within minutes.

"If you feel strong enough, we can go back out front. I think you'll be more comfortable there."

She nodded and stood, feeling his gaze upon her. He extended his hand to steady her, and she accepted it, realizing this is how a new colt must feel. He led the way out of the cell and she followed.

His height amazed her—at least six inches taller than her brothers and they weren't short. If she didn't look up, all she saw was his broad back covered by a cotton shirt. True, he was handsome, with brown eyes hiding under long lashes, and a strong comforting smile, but it was his gentle manner that made her feel she could trust him.

After seating herself in front of his desk, she waited until he walked around and sat in his chair. "Sheriff

Morrow, how did Mr. Woods die?"

He leaned forward, his eyes narrowed. "I won't lie to you. Someone gunned him down. Shot him in the chest five times. Whoever it was made damn sure he was dead."

She gasped. People didn't kill each other for no reason back in Georgia, at least not since the war was over.

"Miss Yeager, what did Mr. Woods tell you about himself?"

"We corresponded by letter after *A Bride for All* mail order catalog matched us up. He wrote he was thirty years old and had never been married. Stated he'd fought for the Confederacy and his family had lost everything in the war. Said they were all dead. He also mentioned he owned a restaurant and a hotel and could provide a good life for me."

Josh clenched his fists. That scoundrel Woods had outright lied to her. Now he was dead and it fell to Josh to tell her the truth.

"Miss Yeager, I'm afraid Woods wasn't exactly honest with you. He didn't own a restaurant or a hotel. He owned the Chances Are Saloon and Social Club."

Her eyes fluttered, but she stayed upright. Her small bow lips formed an 'o'. A sudden urge to touch and hold her shot through him as he felt himself being pulled into her web. Did she know what she was doing to him?

Ever since his fiancée had been raped and murdered when he'd been away fighting for the South, he'd felt overwhelming guilt. His curse in life seemed to be his failure to protect the women dear to him, including his mother and his sister who had died at the end of the war, adding salt to the wound in his heart. Over time, guilt and pain had taken its toll and he'd vowed never to let another woman near his heart. He'd kept that promise, and while some stirred his body, none had stirred his soul.

Until now.

"The eastbound stage won't be here for another five

days. I assume you'll want to be on it." It wasn't his business what she did, but damn someone needed to protect her. "Fanny Appling owns the boardinghouse. Let's get you something to eat, and then I'll go talk to her."

She nodded and accepted his arm. Outside they walked a short distance to Gloria's Cafe. People stopped and stared at the mail order bride. He couldn't help but wonder what she thought about it all.

Annabelle knew she was the object of curiosity. Everyone wanted to see the fool who'd traveled halfway across the country to marry a man she'd never met. It all seemed like a bad dream, one she couldn't awaken from. Barry Woods owned a saloon. She had no idea what a social club was, but, from the look on the sheriff's face when he'd told her, it couldn't be good.

The sheriff left the diner to see Mrs. Appling about a room for her. Confused, she had no idea what to think or do. One thing was certain—she didn't have enough money for a ticket back to Georgia. Besides, there was nothing left for her there. As her ma would've said, she'd burned her bridges and made a fool of herself in the process. This was a chance for a new life and some-how she was determined to make it work. She wouldn't be an unpaid housekeeper to her pa and brothers again.

First things first—she was hungry. She ordered a small meal of steak, mashed potatoes and coffee. Sheriff Morrow returned just as she finished eating and took a seat opposite her.

A man brought him coffee. "Thanks, Ben. This is Miss Yeager. She'll be with us until the stagecoach comes through next week. Do you have any pie?"

Sheriff Morrow turned to her. "Ben and his daughter Gloria are the owners."

She nodded her head toward Ben.

"Mrs. Appling has a room you can rent. Roger'll take your bag over."

"I don't know how to thank you." She faltered, not knowing what else to say.

Ben brought him a piece of apple pie. She was surprised to see a frontier lawman put the napkin in his lap and use the fork, not the spoon.

"It isn't necessary. Mrs. Appling's a fine Christian lady. You'll get a clean room, breakfast and supper. She doesn't like noise though."

"I hope she doesn't charge too much. I don't have much money." *Might as well tell the truth up front.*

"It's taken care of." He ate another bite of pie. "I owed Woods some money on a horse, so I just paid it to Mrs. Appling."

Did he think she needed charity? "I can pay my own expenses, Sheriff Morrow. I won't accept your charity." Her words surprised her. Past experience had taught her it was useless to argue with a man, especially one as large as the sheriff.

"It's not charity. I owed Woods and Woods owes you for what he's done to you," he growled. "I know you were all set to marry the man, but, lady, you should thank your lucky stars someone filled him full of lead. Saved you a bunch of heartache."

He pushed aside what was left of the pie and stalked toward the man at the counter and threw money down. "This should cover my pie and coffee and the lady's meal. Will you see she gets to Mrs. Appling's when she's ready?"

"I'll take care of her, Sheriff."

Stunned, her thoughts and emotions were a jumble. Finally she rose, and placed money on the counter, but Ben politely refused. After another insistence or two, she gave up.

"I'll take ya over to Mrs. Appling's," he said.

"Just give me directions." She could do this—the sheriff had no say over what she did. "I'm certain I can find it."

"I told Sheriff Morrow that I would and Ben Smith keeps his word."

After walking a short distance with him in silence, she was glad to reach the boardinghouse.

Mrs. Appling led her to a room on the second floor.

It contained a lumpy mattress on a simple wood frame, an old discolored three-drawer wooden dresser and a couple of hooks next to the door. *All the comforts of home and she didn't have to cook.*

Returning downstairs, Annabelle broached the topic of rent and was told in no uncertain terms it had been paid in advance.

"I can't allow Mr. Morrow to pay my rent. I'm certain you understand, Mrs. Appling," she pleaded. "It isn't appropriate."

"Call me Fanny since you are going to be living here. Sheriff Morrow is an honorable man. He said he was paying his debt to Woods and I have no problem with him paying for your room."

"I can pay my rent," she protested. "If you won't accept my money, then I'll help with the cooking, the cleaning or the laundry. I'm not afraid of hard work. I kept house for my pa and brothers back home in Georgia."

"I won't turn down help with the laundry." Annabelle wasn't surprised the old lady accepted her offer so quickly.

Fanny explained the bathing policy. One hot bath a week. Any more would cost extra. She heated the water on the stove and emptied it into a bathtub set up in the kitchen. Annabelle enjoyed her first hot bath since she'd left home.

Mr. Woods' death changed her future. Her dream of starting a new life with a husband who could provide for her had been shattered in an instant. She'd almost cried at the sheriff's office, but now, alone in a bathtub with warm water relaxing her muscles, the pent-up emotion of the day ran down her cheeks in a torrent of tears.

She felt better after her bath and before making her way to her room pulled on the new robe she'd made for her life as a married woman.

Sleep was elusive as thoughts assailed her. How could she have been so stupid as to travel over a thousand miles to marry a man she'd never met? She'd believed every line Barry had written.

Now she had to make a decision. She could return home to face Pa's wrath and the ridicule of the neighbors. That meant cooking and cleaning for her pa and five brothers, until Lord knew when. She'd be a worn-out old maid in no time. Or she could stay in Shiloh Springs and somehow try to build a life using what skills she had—cooking, cleaning, washing and some sewing, and she knew how to read, write and do simple ciphering, not that she had used the latter very often.

She still wanted a family of her own—a husband and children. Surely she could find another man willing to marry her. She'd seen plenty of men around town. An image of the sheriff came to mind. The man seemed as demanding as her pa and brothers. He'd told her to think about getting back on the stagecoach. He hadn't given her a choice about where to eat, then paid for her meal. And he'd found a room for her.

On the other hand, if she took a more positive attitude, he didn't have to do any of those things. She wondered if there was a Mrs. Morrow.

When she opened her eyes the next morning, bright warm sunlight streamed into her room. When had she fallen asleep?

She'd worked hard all her life and considered herself as tough as anybody. By God, she was going to make it somehow. She cleaned her face with a washcloth, brushed her hair and put on a fresh dress before hurrying downstairs. Fanny sat in the parlor sewing.

"Don't rush, dear. You had a rough trip with a bad ending, so I let you sleep in. I saved some breakfast for you." The landlady smiled and shooed her into the kitchen. "Just eat what you can."

In the warmer she found biscuits and bacon. A cup sat on the counter and she filled it with coffee. How different food tasted when it wasn't prepared slapdash at stagecoach stations. She ate two biscuits and the bacon. Then she cleaned up after herself and returned to Fanny.

"Which rooms need to have the linens laundered?"

"They were changed the day before yesterday, so

won't need changing for another two days. Ouch!" Fanny yelped, poking her finger with a needle. "Sit a spell and visit with an old lady."

"Would you like some tea?" Annabelle asked.

"Hotter than blue blazes, but tea would hit the spot. Thank you kindly."

Annabelle had just returned with two cups when a knock sounded. She answered and found a small boy standing on the porch.

"I have a message for Miss Yeager."

A message? "I'm Miss Yeager." She took the paper and shut the door. Returning to the parlor she opened the note. "Mr. Landers, attorney at law, wants to see me in his office, today," she told Fanny.

"He's a shyster," Fanny said. "Don't say I didn't warn you and don't believe him unless you see it in black and white."

Whatever it was had to be important coming from a lawyer. Her mind raced. What could it be? Anxious, she had to find out what it was right away.

"I'll go see him now." Annabelle chewed her finger-nail, something she always did when nervous.

"I reckon that's a good idea, or you won't have any fingers left." Fanny laughed as Annabelle walked out the door.

Even without Fanny's directions, Annabelle could have found Mr. Landers' office. A weather beaten sign announcing his name and profession was visible on the front of the building and the dust covered window.

She entered a small office where a man labored behind a desk. "Excuse me. I'm Annabelle Yeager. I'm looking for Mr. Landers. He asked me to meet him here."

"Oh, yes, I'm Sylvester Landers, attorney at law."

He was a stout, middle-aged gentleman with a balding head, who led her into a back office. Fanning his hand, he offered her a worn leather seat across from a huge, dark oak table with fancy carvings all around it.

"I represent Barry Woods' estate, Miss Yeager." He

sat behind the table and opened his dispatch case. "There are some issues of money that need to be settled."

Fear grabbed her and she felt as though her arms were being tied behind her back. He expected her to repay the money to Barry. "I don't have any money, Mr. Landers."

"That isn't a problem." He leafed through his papers.

"I said I can't repay the money Mr. Woods sent me." She wrung her hands. "I don't have it." Panic set in hard.

He peered at her over his spectacles. "What? Miss Yeager, I didn't ask you to come here about the money Mr. Woods sent you. I asked you here about your inheritance."

"Inheritance?" Her heart pounded.

He removed his glasses. "Mr. Woods kept his affairs in order. After you accepted his marriage proposal, he set up a will leaving everything to you."

Her jaw dropped. It was a good thing she was sitting. "Everything?"

"Everything, lock, stock and barrel," he repeated. "The Chances Are Saloon and Social Club, his bank accounts and his personal property. They're all yours now."

"I don't know what to say." Her hands trembled. A man she didn't know, the man she would've married, had left her all his property. Well, she would've made him a good wife, if he hadn't died.

"It won't be final 'til tomorrow when I take it to the judge and get it signed. It's at least a half day's ride to the county seat and I'll be back the day after tomorrow with the signed documents. I just need your signature on a few papers." One at a time, he handed her sheets of paper, briefly explaining them to her. She signed them and handed them back.

He gathered the papers into his case. "I wouldn't advise you telling anyone until I have the signed papers. No sense being pestered by any busybodies."

She stood to leave and he escorted her to the door. "Thank you, Miss Yeager. I'll take care of everything." She walked out onto the boardwalk. Her pa always said life was unpredictable. How quickly her fortune had changed.

Josh wanted to hit something. He'd tossed and turned all night as that little piece of fluff wreaked havoc with his sleep.

He stomped down the boardwalk with a scowl on his face. People stepped out of his way. Those who spoke got a tip of the hat and maybe a terse hello.

Ahead he saw the bane of his existence stepping out of the lawyer's office. What would she be doing there? Maybe she'd inquired about her rights as Barry Woods' fiancée before he died. Maybe even a little money to get her back to Georgia. There was no way to avoid her. "Good morning, Miss Yeager." He tipped his hat. She looked different, not quite like a woman whose fiancé had died suddenly.

Annabelle gifted him with a smile. "Good morning, Sheriff Morrow. It's a nice day, maybe a little on the warm side, but the breeze helps."

Was she actually discussing the weather with him? What had happened overnight? "If you need any help around town, don't hesitate to ask. I'll be glad to show you around." Why did he say that when all he wanted was to be as far away from her as possible.

"Thank you, Sheriff." He detected a fleeting sparkle in her blue eyes.

"Josh. Call me Josh." It sounded so stuffy when she referred to him as sheriff.

"All right, Josh. But you must call me Annabelle." He imagined her warm and inviting smile was just for him. "I need some thread. Where can I find some?"

"Johnson's Emporium. I'm headed that way." He held out his arm and she took it. At that instant he felt her special warmth wrap around his heart and cascade through his body. He could hear his blood rush. The more he tried to suppress his feelings, the more he realized his heart was aching for her and he was hopelessly entangled in her web of innocence. They walked together along the boardwalk until they reached the store. Josh opened the door and ushered her inside. The bell on the door announced their entrance.

"Sheriff Morrow, how can I help you? I'm afraid I haven't gotten in more books." Mrs. Johnson greeted him, then stopped abruptly when she saw Annabelle.

"Mrs. Johnson, this is Annabelle Yeager. She needs some thread." Everyone in town knew about the mail order bride, so the introduction was for Annabelle's benefit.

Josh recognized the sudden coolness in Mrs. Johnson's demeanor. Her daughter, Patricia, had designs on him. He'd been invited to dinner with the Johnsons more times than he cared to remember and he was running out of excuses. They were nice people and she was a fine girl, but he didn't feel that spark or that special warmth he'd felt deep in his heart only once before and not again until Annabelle Yeager walked into his life.

No, this was wrong. He couldn't, shouldn't. The stage was due back in a few days. He just had to keep his distance until then.

"I need some dark blue thread," Annabelle said.

"I'm sorry for your loss," Mrs. Johnson added, clearly devoid of any genuine sympathy.

"Thank you." Annabelle looked at the thread proffered by Mrs. Johnson. "Yes, this will do. Five yards should be adequate."

"Do you plan on staying in town or returning East?" Mrs. Johnson cut to the heart of the matter.

"My plans are unsettled. I may stay in Shiloh Springs."

"I don't have any openings, and I don't think there are any openings in town unless you want to work over at the Chances Are Saloon." Vinegar practically dripped from her fangs as she forestalled any attempt Annabelle might make at finding a job.

"Now, Mrs. Johnson, Miss Yeager isn't the type of person to work at the Chances Are, and I'm certain she'll find a suitable position in town," Josh interjected, "if she decides to stay." The words sounded strange and far away. Did they come out of his mouth? He reminded himself that he wanted her on the stage headed out of town.

She paid for her purchase and he escorted her out the door. He wouldn't make the mistake of trying to pay for her things again.

"Sorry. I don't know what got into Mrs. Johnson," Josh said outside the emporium.

"I need to get back. Mrs. Appling will be expecting me to help with dinner." She smiled at him again and he melted like butter on a hot biscuit.

"Yes, ma'am." He tipped his hat. "I'll continue with my rounds. Good afternoon."

"Good afternoon, Josh," she said before turning and heading toward the boardinghouse.

Josh continued his rounds through town and pondered on Annabelle. She seemed likeable enough, but what had driven her to become a mail order bride? To Barry Woods of all people.

Even now the thought of Woods caused his skin to crawl. The man was bad, no doubt about it. His contacts with Woods had been few and far between. He didn't frequent Woods' establishments except as sheriff. The man defined the words weasel and cheat. The Chances Are Saloon and Social Club demanded more attention than any other business in town. Alcohol combined with card cheating created a volatile situation and kept him busy, particularly on Saturday nights. Throw in the social club, a fancy name for a brothel, and it was a real problem.

Barry Woods had been an enigma to everyone in town. No one knew who he was or where he hailed from. Story was he showed up in town one day with enough cash to buy the old saloon which was on the verge of closing. Business boomed after Lauren Thamann opened the social club on the second floor of the saloon. Cowboys flocked in from surrounding counties. Woods seemed to have a lot of business sense and a lot of money. He was seldom seen outside the saloon. Rumor was he'd made his fortune running Yankee blockades during the war. Needless to say, a man like him had enemies and some thought he was hiding out in Shiloh Springs, but no one knew for sure and Woods wasn't talking.

Annabelle made her way to the boardinghouse. Barry left her all his property! She would use the money to make a new life for herself.

One thing was certain; she didn't have to go home. Did she want to stay in Shiloh? She didn't know, but she owned property now and didn't have to make a decision right away.

Admittedly, accepting Barry Woods' proposal had been a pretty bad idea. He lied to her about owning a hotel and restaurant. Did he lie about loving her? Of course he had, but his marriage proposal was real. Why did he want a wife? What happened that made him secretly make out a will and leave all his earthly possessions to a woman he'd never met? She'd never know what kind of a man he was or the husband he would've made, but one thing was darn sure—his gift was real and had no strings attached. Woods must've loved her in his own strange way. Silently, she thanked him.

The boardinghouse loomed before her. Fanny sat on the porch snapping a pan of beans. Annabelle pushed all thoughts of men to the back of her mind.

"Let me help you." She sat beside Fanny, picked up a handful of the beans and began to work on them. Her younger, agile fingers worked more quickly than the older woman's.

"You have a nice trip around town?" Fanny was clearly fishing for information on her business with Mr. Landers. Annabelle avoided it.

They discussed the Johnsons at the store. She learned Patricia, the daughter, thought the sheriff would marry her. For some unknown reason that bothered her, but it explained Mrs. Johnson's hostility toward her.

Annabelle finished snapping the last of the beans.

Fanny picked up the bowl and started inside. "Better get these on if we're gonna eat them for dinner."

Together they fixed supper. It wasn't any different than meals back home. Annabelle volunteered to do the dishes and help straighten the kitchen.

"Goodnight, Fanny," she said after they'd finished. "I'm going to bed."

"Go right ahead," Fanny replied. "You need to peel potatoes in the morning."

She gave Fanny a quick smile as she stopped on the stairs. She squeezed the banister so hard her knuckles were white. What had just changed? Was she a paying tenant or a charity case?

The next two days, Annabelle stayed at the boardinghouse and Mrs. Appling treated her like the hired help. Her patience was beginning to wear thin when Mr. Landers sent for her.

She put on the only clean dress she had and told Mrs. Appling she was going out. Before she got out the door, Mrs. Appling handed her a shopping list. She shoved it into her reticule.

At the lawyer's office, Mr. Landers ushered her to his desk.

"Thank you for coming, Miss Yeager. The Judge signed the papers and you're now the legal owner of the Chances Are Saloon and Social Club. Money at the bank has been transferred to an account in your name. All that remains is my fee." He presented her with a bill.

It was over a hundred dollars. "I don't have this much money," she lamented.

"Yes, you do—at the bank. We can go there and I'll introduce you to Mr. Webber."

"I'm not sure what to do next." She pushed the panic away, certain he'd tell her.

"You're the owner of the saloon and social club. The employees work and have to be paid. Rufus, the bartender, has been paying them out of the daily receipts. I'll take you there and introduce you to him, too." He pulled his watch out of his vest pocket. "We can do it now."

"Now?" she stammered.

"Yes, it's a perfect time." He gathered up some papers and put them in his dispatch case, then led her to the door and locked it behind them.

At the bank, Mr. Landers introduced her to the bank employees. Mr. Webber wasn't in. To her surprise, over five hundred dollars was in an account with her name. She arranged payment for Mr. Landers and thanked the attentive clerk.

Mr. Landers then led Annabelle to the back entrance of the saloon and knocked on the door. A fat man with greasy hair answered. "Mr. Landers, come in." The man stared at her.

"Rufus, this is Miss Annabelle Yeager, Mr. Woods' fiancée." They went inside to a small office. "Mr. Woods made a will out after Miss Yeager agreed to marry him. It was important to him to provide for her. He left the saloon, the social club and all his assets to her."

Rufus sat as if he had been pole-axed. "What does that mean?"

"This young lady is the new owner of the Chances Are Saloon and Social Club."

Rufus' jaw dropped. "The new owner? I work for *her* now?"

"Yes, you do, Rufus, and I expect Mr. Woods would want you to extend every courtesy to her. She doesn't know anything about running a saloon, so we're going to have to help her."

Rufus' stare cut through her. Maybe he expected to end up with the business after Mr. Woods' death. "I know this is a shock to you; it was for me, too. I'd appreciate your help as you obviously know how to run a saloon." She added quickly studying Rufus' reaction.

"You do know this is a saloon and uh—social club?"

"Yes, I know, but I'm not certain what a social club is. Is it a hotel?"

The men looked at each other. Rufus finally spoke. "It's a brothel, Miss Yeager. Lauren Thamann is the madam. She pays rent and a percentage to the house,"—

he pointed a finger at her—"which is you."

She owned a brothel! A whorehouse! What had Barry Woods done to her?

"Of course, you can always sell the business and the buildings," Mr. Landers volunteered.

"Lauren isn't going to be happy about this. She thought Barry was going to marry her." Rufus furrowed his brow. "I don't know how she's going to take this news."

"She doesn't have a choice," Mr. Landers said. "Judge already signed the papers."

"What papers?" a female voice asked.

Annabelle stared at the tall woman dressed in what appeared to be an expensive day gown. Her long red hair hung loose down her back. Red tint colored her cheeks and lips. A little on the stout side, maybe even chubby, an air of arrogance and authority surrounded her.

"Miss Thamann, this is Miss Annabelle Yeager, Mr. Woods' fiancée," Mr. Landers explained. "Miss Yeager, this is Miss Lauren Thamann."

"Nice to meet you." Annabelle offered her hand.

"I don't believe it." She rested her hands on her hips, ignoring Annabelle. "Barry loved me and we were planning to be married. She's lying."

"No Lauren, she ain't lying. Mr. Woods told me about it. Sent for her from Georgia," Rufus said.

"Mr. Woods also made provisions for Miss Yeager in the event of his death. He left her all his property, including the saloon and social club," Mr. Landers added.

Lauren clenched her hands into tight fists and her mouth tightened. "Barry wouldn't do that to me. The Chances Are is rightfully mine, she can't have it."

"The will was offered for probate and the judge already signed the papers. There's nothing you can do," the attorney explained.

"We'll see about that." She spun on a heel and clomped out of the office. Her heavy footfalls on the steps echoed through the building as she stomped upstairs.

Rufus opened a drawer and pulled out a book. "This is the ledger. You can read and write?"

"Yes, I can read and write and do my numbers." Obviously Rufus didn't have a very high opinion of women.

"I reckon you better start learning the saloon business. This'll give you a good idea of what goes on. We sell alcohol-liquor-all kinds. There's gambling and each table pays the house fifty percent of the take. Lauren runs the social club and pays fifty percent of those proceeds to the house." Rufus tapped the books and gave her a short lesson about running a saloon.

She looked at the ledger, but her head hurt so much the numbers danced on the pages. "I'll look at this later. You'll stay on won't you?"

"For the time being. I need to order whiskey and beer. There's enough for the next two weeks, but it takes a week for an order to get here. The barmaids have been paid and I drew my pay last week. Mr. Landers has been overseeing the books since Barry died. The piano player needs to be paid."

"By all means, pay him, please. What about the... er...ladies?"

"Lauren handles them. She hires and fires the girls, collects the payments and pays them. The house takes care of the furnishings and linens. The girls pay a re-duced weekly rate for their rooms."

"Oh." She sat, numbed.

"Why don't you show her around?" Mr. Landers said.

"It ain't proper for a lady to be in a saloon," Rufus protested.

"She owns it, she should check out her property," snapped Mr. Landers, clearly losing his patience.

"Well, I reckon," Rufus conceded. "We're in the office. Out there is the saloon and upstairs is the social club."

"I think we would like to see it," Mr. Landers said, looking at her.

"You've been here before, Landers, including

upstairs," Rufus challenged.

Mr. Landers' face flushed with embarrassment until he looked like a ripe tomato. "Miss Yeager hasn't seen it," he stuttered in protest.

"All right," Rufus stood and led them into the bar. "This is the saloon. Customers drink at the bar or at tables. Those tables back there are reserved for gambling." He walked to the door next to the office and unlocked it—the supply room. Next, he showed her the bar and all its bottles, before he pointed out a piano sitting in a darkened corner of the hall. Unless you knew it was there, it could've been just another piece of furniture.

"Do you serve food?" Barry had written about a restaurant in his letters.

"No kitchen," Rufus said. "This is the grand tour unless you want to go upstairs. All the girls are sleeping, except for Miss Lauren."

"I think I'll wait 'til another time. Is it always this dark in here?"

"No need to light the place when it's empty, and drunks don't much like bright lights," Rufus explained. "The gaming tables are lit to keep down the cheating. Mr. Woods didn't tolerate cheating."

"I don't condone cheating either."

"Thanks for the tour, Rufus. I think Miss Yeager is a little overwhelmed. I better get her back," Mr. Landers said.

Hurrying down the street, they returned to the front of his office.

"If you need anything at all, just let me know. Rufus and I will help you through it the best we can." He started to go into the office. "Maybe you better come inside a minute."

He took a seat at his desk. "I better warn you. Barry told me someone wanted to buy him out and was trying to cause problems." Mr. Landers leaned back in his chair. "If someone offers to buy you out, check with me first. They may make a real low offer hoping you don't know the value."

"I will, and thank you so much," she said shaking his hand.

Annabelle left and went by the mercantile for some tooth powder. The doorbell announced her presence, and Mrs. Johnson and an older lady stopped talking. Annabelle felt their long hard stares. She made her purchases and left the store.

A soft afternoon breeze caressed her skin and a sudden memory of a carefree little girl frolicking in the mountain streams of Georgia on a hot summer day came to mind. The war had snuffed out her dream of a home and family as one by one young men marched off to war, never to return. She came to Shiloh Springs in an attempt to resurrect that dream, but it had been extinguished again. It was only a few days ago she faced either going back to Georgia and its hardships or trying to make it on her own. Now she owned a business and her future looked bright. But deep in her heart, she still wanted that little girl's dream.

Before she could get to the boardinghouse, Fanny came storming up the street toward her like the Confederates coming out to meet the Yankees.

"Miss Yeager, I heard you inherited the Chances Are Saloon and Social Club," she snapped.

"Yes, Mr. Woods was kind enough to provide for me, despite our not being married," she stammered. What good would it do to deny it?

"I won't have it in my house. You have to leave right now."

Mrs. Appling was kicking her out. "You can't do that, I paid for a week in advance."

"You didn't tell me you owned the saloon. I don't allow people like you in my house," she ranted. "Pack your things and get out."

It was senseless trying to argue with her, so Annabelle returned to the boardinghouse and packed her meager belongings. Normally she would have removed the soiled linens from the bed, but she saw no reason to do so now.

"Do you know another place in town where I—" She

stopped, realizing she shouldn't have asked.

"Why don't you sleep at the social club, since you own it?"

Surely there had to be some place for her to stay.

Minutes later Annabelle stood in the middle of town carrying her bag. There was no hotel. Perhaps Mr. Landers would know where she could stay. She hurried to his office, but found the door locked and he didn't answer her knock.

She was still standing there when Sheriff Morrow appeared. Her heart skipped a beat in anticipation of his touch. If he was going to order her around again and try to get her to leave town, he better think again.

"Miss Yeager, is something wrong?" He stopped a respectable distance away.

"I was hoping Mr. Landers could tell me some place to stay."

"I thought you were staying at Mrs. Appling's." A smile quirked the corner of his lips.

"She threw me out because I inherited Mr. Woods' property—lock, stock and barrel."

"You what?" Josh removed his hat and wiped his brow.

"Mr. Woods executed a will leaving everything to me, including the saloon and...social club. So Mrs. Appling won't let me stay at her house any longer." Annabelle really didn't want to discuss it standing on the street, but had no choice.

"There isn't a hotel in town and she has the only boardinghouse." His eyes narrowed and a facial muscle twitched. "Why don't you wait at my office and I'll see what I can find."

Carrying her bag, he started walking toward his office as she struggled to keep up with his long stride. The squeaking boardwalk seemed to mock her.

Sheriff Morrow dropped her bag and lit a small lamp on his desk. "Wait here 'til I get back." The grim set of his jaw portrayed a man who didn't take his job lightly. It would've frightened her a few days ago, but she'd seen how people in town respected him. Clearly, he was a good man.

"Thank you. Seems like you're always coming to my rescue." She felt safe when he was around, like how he helped smooth away the bad things that had happened to her.

Josh left Annabelle in his office. Mrs. Appling was in her rights not to rent to her, but it wasn't fair. He just had to find another place for her to stay since she couldn't sleep on the street and didn't know anyone in town. He didn't want to be responsible for another woman getting hurt when he could stop it.

He entered the Emporium and approached Mrs. Johnson. "I need your help," he began. "Seems Miss Yeager inherited Woods' property, including the saloon and social club. Mrs. Appling told her to leave. Do you have a room she could rent?"

"I'd lose business if I let a woman like that stay here. Why can't she stay at the Chances Are? They have rooms there." A wicked grin crossed her face. "Maybe she and Miss Lauren can share a room. Excuse me, I have work to do."

Damn, he should've expected that kind of response.

He tried several other places, including the pastor, all without success. They couldn't let a woman who owned a saloon and social club in their home or business. Mrs. Huddleston strongly lectured him on why God's people should stay clear of people like Miss Yeager and how the sheriff should be ashamed of getting involved with her. Josh trudged back to the jail. It surprised him how fast everyone passed judgment on Annabelle when she hadn't done anything wrong.

Annabelle sat at the desk reading a Mark Twain book he'd left there.

"I'm sorry, Annabelle. There isn't a room to be had in town. I was told several times that you could stay at the Chances Are." His gut wrenched as her face paled. "There is one other place, but I don't think I could let you stay there."

"I'd be happy to stay anywhere but the Chances

Are," she said, "including here at the jail."

A smile crossed his lips. "Well, that was the spot I was thinking about." Did he have the right to offer it? The town owned the jail. Annabelle owned property and that made her a citizen, didn't it. Oh hell, what difference did it make?

"You haven't changed your mind?" Annabelle asked. Worry lines creased her young face.

He couldn't raise her hopes and then dash them. That would make him the worst kind of a heel.

"No, but only because we don't have any prisoners right now. When we get one, you'll have to leave. All I can offer is the bunk to sleep on. You'll have to take your meals elsewhere and other things, too."

"What other things?" Her innocent blue eyes did him in.

"You know." He couldn't say it. "Uh, well, er, ladies things." Lord, what the hell had he gotten himself into?

"No, I don't know."

He willed someone, anyone, to come through the door, but it remained resolutely shut.

"Bathing and washing and such." Damn, now he'd done it, he'd mentioned the unmentionables. If his cousins heard about it, he'd never hear the end of it.

"Fair enough. Who's here at night?"

"No one unless we have a prisoner," Josh answered. "I'll lock up the jail when I leave. Roger has no business here at night unless something happens and I require his help. You'll know it's me when I come around. People know where to find me if they need me at night."

Josh admired Annabelle's spunk. It took a lot for a woman to come west by herself to marry a stranger. She was not only beautiful but brave. Still he was reluctant to leave her in the jail by herself. Hell, what could happen? Well, there could be a fire, but that could occur anywhere. Would he worry about a man, say his brother, staying in the jail? No, but damn it, she was a woman, and a damn fine woman at that, and he just couldn't ignore that fact. He hadn't felt this way since he met his fiancée back before the war.

"I understand, Josh," she said.

If she did, she was the first female in the history of mankind to understand a man.

"I can't stay here if there is a prisoner. I'll eat at the diner, and do ah—other things some place else." She sat down heavily in the chair. "I might as well leave town."

To his surprise, he no longer wanted her on that stage out of town. "It's late and I'm hungry." He had to stop her before the tears came. "I bet you are, too. We'll just go over to Gloria's and get dinner." He didn't give her much choice, grabbing her elbow, picking up her reticule and pushing her out the door.

The long shadows of evening were falling. On the way to the diner, they passed Mrs. Appling. Annabelle stiffened while he glared at the pompous old woman, forcing her to remain silent.

At Gloria's, he held the door for her. As she entered Gloria rushed forward, evidently to shoo her out of the restaurant, but stopped short when she saw him. So this was the way it was going to be.

Gloria escorted them to a table in the rear where *decent* folks wouldn't see Annabelle, but Josh stopped at a table in the middle of the room. "This one will do just fine," he said, pulling out a chair for Annabelle and sitting down himself. He could almost see steam pouring out of Gloria's ears and lightning bolts shooting out of her eye sockets.

He ordered steak and potatoes for them. Gloria's discomfort about Annabelle's presence was evident because the food arrived in record time.

"Eat up," he said when Annabelle hesitated. "She won't turn down money. Nor will she serve any food left on your plate to others, so eat up.

"I suppose not." She cut the steak and ate a bite. "This is very good."

All conversation ceased as her fork remained in constant motion from her plate to her mouth until the plate was empty. He couldn't remember watching a woman eat so much at one time. And he didn't remember eating his own food when he found his plate empty, too.

"Would you like some dessert?" he asked. Personally, he couldn't get enough of Gloria's apple pie.

"I shouldn't," she said biting her lower lip. "Do they have good desserts?"

"Gloria has the best apple pie in Texas. I'm going to have a piece."

"Then I will, too." Annabelle laughed.

Gloria took his order and returned with two slices. She stood nearby as he savored the taste of the pie. "Wonderful as always." Despite her pique, she puffed out at his praise.

Annabelle took a tentative taste. "This is very good." He wasn't sure if she meant it, but clearly Gloria thought she did. The woman fairly beamed.

"Won first place at the Fourth of July Celebration five times in a row."

"I can see why." Annabelle finished the last of the pie. "That was delicious," she said to Gloria.

"Thank you." Gloria replied with a smile. He pulled out a few coins and paid the bill. Then he escorted Annabelle back to the jail.

He unlocked the door and led her inside. How could he leave her here alone?

"Annabelle," he said, "I don't feel right leaving you here by yourself."

"I'll be all right, Josh. I've stayed in worse places. It was pretty bleak on the farm at times, particularly during the war."

He took a seat at the desk while she sat in the chair on the other side. "Don't tell me you were in the fighting?"

"No, but they fought all around us. Troops from both sides moved through so often we didn't pay attention to them anymore. It wasn't too bad until Sherman came through and torched everything for miles, including our house. Pa hid me in our root cellar. He'd built a false wall to hide me. It saved me from the Yankees. My best friend Miranda killed herself after they had...all had her."

By her expression, he could tell the memories were

painful.

"The soldiers beat Pa before they burned the house around me. After that he was never the same."

Getting up and taking her in his arms, he held her until the body shaking sobs died. He wiped her eyes with his bandana. "That's over and you're in Shiloh Springs now. You got a new life and a future ahead of you."

"Some future. The only restaurant in town serves me only when you're with me. The only boardinghouse throws me out and no one else would even consider renting me a room. All because I inherited Mr. Woods' properties. I've been in them once, and never met him."

"They don't know anything about you." He stepped back. Holding her caused too many problems and one big problem he didn't want her to see. "They only know about Barry Woods and the kind of businesses he ran in town. You just have to give them a chance to know you. You'll see changes in people once they know who you are."

"It's difficult to do when they're shutting doors in my face."

"Why don't you get some sleep and things will look different in the morning?" He still felt uneasy about leaving her alone in the jail.

"You're right. I'm keeping you from your duties." She moved to the cell and tested the mattress. "I've slept on much worse. Thank you, Josh." She bounced on the bed a few times. He needed to get out of here before he lost control.

"I'll make my rounds and check on you before I go home." When he left, he locked the door behind him.

Annabelle plopped onto the cot. Tears that never fell during the years of war and deprivation burst forth. Damn Barry Woods and the Chances Are Saloon and Social Club. Damn the townspeople of Shiloh Springs.

If it wasn't against her nature, she'd take all Barry's money, sell the properties and leave town. She'd survived the war, the Yankees hadn't driven her from her home and a few narrow-minded bigots wouldn't drive her away from this town either.

She wiped the tears and steeled her spine. No longer penniless, she was now a businesswoman. She'd take things one day at a time. Worrying wasn't going to do her any good.

Closing the saloon and social club might satisfy the town busybodies, but she needed to generate money. Barry told her he owned a restaurant and hotel. The town had a restaurant, but there was no hotel. The idea had possibilities. The girls in the social club used the rooms upstairs for their—uh, business. She could turn them into hotel rooms. Her mind was mulling over the prospect when she heard a key in the lock.

Relief filled her when Josh entered. She entertained running to meet him, throwing her arms around him and enjoying his warm embrace. But perhaps he wouldn't like her touching him.

"Just making sure you're all right." The shadows played across his face emphasizing his stubble. His maleness threatened to overwhelm her.

"I'm fine. Just one thing." She didn't want to say it, but had to. "I need to use the necessary."

He led her to the back where a heavy bar lay across the door. After removing it, they stepped into the alley. He pointed her in the direction of the privy. "I'll wait over here. Call out when you're done."

She entered the small wooden structure and used it as quickly as possible. "I'm ready."

Josh placed his hand at the small of her back and ushered her back into the jail. Once inside he relocked and barred the door. "The cell won't lock unless you use the key. So you won't be locked in. If anyone comes to the door, don't answer it, don't open it, and don't say anything. Do you understand?"

"Yes. No one is to know I'm here."

"Right, I'll lock the door behind me like I always do. Keep the light low and in the back." Josh walked to the door. "When I come back, I'll knock, then unlock the door. Good-night, Annabelle."

She wanted him to stay. But before she could utter a word, he was gone. "Good-night, Josh," she whispered to herself.

She made her way back to the cell and changed into her nightclothes. The cool sheets soon warmed. The lights and shadows dancing around the room made her uneasy.

Her thoughts turned to Josh. He seemed like a good man who took his responsibilities seriously and the townspeople clearly respected him. For all his ordering her about, she realized it was for her own good, not to get something for himself. A handsome man, he bore few visible scars on his face and hands. His touch left her breathless and light-headed. Her head swam, her breath caught in her chest and an ache formed low in her abdomen, driving her to yearn for his touch. She'd known him for only a few days and here she was—wanting him.

Violent pounding on the door woke her from a deep sleep. It was still nighttime. Someone was outside the door. She lay still, refusing to breathe lest they know she was inside.

"Sheriff, you in there with that little girl? We want some of that, too."

Oh no! If Josh were here, he'd know what to do. All she had to protect herself was a broom. She slipped from the bed as the man continued to yell. Crawling to the desk, she grabbed the keys and took them back to the cell as the man continued to pound and tried to peer in the window.

Inside the cell she pulled the door closed behind her and fitted the key in the lock until she heard it click.

She slid under the bed with the blanket. She whispered, "The Lord is my Shepherd, I shall not want." The Twenty-third Psalm, which she'd recited repetitively while hiding from the Yankees during the war, poured from her lips. Violent smashing of the window caused her to cover her ears and shudder with fear. They were coming through the window!

"Well, that bitch has to be here. We ain't found her

no place else in town."

Annabelle held her breath.

"The boss says to kill her, but nothing says we can't have fun first."

"Ain't no other place in town would take her. She being a whore and all."

How could she be a whore? She'd never even been with a man. Pain and fear gripped her. Would they find a way into the cell? She didn't dare breathe.

"Where you at whore?" one called out. "Finished servicing the sheriff? We're next."

They moved through the jail. "Come on out here, girl, we want some, too. Just give us some of what you gave the sheriff."

She pulled herself as far into the corner as possible. Memories of the war spiked through her. The blanket filled her mouth to muffle any sounds she might make. Only the scarcest of breaths reached her lungs.

The men rattled the cell door. It held. "Come on, whore, open up." The door rattled violently. "We'll get you one way or another."

"Step away from that cell!" Josh's thundering voice filled the jail and chased away her fear. "Turn around and put your hands on the wall."

"We ain't doin' nothin'." The cell door rattled again. Gunshots filled the air.

Did they kill Josh? Her heart sank until she heard his voice.

"Annabelle! It's Josh. Where are you?" Footsteps moved toward the cell. The door rattled. She looked out from under the cot. Josh stood at the cell door. She thanked God.

"Annabelle, are you hurt?" He rattled the door. "Where's the key?"

"I have it."

"Josh, you in there?" She recognized Roger Miller's voice.

"Yeah. We have two dead in here." He looked at her. She saw anger in his eyes, but it wasn't for her.

"What happened?" Roger asked.

"These two broke into the jail. Miss Yeager locked herself in the cell to protect herself." Both men eyed her, standing there in her nightgown and bare feet. "They refused to surrender and drew on me."

"He was one bad hombre," Roger opined, craning his neck to look at one of them. "Kicked dogs and kids for no reason."

"Would you open the cell, Miss Yeager?" Josh asked.

She retrieved the key and shakily unlocked the door. He wrapped a strong arm around her shoulders and used his body to shield her from the dead while ushering her into the front office. She sat in one of the chairs, her head in her hands. Josh got a blanket and wrapped it around her. His hands rested on her shoulders for a few moments reassuring her.

"Roger, go find the undertaker and get something to board up this window. I want them out of here," he gestured toward the bodies.

"What happened? Don't leave anything out." Josh asked her.

"I was asleep when someone knocked on the door and started yelling. I did like you said and ignored it." She pulled the blanket closer. "He continued to pound. I got the keys and locked myself in the cell. They broke the window and came in. I hid under the bunk."

"Did they say anything?"

"They said they wanted what you got." She stiffened. "They called me a...a whore. One said the boss wanted them to...to kill me, but he wanted to have fun first." Just having Josh close calmed her. He would protect her.

"Well, you can't stay here now. Once Roger gets back, I'll take you to my place and you can stay there. I'll stay here." He looked around.

Damn. This was his fault. Josh knew he shouldn't have left her alone. Someone had killed Barry Woods and now someone had attempted to kill her. It had to be connected to the Chances Are. Once again, a woman he cared about had been hurt because he hadn't protected her. This was the last time. He would keep her safe and find the culprit.

Moments later others arrived and he sent them away. He had no patience with people who were just too nosy for their own good and besides he didn't want people gawking. Reverend Huddleston showed up uninvited and went to the back to pray for the not so dearly departed.

"Reverend, I would appreciate it if you'd put your efforts into comforting the living." He motioned at Annabelle. Although he wanted nothing more than to take her into his arms, it wasn't proper. How had she gotten under his skin so fast?

The Reverend moved over to Annabelle. She looked up at Huddleston. Her eyes, how Josh loved her eyes.

"Oh dear, what a trial you've endured."

"Thank you, Reverend, but I'm quite all right. You can return home."

Thank God she dismissed the windbag. Josh ushered the man to the door. "Thank you, Reverend. I'm sure Digger will let you know about the funerals." Recognizing the man's reluctance to leave, he quickly added, "I'm certain Mrs. Huddleston is worried."

"Yes, yes, I'm sure she is." The minister rushed out of the jail like the devil was on his coattails.

"We didn't need him," Roger said as he showed up with Digger, the undertaker.

Josh walked to the cell area with them and picked up the dead men's guns. "They won't be needing these now. Take them out the back door." He unlocked it.

"Yes, sir," the undertaker responded. "I'll just move the wagon around back." He left through the front door only to enter through the back a few minutes later.

"I'm going to take Miss Yeager to my room. I'll be back directly." He took her arm and thought more about his decision to let her stay first at the jail and then his room. "Don't anyone go thinking bad things about Miss Yeager and me. I'll be bunking here at the jail, like I should have in the first place."

As he spoke, he found himself staring at Annabelle.

The blanket had slipped loose and the silhouette of her curvaceous body in her nightgown danced eerily against the dimly lit lantern as it mesmerized him beyond redemption. Without hesitation, he rewrapped the cover around her.

He slammed the door behind them and walked her through the dark, deserted street.

At the blacksmith's shop, he took her to his room. The room was neat because he had yet to sleep in it that night. No matter how hard he'd tried, he couldn't get Annabelle out of his mind—her eyes, her lips, and her body. He'd imagined her softness, her fragrance and the taste of her sweetness. He'd wanted to be near her and was making rounds for the third time when they'd broken into the jail.

Now he wanted to stay and hold her, but he couldn't. She had to have been scared out of her wits just like in the war. How could such a fragile looking beauty be so brave and tough?

She crawled up on the bed, her legs hanging over the edge.

"You stay here. Do you know how to use a gun?"

"Yes. Pa and my brothers made sure I could use a pistol and shotgun."

"I've got a shotgun." He pulled it out of a corner. "Keep it by the bed. If anyone you don't know shows up, shoot first and ask questions later."

She nodded.

"Go to sleep, no one will bother you here." Of course, he'd said the very same thing about the jail. Josh tucked her in his bed and watched her close her angel eyes. His pants tightened as he hardened. He stepped out the door, locking it behind him.

When he returned to the jail, the bodies were gone. He'd scrub the blood stains later.

Stretched out on the same bunk where Annabelle had slept, he thought about what she'd said. Someone wanted her dead. Why? The answer kept coming back to the Chances Are Saloon. Barry Woods owned it and someone murdered him. Annabelle had saved herself from the same fate.

He was too tired for serious thinking. Changing his mind, he arose, found the brush and a bucket in the backroom and started to scrub the blood. Damn, they hadn't given him any choice. He'd much preferred capturing them so he could find out who hired them. No doubt there would be another attempt on Annabelle's life. Much as he wanted to kill the person who hired them, he'd let him meet Judge King who didn't have a compassionate bone in his body. He scrubbed harder.

Finished with the cleanup, his mind drifted as he drank another cup of coffee. Annabelle kept invading his thoughts. Her cute little bare feet under the nightgown, tousled hair, pretty face and bow lips caused his body to hum with anticipation. He wasn't a randy schoolboy, but a twenty-eight year old man who wasn't celibate. The last time he'd given away his heart had been to his fiancée, but heck, he wasn't giving it away this time—Annabelle was stealing it.

Earlier, he'd sent Roger to the hardware store about the broken window. While Josh was making his rounds, Doug Tipton, the hardware store owner, made the repair. Everything seemed normal in town except for women raising their noses at him, which he took in stride.

Doug met him on the sidewalk. "You want me to put that wender on your bill?"

Hell no. "No, it's the county's window. Send the bill to them." He took two steps and stopped. "Why would you think I'd pay for it?"

"Guess because it was yor girlfriend sleepin' in the jail. Wender wouldn't gotten broke if she hadn't been in the jail." Doug rubbed the back of his neck as he leaned on his broom. "She should've gone to the Chances Are. There's plenty of room there."

He grabbed Doug and slammed him up against the wall. "Miss Yeager is a lady. She couldn't stay with whores and have any hope of ever holding her head up in Shiloh Springs."

A crowd quickly gathered and he turned to face

them. "She came here with only one intention—to get married. Woods died and left her a way to survive—the saloon." He saw the preacher standing in the crowd. "I ought to rip down that cross on the church because it doesn't mean a thing in Shiloh Springs. Not one of you has followed the golden rule. I'm ashamed of being sheriff here." He took off the badge and handed it to Mr. Landers.

Then he saw Annabelle standing at the edge of the group, fear pooled in her eyes.

Immediately he strode over to her. "Miss Yeager, may I escort you to breakfast?"

The crowd parted and he walked her to Gloria's.

Annabelle felt sick at heart as she picked at her food. She'd been nothing but trouble to Josh since she'd arrived in town and hated herself for it. Maybe she *should* get on the next stage out of town after all.

"I think you ought to sell the Chances Are Saloon. It ain't nothing but trouble." He cut into a stack of flapjacks and lifted the fork to his mouth. "In fact, you should do yourself a favor and just close it."

"I can't afford to close it." She wasn't sure how much money she had left and the place had lots of customers.

"It's a nuisance. Why I'm, or was, over there at least once a day and more on weekends." He took another bite of flapjacks.

"I asked Mr. Landers about selling it, but he said there weren't any takers. I have another idea, though." Her throat was dry so she sipped some more coffee. "I could turn the social club into a hotel and make the Chances Are a restaurant."

His fork stopped mid-air. She thought he'd started to say something, but didn't.

She continued with her idea. "The ladies will have to move out, of course. And I'll have to replace the beds and fix up the rooms. It could take a week or two."

"Personally, I still think you ought to close it." He took another bite. "But it's yours. Talk to Mr. Webber at the bank and Mr. Landers. Meanwhile you'll stay in my room. The sooner you do something, the better."

Annabelle struggled to understand him. She thought he'd like her idea. Last night he'd held her and made her feel safe, but now he treated her like a stranger. She needed to hold him, touch him, and feel his quiet strength. What had she done to lose her only friend?

"I'll walk you over to the bank." Josh stood and paid Gloria. When Annabelle followed him out the door, he took her arm and led her to the bank. It wasn't the closeness she wanted, but she'd take what she could get.

Ted Webber sat in his office. "Sheriff. Miss Yeager. Mr. Woods was a valued customer. Mr. Landers brought the documents and opened an account in your name. I transferred Mr. Woods' account into yours." He pulled out a small booklet and handed it to her. She looked at it. Her balance was over four hundred dollars. A gasp escaped her.

Josh took it. He lifted a brow before returning it to her.

"How soon can I have some of the money?" Anticipation filled her. She had enough money to make her plan work.

"Whenever you want it. Just bring the book and tell Mr. Smiley how much you want." He rose. "Now if you'll excuse me, I have a prior engagement. Thank you, Miss Yeager."

Josh ushered her out to the lobby. Lauren Thamann blocked the door and stared at her.

"Lauren." Josh acknowledged her presence.

"Sheriff," the madam said, walking toward the banker's office.

Josh's hand rested on Annabelle's back as he guided her outside. She savored his touch.

"I need to speak to Mr. Johnson," she said.

"And I need to see Landers. He's president of the town council and I need to give him the keys and make it official. I expect I'll see you later." He tipped his hat, turned and walked away.

She felt his loss and walked to the Emporium. She met with Mr. Johnson and ordered a bed, linens, and a small chest for each room in her hotel and other supplies with delivery in a week. He practically rubbed his hands together in glee as Mrs. Johnson sneered at her.

Like a woman off to the gallows, she walked to the Chances Are Saloon. Tired, cranky and covered with dust, she was in no mood for an argument, but knew she would get one.

She couldn't bring herself to go through the front door and the back door was locked. When she knocked, she got no response. In frustration she kicked the door, gaining nothing but a sore foot. Limping, she went back to the front and entered. She caught Rufus' eye and headed for the office. The two customers paid her no mind.

She sat in the small office. A vision of her mother loomed in her head.

Annabelle Dallas Yeager, what has got you so down in the mouth? You made your choice. So it didn't work out like you expected. Didn't I teach you to pick yourself up and move on? Now you own a saloon and brothel. You didn't ask for them, but they is yours. You either throw it overboard or make it work for you. These people work for you. You just gonna hand it o'er to them? Where is your pride? The Yankees take it, too?

She heard it as clear as she heard the tinny piano in the saloon. Well, she'd come here in search of a new life and while this might not be the one she thought, it was a new life. *Her* new life and she'd make the best of it.

Rufus entered the office without knocking. "What do *you* want? I'm busy."

"I'm busy, too. From now on, knock when you enter my office. Second, give me keys to all the doors, so I can get in. Third, tell Lauren that she and her girls have to be out in three days. I'm converting the social club into a hotel, something the town desperately needs. Once they move out, I'll refurbish the rooms."

"You want *me* to tell her and the girls to leave?" His face paled.

"Yes, you are the manager aren't you?" She studied

him a moment. Would he do it? "Once they vacate the rooms, I'll clean and paper them before the new furniture arrives."

"Where are they supposed to go?"

Josh and Rufus were wearing on her. "Lauren's a resourceful woman. I'm sure she can find a place."

"I just don't feel right doing that." He shifted from foot to foot. "She ain't never hurt anybody. Nope, it ain't right. I can't work for a woman." He started to remove his apron.

Panic set in. After all, she needed him to run the saloon. "Wait! I'm sorry, Rufus. I didn't mean to step on your toes." Hell, it was her saloon and she needed to learn how to run it in case Rufus decided to quit. "Maybe we can work out a compromise. You teach me how to run the Chances Are and I will pay you an extra ten dollars per week."

Rufus didn't move, but he didn't say yes either. She watched him mulling the idea over.

"I want a rent-free room in the hotel as long as I work here."

Good, she could do that. She was willing to pay more and a room would be a breeze.

"Deal." She stuck her hand out.

"Deal," he said, walking over to the desk and taking her proffered hand. "We need some whiskey ordered."

"How do I order it?" She doubted it was purchased from the Emporium.

"You send a telegram to the distributor telling him what you want. You pay when they deliver. Name should be there in the desk." He paused at the door. "Do you want to learn to tend bar, too?" he asked, leaning against the doorway.

She hadn't considered that. The idea intrigued her. "Is it hard?"

"No. You have to pay attention. They start yelling, you ignore it. Just keep filling the glasses and take the money. Why don't you start this afternoon? Won't be too busy and I'll be here."

She liked the idea of seeing customers spend money

at her saloon. "I'll do it."

"After lunch I'll show you how to determine what stock you need to order," he said, pushing away from the door. "You might want to dress in some clothes other than that fancy dress." He jutted his chin at her and was gone.

She wasn't wearing a fancy dress. She wouldn't do housework in it, but it wasn't a party dress either. She'd slip back to Josh's room and change.

A knock at the door interrupted her thoughts. "Come in."

"Miss Yeager, you still staying at the jail?" Rufus wiped his hands on his apron.

"No. After the attack, Sheriff Morrow moved me to his room. I really can't stay there much longer."

"I was thinking. Mr. Woods has rooms upstairs over the saloon. I don't see why you can't use them. He certainly won't, and he fixed it up for you. It's got a separate entrance from the alley and it ain't connected to the social club."

How come no one thought about where Barry lived before? "Do you have a key?"

"I suppose Mr. Landers has it," he said. "There might be an extra one in the desk."

She began rifling through clean, organized desk drawers. In one she found the ordering records and other business papers and a small key.

"It might be in the safe behind you. I have the combination."

He pointed behind her to a small table with a skirt around it. She lifted the skirt and discovered a safe. "What's in it?"

"I put the receipts and the day's take in there. Barry took everything out in the morning but what was needed for the next day. He'd put part of it in the bank, but I don't know about the rest."

"How much money is in here?" Her breath hung in her throat.

"About four hundred dollars or so. I took money out for expenses, such as my pay, pay for the waitress, and things like that." He opened the safe. Money lay in neat stacks. She counted four hundred and twenty seven dollars. It was a fortune. She hadn't seen that much money in her whole life!

Inside the safe she spotted a locked drawer and remembered the small key in the desk. Once opened, she found a larger key–it had to belong to the rooms upstairs. She fingered it.

Now she would have a place of her own, separate from the saloon and the social club. "How do I get upstairs?" Excitement and disappointment at leaving Josh's room welled up in her fighting for control. She closed the safe and rushed after Rufus.

Stairs leading to the second floor were on the side of the building. Why hadn't she seen them before? At the top of the steps, she fitted the key into the lock. The door creaked as she pushed it open.

She stepped into a small, well-furnished parlor. A large woolen rug absorbed her footfalls as she moved around the room, looking in awe at the new furniture, the heavy lace curtains, crystal and china. A slight coating of dust had settled on the furniture in the parlor and an attached kitchen area. Of course, since no one had been here since Barry's death.

She spotted a door off to the side and paused. It would be the bedroom. Composing herself, she turned the knob and opened it.

Another plush rug covered the floor. Her breath caught in her throat at the sight of a large, carved sleigh bed with lace edged linens and comforter. They would have lain together at night and she would have borne their children on this bed. Her legs threatened to fold. Tightness filled her chest feeling the loss of her dream.

"Annabelle, are you in here?" a voice called from the front room. "Are you all right?"

She turned and saw Josh standing in the parlor. "Yes."

"Rufus said you were up here. I'd forgotten about these rooms. Woods kept the carpenter busy getting it ready for you." His eyes traveled over the room before resting on her again.

"Yes. Rufus just remembered to tell me. I found the key. A little dusting and I can move right in."

"I reckon so," Josh sighed. "Annabelle, be careful. That alley can be extremely dangerous."

"I suppose it could be." She didn't want to think about that right now.

He shrugged. "Landers talked me into taking the badge back. I could escort you to the door every night. That way you won't have to worry about the drunks."

Josh cared for her. Her feet barely touched the floor as she moved toward him. She stood on tip-toes with her hands on his chest and kissed him on the cheek. It wasn't enough for her.

His arm wrapped around her waist and pulled her close. Excitement danced in his eyes, as her breasts pressed against his broad chest. He leaned down to take possession of her lips. Her eyes closed and she uttered a contented sigh. Her surrender allowed him to caress her and she wanted his hands to touch her all over. Though it seemed like an eternity before they broke the kiss, it was over too soon.

He rubbed the back of his fingers over her cheek. He kissed down the column of her neck. His hand found her breast through the layers of clothing.

Her fingers moved over his chest and back. How had she become so lost in him?

"Annabelle," he said before kissing her again. "Sweetheart, we have to stop."

"I know," she whimpered between kisses. "We have to stop." She continued to kiss him.

Finally he broke the kiss. "I'm not sorry I kissed you."

"I'm not sorry you did either." She continued to lean against him. "I'd better go downstairs. I told Rufus I'd help him tend bar and I have to tell Lauren I'm closing the social club."

"Why don't you let Rufus do it?" He planted kisses along her jaw and ear. "She ain't going to go willingly."

"I told him to tell her, but I really think I should do it." She stepped away from him and moved to the door. He followed, stepping out first so she could lock up. "I can't have Rufus doing my dirty work while I sit back and rake in the money." He stood on a lower step putting him eye-to-eye with her. Without thinking, she leaned forward and kissed him again. She wrapped her arms around his neck as he wrapped his around her waist. "Should we be standing here doing this?" she asked before her lips met his again.

"Probably not." He kissed her once more before he carried her down the steps and escorted her back into the saloon.

"Rufus," she said, "do I have time to go back to the sheriff's place and change clothes before I start learning how to tend bar?"

Josh watched her hips sway as she walked over to the bar and felt himself harden all over again.

"Yes, ma'am." Rufus eyed him with a smirk. "Take your time."

Annabelle walked out the door. Instead of following, he turned to Rufus. "Do you have something you want to say? You're grinning like the cat that caught the canary."

"Never noticed 'til now how pretty Miss Annabelle is." He grabbed the rag and started to wipe the counter. "I expect you already know that. I bet she's a screamer in bed."

Josh grabbed Rufus' shirt and pulled him onto the counter. "Rufus, I don't think I heard you right. I thought I heard you insulting Miss Yeager and casting aspersions on her. Did I misunderstand you?" His clenched fist itched to wipe the smirk off his face.

"Why...yes-yes you did, Sheriff. Miss Annabelle is a lady." The man squirmed as sweat broke out on his brow. "She's a fine lady and I don't know what got into me. You're one fine gentleman, helping her out."

"I thought I might've misunderstood you. When Miss Annabelle gets back, I expect you to treat her with kid gloves and protect her like your life depends on it, because it does." He released Rufus who slid off the bar. "Do you understand me?"

"Yes, sir." Rufus wiped his brow.

Josh didn't want to care so much, but he did. In just a few days Annabelle had managed to get deep under his skin.

He exited the bar and headed to his room. The door was closed, so he knocked.

"One moment, please." After two or three minutes she opened the door wearing a simple white blouse and dark skirt with her hair pulled up into a tight bun. He imagined pulling the pins out and letting it fall down her back. Damn, if she wasn't more attractive than ever.

"I'll have my things packed in a few minutes." She flitted through the room stuffing clothes into a carpetbag.

It seemed so natural for her hairbrush and mirror to be on the dresser. The cool silver burned his hand when he picked them up. "Don't forget these."

She took them and scanned the room. "I believe that's everything."

Once the carpetbag was closed he grabbed it before she could pick it up. "I'll carry it for you."

She didn't argue, but graced him with a smile. She reached up and kissed him. His lips tingled from the contact. For a moment he considered dropping the bag and forcing her back on the bed. She'd be willing, he was certain. He'd also be a first class rounder if he did that. So, with every ounce of his willpower he stopped himself. "Annabelle—"

Her finger on his lips hushed him. "Don't say a thing." She licked her lips. "I like kissing you." With that she turned and walked out the door. The little minx had him wrapped around her finger and she knew it.

At the saloon, he left her with Rufus. "Remember, when you're ready to go upstairs, send for me. I don't want you in the alley alone." She nodded and he took her bag upstairs. He didn't feel right about her moving in here. He liked it better knowing she was in his bed at night, even if he wasn't there.

Annabelle's heart sank when he left. She'd come to town to marry one man and fallen in love with another. Did love happen that quickly? It wouldn't do any good to moon about it all day.

"Rufus, could you go tell Miss Lauren I want to talk to her?"

"Don't bother, Rufus. Miss Lauren is here." Dressed in a robe and slippers, she slid to a table. "Bring me a drink."

Rufus looked at Annabelle, undecided about what to do. She nodded her permission. He poured a whiskey and set it before Lauren. Annabelle took a seat at the same table.

Eyes pinned on Annabelle, Lauren gulped the drink down. "You don't belong here," she slurred.

"Doesn't matter whether I belong here or not, I'm the new owner of the Chances Are. You, on the other hand, just work here and your services are no longer needed." She sat straight and unflinching. "I'm converting the social club into a hotel and giving you three days to vacate the property."

"You can't do that. The Chances Are is nothing without me." Daggers shot from the madam's eyes while her knuckles went white around the glass. "We won't leave." She threw down the dare.

"Yes, you will. I own this place and if you don't leave in three days' time, then the sheriff will remove you." Annabelle stood and turned away. Lauren leaped from the chair and tackled her. All those years wrestling with her brothers taught her how to pin the drunken whore to the floor. "Three days, Lauren. I suggest you all start packing. Now."

Within three days, the *ladies* moved out of the social club, though Lauren complained loud and long to everyone. They left a mess for Annabelle to clean up. The following three days she thoroughly scrubbed the rooms. It didn't matter how tired she was, they were gone and that had to count for something with the townsfolk.

Tiredness quickly claimed her. Every evening Josh came at seven and walked her to the stairs. Tonight, however, it was seven-thirty and he still hadn't shown up. She decided not to wait any longer. Bone weary, she wanted to go to her room. Rufus was working behind the bar. All she had to do was go out the back door and climb the stairs. Surely she could make it on her own.

She slipped into the alley with the upstairs key in hand. There was no light in the back, but she didn't see anyone as she hurried to the steps. No sooner had her foot hit the second step when a hand clamped over her mouth and someone grabbed her around the waist. She kicked her feet back to beat on his legs and bit his fingers. Hard.

She tasted blood and the hand left her mouth. Her hands clawed at her attacker and he fell backward losing his grip. On the ground she rolled away from him and scrambled to her feet, screaming as loud as she could.

Rufus came running out the back door, shotgun in hand. When her attacker saw him with the gun he started running. Oddly, Rufus seemed dazed and con-fused. She tried to take the shotgun from him, but he held firm. He raised it straight up in the air and fired a shot as the man disappeared around the corner.

"You hurt, Miss Annabelle?" Rufus asked.

She brushed her dress off as Josh rounded the opposite corner, gun drawn.

"What's going on?" He quickly surveyed the alley.

"Someone attacked Miss Annabelle. I was tending bar when I heard her yelling. I grabbed Old Jake here and run out. She was on the ground and a man was standing over her. He vamoosed when I let Old Jake go."

Josh holstered his gun and placed his hands on Annabelle's shoulders. "Are you hurt?"

"No, just frightened." She trembled from head to toe.

Josh pulled her to him, wrapping her in his arms.

She welcomed his embrace.

"I told you to wait for me before you left the saloon," he admonished, then led her back inside. "Rufus, get her a brandy to settle her nerves."

"Sure thing, Sheriff. I need one to settle my nerves after seeing him go after her like that." He stopped in the doorway blocking their way. "Who would do something like this?"

"I don't know, but I intend find out." Josh's jaw set in determination.

Josh helped her into her office. Annabelle sat shaking. Rufus brought in a bottle of brandy and a glass. Josh poured in a healthy amount. "Here, drink this." His emotions were wound tighter than an alarm clock and he was ready to tear up stumps.

Squatting next to her, her blue eyes got to him. It would be a pleasure to watch those eyes open up every morning and stare at the world in wonder. It nagged at him that this was the second time he wasn't there for Annabelle. He couldn't lose her.

"Josh,"—he didn't like the edge of fright in her voice—"can you take me to my room? I don't want to stay here."

"Good idea, but finish your brandy first." As she sipped the last of the golden liquid, he told Rufus to keep his shotgun close by. He grabbed the brandy bottle in his left hand and wrapped it around her waist to hold her up, freeing his right hand in case he needed it. A quick look up and down the alley showed it was safe to leave. When they reached the door at the top of the staircase, she opened it and he all but shoved her inside as he followed.

"Wait here while I look around." He checked the rooms before holstering his gun. "All clear," he said returning to the parlor.

They faced each other without speaking. His need grew just looking at her. She was an innocent and he shouldn't do this, but he couldn't stop himself. Their breathing grew heavier and louder. His lips brushed hers lightly, then burst into full-fledged passion. His tongue teased her lips apart and tasted the brandy. She intoxicated him in more ways than one.

He was lost and wanted nothing more than her. He wanted her by his side and in his bed for as long as he breathed. His hands roamed over her body. He cupped her butt and pressed her closer. Surely she felt his erection pressing against her belly. He didn't remember ever being this hard for any woman. He was losing control—no, he'd lost it long ago and only the matter of surrender still remained unresolved. His desire for her was now becoming too painful to endure.

Annabelle returned his kisses and wrapped her arms around his neck. Her naiveté excited him even more, if that was possible. That's when he recalled she was probably a virgin. This wasn't how he wanted to make love to her. He wanted it to be unhurried and gentle. He wanted it tonight. She was his woman and he wanted to share with her all the wonders and pleasures two people in love could feel.

"Annabelle. Annabelle, honey." He broke the kiss. "We have all night. First I have to finish my rounds. Have you eaten yet?" Her lips showed evidence of his branding. She shook her head. "I don't want you going out. Do you understand me?" Why did he think she would listen this time?

"Yes." She nodded.

"I'll stop by Gloria's and pick up two dinners. I won't be gone long. Don't open the door for anyone. I'll use the key. Do you have a gun?"

"Yes, Pa gave me one during the war. I brought it with me." She reached into her skirt pocket and handed him the key.

"Get it." She went to the carpetbag and removed an old Navy Colt covered with rust. The likelihood of it misfiring or exploding in her face was something Josh didn't want to chance, no matter how small. He removed a Colt from his left holster and handed it to her. "Use this. Just pull the hammer back, point and pull the trigger." Another peck on the lips and he was out the door. "Lock it behind me."

Stepping outside, he waited until he heard her turn the latch. He stopped at Gloria's and ordered two meals and said he would return for them. On his rounds he paid particular attention to every man he passed. Each was a suspect, but he had nothing to go on.

At the jail he found Roger sitting at the desk cleaning his gun. Josh filled him in on the trouble at the Chances Are. "If you need me, I'll be there." Josh just didn't mention he would be upstairs with Annabelle.

He picked up the dinners from Gloria's and headed back to Annabelle's room. He stood by the building and watched the alley for a few minutes before climbing the stairs. He unlocked, then opened the door and stepped into the front room. He could see the soft flickering light dancing on the wall from a kerosene lamp she'd lit atop the mantle.

Annabelle lay asleep in one corner of the sofa, a book in her lap. The brandy must have relaxed her. Placing the dinners on a chair, he knelt next to her. "Sweetheart?" His fingers caressed her cheek. "Wake up. I'm back." She mumbled and her arms went around his neck as she woke up.

"Umm." The little temptress pulled him toward her, wielding her newfound power over him.

His hand squeezed her breast and she moaned her approval. He sat on the sofa and pulled her across his lap. Waves of golden hair cascaded over her shoulders and back when his fingers pulled out the pins holding the tight little bun.

"You make me feel like I'm important, not just someone to look after you," she whispered in his ear. Her stomach growled.

"Sounds like you need to eat. I picked up two dinners from Gloria."

The aroma of warm roast beef and potatoes pulled her off the sofa into the kitchen. He watched as she picked up two plates and silverware, and fixed two glasses of water.

The roast beef was tender and the potatoes were

lumpy. He sopped up the gravy with the biscuits. Annabelle seemed to perk up a little as she ate heartily. She would need her strength for what he had planned for tonight. After eating she set the dishes in the sink and returned to the sofa.

She sat on his lap and wrapped her arms around his neck. "How can I thank you? You watch out for me, see me home, and bring me dinner. Make me feel like I never felt before. Like I'm alive." She took his face in her hands.

"And you, little one, scare the wits out of me, but no matter how hard I try, I can't stay away from you." His hand worked the buttons on her blouse until it was open below her breasts. Their creamy, rounded tops gave hints of the joys that lay beneath her chemise and corset.

Her fingers worked the buttons of his shirt, pulling it open and sliding her hands over his undershirt before working her hand underneath to his skin. The feel of her fingers almost undid him.

With little effort, he scooped her into his arms and carried her to the bedroom. He stripped her clothes off. The sight of her naked body intoxicated him. Raw passion engulfed him. She was more beautiful than he imagined. Her breasts were large and perfectly shaped, tipped with raspberry nipples. He suckled first on one nipple and then the other, and was rewarded by more mewls.

In a matter of moments he had his clothes off and lay next to her. He laved one breast as his free hand dipped lower and teased her curls and he felt her desire. Their breathing quickened as their bodies trembled, demanding immediate union. Her moaning became louder and more frequent as they continued touching and kissing. He could no longer delay the inevitable.

Josh slid his body over her and settled between her legs. He positioned himself and moved to sheath himself. Her body stiffened and she yelped in pain as he breeched the barrier to her body. How could he forget she was a virgin? "The pain will pass in a moment, sweetheart." He forced himself to remain still, kissing her and rubbing her breast to distract her. He didn't really know that for a fact, but hoped it would. He was right, judging from Annabelle's response.

"Don't stop," she begged. His shaft throbbed within her. "It hurt for a moment. Is that all there is?" She slipped her arms around his neck.

"No, honey, this is just the beginning." He spent the night in her bed showing her how a man makes love to the woman he loves. Yes, he loved her.

Annabelle woke early the next morning to see Josh propped up on one elbow studying her. He leaned over and kissed her.

"I was hopin' you'd wake up. I need to go make rounds."

"You should've awakened me," she scolded as she stroked his arm. The powerful muscles that wielded big, deadly guns had patiently changed her from a girl into a woman. "I'll fix breakfast."

"Mmm, breakfast. I'd like that." Before she could speak, Josh kissed her and positioned himself between her legs. She gasped at his entry into her body. Once again she responded to him, threatening to fly into a thousand pieces. She never dreamed it could be like this between a man and a woman.

Feeling every bit of pleasure having him deep inside her, she took his unshaven face between her hands and kissed him. He crushed his mouth against hers as he poured his seed into her.

"I love you," he whispered in her ear. Her heart skipped a couple of beats. He loved her!

She lay wrapped in his arms as he dozed. Her prayers had been answered. This was the life she'd always dreamed about—wrapped in the arms of the man she loved.

She slipped out of bed, careful not to waken him and pulled on a wrapper. She built the fire and put on a pot of coffee before slicing some bacon and bread. The bacon sizzled as she mixed the eggs together with a bit of cheese. Josh came up from behind her and wrapped his arms around her and nuzzled her neck. "You should've wakened me."

She turned in his embrace and slid her arms around his neck. "I wanted to fix breakfast for the man I love. I do love you, Josh." The words hardly left her mouth before she felt his body responding to her and his erection press against her belly. He whooped and lifted her in his arms and spun her around.

He reached behind her and using the fork, he turned the bacon. "It's too late to go back to bed, so you'll have to wait 'til later. You aren't too sore are you?"

"No, I'm fine." She laid out the bread to toast it and removed the bacon. Then she poured the egg mixture into the skillet. Josh got out the cups and poured coffee for them both.

"I don't want you in the alley by yourself. I'll be back to take you to the office." Clearly, he was serious and he wanted her to know it. "I mean it. Someone killed Barry Woods. Twice someone has tried to kill you. I don't want them to succeed." He put his fork down and used his thumb and forefinger to turn her face toward him. "I don't know what I would do if something happened to you. I couldn't live with myself if I lost another woman I loved because I wasn't there to protect her."

What was he telling her? Had there been another woman in his life who died? A wife? He must have seen her puzzled look.

"Her name was Connie. I joined the army when I was seventeen and went off to fight the Yankees. Before I left, I asked her to marry me. Yankee stragglers raped and murdered her while I was gone. The same thing happened to my mother and sister. I wasn't there to protect any of them." He leaned forward and rested his elbows on the table, his fingers pinching the bridge of his nose.

"My dad died from heart trouble when I was a boy. I promised him I'd take care of my mother and sister." He remained still. "But I wasn't there to protect them when they needed me. I searched for the bastards, only to find somebody else got to them before I did." He couldn't tell her that he vowed to never love again, never to have that responsibility again. That was before he'd met Annabelle. How could he not love her?

"I know it doesn't help, but I'm so sorry." She took his hand in hers and kissed it. "I promise to be careful and wait for you. I want you to swear you'll be careful, too."

"Always. I better make my rounds and then I'll come back for you." He cupped his hand behind her head and gave her a tender kiss. "Lock the door behind me." She followed him to the door and locked it.

While waiting for Josh to return, she cleaned the room and washed the dishes. She found herself smiling, suddenly unable to imagine life without Josh. Despite his tendency to give orders, he was everything she wanted in a husband. She knew she loved him and he said he loved her, too. Her dream was coming true after all.

Josh returned as promised, and she rushed into his arms. After a kiss and brief conversation on safety, he opened the door and scanned the alley. Ushering her out, he escorted her to the saloon and gave orders to Rufus that she wasn't to leave alone. "I'll come by about one. Gloria is putting together a dinner for us."

In her office, she settled in her chair and drank the tea Rufus brought her. It took her a couple of hours to do the books, and discovered she'd made money without Lauren and her girls. The hotel awaited its first guests.

Annabelle decided there was too much money in the safe. She prepared the deposit and went out into the saloon and found Rufus counting whiskey bottles. "Rufus, the receipts need to go to the bank. Josh doesn't want me to leave the saloon. If you take them, I'll watch the bar."

"Sure thing, Miss Annabelle. Simpson has a tab of two seventy-five and I cut him off."

"Got it." She handed him an envelope. "The money and the bank book are in here. Don't let Mr. Smiley try to tell you it's less. I wrote down the number of bills. Would you stop at the Emporium and pick up some cigars to sell?"

"That is a dandy idea, Miss Annabelle." He removed his apron and took the envelope. He retrieved a small pistol from under the bar and stuffed it in his pocket before leaving.

Annabelle grabbed the rag and wiped down the bar. She heard the bat wing doors squeak and saw Lauren standing in the doorway.

"You didn't waste any time changing things. Can't say I like them, but I'll change them back when this joint is mine."

What was she talking about?

The woman walked to the middle of the room and continued her tirade. "Barry wanted to marry *me* and he promised me this joint. Believe me, it's mine and you won't be here much longer."

Annabelle had had enough of Lauren Thamann. She walked around the bar to face her. "Lauren, what are you raving about? Barry asked me to marry him and paid for me to come from Georgia. He made out his will leaving me all his property before I got here. From where I stand, you don't have a leg to stand on."

She saw Lauren flexing her fingers wildly against her skirt, but Annabelle wasn't finished yet. "Now why don't you slither back under whatever rock you came out from? I have work to do." She turned back toward the bar, but was stopped short when Lauren grabbed her hair.

"You have no right to what was promised to me," Lauren whined.

Annabelle threw her foot back as hard as she could and it connected with Lauren's leg, causing the madam to yelp in pain and release her hair. Turning, she saw Lauren rush her. She sidestepped and stuck her fist out. It landed squarely in Lauren's face.

Blood ran down Lauren's dress. Her hands covered her face and she grimaced in pain. "You bitch," she hissed as she grabbed a bottle and smashed the end of it on the edge of the bar. She waved the jagged bottle and jabbed at Annabelle, whose only choice was to retreat.

"Put the bottle down and get out," Annabelle shouted as she backed away from her. She threw a chair at Lauren who brushed it aside. The chair broke apart upon hitting the floor. If she could only reach one of the broken chair pieces, she could protect herself.

Lauren charged Annabelle again, cursing.

Stooping, Annabelle grabbed a chair leg.

"Not until I cut your face to ribbons so no man will ever want you again." Lauren smirked through the blood.

"I don't think so," Josh's voice boomed over the room. Thank God he was here. "You try that and I will drop you where you stand. You being a woman won't make a bit of difference." Josh's gun was pointed at Lauren's heart.

Annabelle dropped the chair leg, wondering how he'd drawn the gun so fast.

Long moments passed before Lauren dropped the bottle and it shattered on the floor. She stalked out of the saloon passing Rufus on the way in.

Josh holstered his gun before he wrapped his arms around Annabelle. "Did she hurt you?" He pressed her head to his chest.

"Not really. She pulled my hair that's all." Her controlled regular breathing belied the pounding of her heart in her ears.

"What in tarnation happened?" Rufus asked. "Are you all right, Miss Annabelle?"

"I'm fine, thank you, Rufus." She leaned into Josh and he held her up.

"Rufus, get some coffee for her." He sat her in a chair and took a seat. "What happened?"

She told him what Lauren had said and done. "Thank God you arrived when you did. I think she would've killed me."

Rufus set a cup down, but she saw something shiny lying on the floor and leaned over.

"What is it?" Josh asked, leaning closer to see the

item.

"It must have come off Lauren's dress." Annabelle picked up a gold button and handed it to Josh. "It's an unusual button and looks expensive." She looked at the button as he held it out.

"I've got to run over to the office," Josh said. "She's gone now, but I don't trust her." He pocketed the button. "I'll see she gets it back. Do you want me to take you upstairs now?"

Enticing thoughts danced through her head. "I'll be fine. See you about one."

"Rufus, send for me if Lauren comes back." He stood and left the saloon with his usual confident stride.

She couldn't believe she loved him and he loved her. Anticipation for an afternoon with Josh made her feel warm and tingly like a schoolgirl.

Josh finally had a break in the murder of Barry Woods. He fingered the button in his pocket. Upon returning to his office he removed an envelope from his desk drawer. The button inside was an exact match to Lauren's whalebone button with a gold inlay. The first button had been found clutched in Woods' hand when the body was discovered.

The Emporium wouldn't sell anything like it. Stashing the first button back in the drawer, he decided to talk to Hiram Johnson to make sure. The bell announced his entrance and he found Hiram behind the counter looking at a catalog. "What can I do for ya, Sheriff?"

"I need some information. Do you sell buttons like this?" Josh held the button out.

Hiram looked at it, turning it over. "I ordered two dozen of these in special for Lauren Thamann a few months ago."

Josh slipped it back into his pocket. "Thanks, Hiram." He had a suspect in Woods' death—Lauren. She might not have killed him, but she was there. As he faced death, Woods had pulled the button off Lauren's clothes.

Josh went looking for the madam. She wasn't at her new house and they didn't know when she would be back, so he went to the barbershop for a bath and shave. On the way, he reminded Gloria about the picnic basket.

At one, he presented himself to Annabelle at the saloon and escorted her upstairs for her to change clothes. She tried to ferret out his plans, but he stood firm and ushered her into the buggy he'd arranged earlier. After picking up the basket, they rode out into the country until they reached his ranch and stopped along a creek.

"This is beautiful. Are you sure it's okay to be here?" He lifted her from the buggy and she spread a blanket on the ground. "The owner isn't going to run us off with a load of buckshot?"

"No, the owner gave his permission, but if you want to ask him, go ahead." He lay on the blanket and patted it.

"We should have asked before we got here." She sat close to him and spread her skirt around her, but not before he saw her shapely legs and felt a response below his waist.

"Just say it out loud," he teased. "You never know where he might be."

"Sir, can we use your property for a picnic?" Her throaty laugh excited him.

"Be my guest," he answered. Her head jerked around.

"Really, Josh. The owner might get upset." She gently put her hands on his chest and shoved him on his back. When she leaned over, her breasts pressed against him. He wrapped his arms around her.

"Who says I'm not the owner? Actually, I bought it about a year ago. I had a well dug, but haven't gotten around to building a cabin yet, although I'm working on it. A couple of times a month I come out here and hunt."

"This is your ranch?" Pink splotches colored her cheeks and wonder filled her eyes. "You tricked me."

"Yep, I own it. There's a special reason I brought you here." He sat up and pulled her around to sit facing him.

"This place is special and so are you." Her little hand was warm and soft in his big calloused hands. He reached into his vest pocket. "I love you, Annabelle, and can't imagine life without you. Will you marry me?" He pulled out an engagement ring. She squealed and threw her arms around his neck.

"Yes, I'll marry you. I can't imagine a life without you either." He slipped the small diamond ring onto her finger. "I love you so much." She held out her hand and stared at the ring. "It's perfect."

They kissed and he felt her breasts pressing against him. He could no longer deny his body and lay her down on the blanket. In moments he had her undressed. His eyes feasted on her smooth delicate body. "You're so beautiful. I can't wait to make you my wife." After spreading kisses over her body, he shed his clothes and slowly entered her, savoring their passion until finally they exploded with pleasure.

After dressing, Annabelle opened the picnic basket. "Do you want chicken or ham? There are some hard-boiled eggs, too." She fed him chicken and he fed her ham and they laughed. Soon he helped her to her feet and interlaced fingers with her. They planned the house he would build for their family. Standing at the crest of the hill, he wrapped his arms around her and caressed her. She touched her stomach and imagined their child growing there.

Josh held onto her, stealing kisses, as he drove back to town. He wanted to get married as soon as possible and get her out of the saloon business.

At the livery, Josh stopped the buggy and helped her out. "Let's get you into the saloon before someone takes a shot at you." Solving Woods' murder had suddenly become urgent; his future wife's life depended on it.

He left her in the office with the order, "Stay in here. Things might get rowdy out there and I don't want you exposed to danger. Keep that gun close by at all times and if in doubt shoot first and I'll ask questions later. I want us to grow old together." She pressed herself against him and slid her arms around his neck. "I love you, Annabelle. If anything happened to you, I would die."

"I would die without you, Josh. I'm certain I can find something to do around here until you get back." She gestured at the general disarray around her.

A quick kiss and he departed, closing the door behind him. Once again he headed to Lauren's place to question her. Her girls denied she was there, but he searched the establishment. He failed to find her, but he found a dress with the same buttons with one missing and the dress she'd worn this morning with a button missing. He found a gun, but it wasn't the same caliber that had killed Woods. Lauren could have disposed of it. He took the dresses to his office and left them there.

When he came out of his office he saw smoke bellowing from the other side of town and broke into a run. Flames shot from the saloon high into the air. His blood pounded through his ears. Annabelle promised to stay in her office in the center of the saloon. He had to protect her. He wasn't going to fail this time.

He slid to a stop across the street from the saloon. Flames licked the sky from the upper rooms and the roof and spread to the front of the saloon. There was no way to stop the fire; it would burn the building to the ground. Judging from the flames, the back seemed still intact and he ran around to the alley. The back door was locked. He tried kicking it with all his strength, but it wouldn't budge. He should've known Woods would put the heaviest and strongest door in the rear. He moved to the front of the saloon and to his amazement found it still intact.

Lauren stood in front of the saloon yelling, "Burn. Burn." Rufus appeared in the doorway. When he tried to come out, Lauren raised a pistol and fired a shot at him.

"What the hell you doing, Lauren?" Rufus shouted. "I have to get out. The damned building is on fire."

"The Chances Are Saloon is rightfully mine. If I can't have it, no one can," the mad woman shouted. "I want that bitch to die just like that two-timing son of a bitch

Woods did. The Chances Are was supposed to be mine."
She fired another shot at the door. "The lying bastard
promised to marry me, not her. After everything I did
for him she took him away from me. The bastard
deserved to die and I'm glad I killed him."

"Drop the gun, Lauren," Josh shouted over the
crackling of the fire. She turned to face him and fired a
shot in his direction. His pistol easily slid from its
holster and he pulled the trigger. Her legs folded as a
bright red stain over her heart spread across her chest
coloring her white blouse. She fell to the ground.

With a tinge of regret Josh holstered his Colt.

Rufus ran out of the saloon violently coughing as
soot shimmered through the air. "Annabelle's trapped
inside her office. I tried to get her out, but part of the
building collapsed blocking the way."

Josh crashed through the front door and a
seemingly impenetrable wall of fire. He fought his way
through popping wood, intense heat and fire that
blistered his skin. The pain failed to register as he made
his way to the office. "Annabelle. Annabelle! Talk to
me!"

He heard Annabelle's screams for help over the fury
of the fire. She was alive.

"I'm here, Annabelle," he shouted. A huge burning
timber blocked the door to her office. Strength rushed
through his veins as he tossed it and other debris to the
side. Heat had warped the frame and the door wouldn't
open when he pushed on it. No! This wasn't going to
happen again. He wouldn't survive losing Annabelle.

"Stand back, I'm coming in!" He lifted his leg and
crashed his boot against the door. It gave a little.

"Josh, help me." Annabelle coughed on the other
side.

Putting his shoulder to the door, he heaved his body
against it. This time it sprang open and hot air rushed
into the room. Through the dense smoke, he managed
to find Annabelle sitting on the floor coughing. He
struggled to breathe—he had a promise to keep and he
wasn't going to fail.

"We have to get out of here. The building is coming down around us." He pulled her to her feet, but she couldn't stand on her own. Scooping her into his arms, burying her face against his chest, he made his way to the front door of the saloon, dodging flames and falling debris. Her skirt caught on fire, but he quickly pulled it up and smothered the flames. Moments later he saw the wall of fire at the door separating them from safety. He shielded her from the flames and with one last burst of energy ran through the flames and broke out into the street.

In the safety of the open air, he took a long, deep breath of fresh air before he set Annabelle on her feet. They held onto each other and watched in silence as the building collapsed. Her hand flew to her mouth when she saw Lauren's body on the ground. Mr. Webber was kneeling next to the corpse, tears streaming down his face.

The banker staggered to his feet with Lauren's gun in hand. "Who killed her?" The crowd watched in silence. "I want to know who killed her." No one answered. "Who killed my sister?" he yelled. A collective gasp filled the air at Webber's rant. She was his sister?

Josh led Annabelle over to Rufus, never taking his eyes off Webber. "Watch her." He slid the Colt from its holster and held it at his side.

"She set fire to the saloon, and when Rufus tried to escape she fired a shot at him." Josh moved away from Annabelle and toward Webber. "I told her to drop the gun and she fired at me. I had no choice."

"Lauren only wanted what was hers. The no good son of a bitch broke the engagement, saying he couldn't marry a whore. Said he needed a respectable wife and laughed at her. The Chances Are would have been hers after she killed him, except for that damn will." Webber raised his arm and pointed the gun at Annabelle. "He left it all to that tramp."

Josh tamped down his anger; it wouldn't help him in a gunfight.

Webber continued to rant. "*She* didn't leave town;

then Monty and Randy didn't kill her at the jail. Lauren went crazy after that bitch made her leave the Chances Are. Everyone here knows Lauren deserved this place more than anyone. *She's* responsible for the death of four people." He pointed the gun at Annabelle. "I intend to kill her, Sheriff. The town will thank me for it. If it wasn't for her, Woods and Lauren wouldn't be dead." Webber played to the crowd. "That bitch has got the sheriff on her side and stole everything that should've been Lauren's."

"I can't let you do that, Webber. Which one of you killed Woods?" Josh shut out everything but Webber. "I suggest you walk away from this now before any more blood is shed."

"Lauren did. She shot Woods when he said he was marrying that bitch." Josh's blood ran cold. "Once that bitch died, Lauren could have gone back and taken over the Chances Are. Things would have been the way they were supposed to be. Lauren would own the Chances Are, I would own the bank, and our brother Carl would be back to run the gaming tables. Now I have to kill you both." Carl was their brother?

Josh saw Roger off to the side. One way or another, the banker wouldn't survive if he decided to fight it out.

"Drop the gun, Webber. If it was all Lauren, then I have no problem with you walking away from this." *It's not too late* he whispered under his breath. The barrel of the pistol pointed at Annabelle started to rise as Webber began to squeeze the trigger. Josh's shot hit him in the heart. The man pitched forward to his knees. He tried to raise the gun, but he fell forward and landed face down in the dirt.

Annabelle ran to Josh and slid underneath his arm. "I'm so sorry."

"It wasn't your fault." He wrapped his arms around her. "They were bad seed."

She buried her face in his chest. "I was so scared he would kill you and I don't know what I'd do without you."

"When I saw the flames and realized it was the saloon, I almost went crazy thinking about losing you." He kissed her right there in the middle of the street. "It scared me to think you depended on me and I'd let you down."

"You would never let me down. I knew you'd come for me." He kissed her again.

Mrs. Johnson approached them. "I'm sorry you lost everything, Miss Yeager. Why don't you come on over to the store and I'll help you replace your clothes and things." Annabelle turned to Josh whose mouth had fallen open. Now that the Chances Are was gone, Annabelle was respectable again and Mrs. Johnson wouldn't miss making a sale.

Mr. Landers stood next to Mrs. Johnson, "On behalf of the town, we're real sorry, Miss Yeager. Appears some people misjudged both you and Webber and put their faith in the wrong person. We hope you'll stay in town and give us another chance."

The words touched her and she turned to Josh. He draped his arm over her shoulders and pulled her close. "Thank you, Mr. Landers. I'll do whatever Josh says."

"I'd thought about moving, but there's a ranch outside town with my name on it. So I guess we'll stay around awhile and see how things work out." Josh shook Mr. Lander's hand.

She looked at the burning rubble of the saloon. "I might have to spend the night at the jail again."

"Oh no, you won't. As soon as I find the preacher, we're getting married and you'll spend the night with me at the ranch out under the stars. Looks like we need to get started on that house right away, because I want a house full of young'uns to keep you out of trouble."

Annabelle stood on the porch of the ranch house and watched her husband ride up. He slid off his horse and bounded up the steps. He bypassed her, went straight to the cradle, and picked up the sleeping baby. "How's our boy?" He tucked Tyler in his arms close to his heart, then wrapped an arm around Annabelle before kissing her. "I missed you both. Seems like I've been gone a month."

"You were gone less than five days." She leaned against his strong body. "Yet it does seem like months. Did you catch them?"

They sat on the porch swing. "The tip we received was good this time. We caught Carl Thamann and his gang outside Temmings. Carl died in a shootout and the posse took the other three to jail. The Judge'll be there next week so they should be off to Huntsville right after that."

"We were worried about you." The baby scrunched his face and waved his fists as he started fussing. "I think he's hungry." She undid her bodice and Josh handed her the baby. Tyler settled at her breast.

"This is a sight I missed seeing." Draping an arm over her shoulders, he said, "If someone had told me a year ago, I would miss being home with my wife watching her feed our son, I would have locked him up as crazy."

He watched his son suckle at her breast and brushed his cheek.

Annabelle looked up at him with her beautiful, loving eyes. "This is what I truly wanted when I came west. I'm so thankful I found you."

"So am I, sweetheart." He tickled the little baby toes of his son. "So am I."

The Authors

Michele Ann Young

Michele Ann Young grew up in England, and now lives in Canada working as a full-time writer after an interesting career in university administration. She lives with her husband, two lovely daughters and a dictatorial Maltese Terrier. When not creating stories, she enjoys the ancient arts of tatting and smocking.

The Brides of the West story struck a particular chord with her, since her heroine Tess, is new to North America, and Michele Ann had fun recalling some of her own surprises about the differences between the Old World and the New when she first arrived on these shores.

www.micheleannyoung.com

Kimberly Ivey

Kimberly Ivey began her career as a freelance writer more than twenty-five years ago. Since then, hundreds of her nonfiction articles, poetry, short stories and essays have been published throughout the U.S. and Canada. She is the author of one children's book, a romantic suspense novel, two novellas, and several short stories in print anthologies.

She has served on the board of professional writing organizations and literacy committees, and enjoys presenting workshops at conferences and to local groups. She is a creative writing instructor at a southeast Texas college.

A mother of three and grandmother to four, Kimberly resides in her home state of Texas with her husband of 31 years, the youngest of her three children, and several spoiled, and demanding pets.

http://hometown.aol.com/kimberlyivey2/index.html

Billie Warren Chai

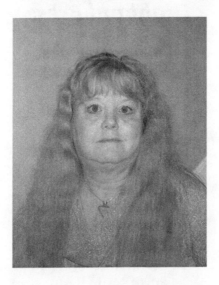

Billie lives in Ohio with her husband whom she met while attending the University of Louisville. They have two teenage sons. After graduating, Billie and her husband had several successful business ventures and are now retired.

Billie's stories appear in numerous Highland Press anthologies: *Secret of the Blue Moon* in Blue Moon Magic and *Operation Family* in Christmas Wishes. *Keeping Hannah Safe* appears in the Recipe for Love anthology and *Calling Hailey's Bluff* in Love Under the Mistletoe. Her story *Hitting Paydirt* will appear in the Love on a Harley anthology. Billie is currently working on two full length manuscripts.

She and her husband love the freedom of touring the country on their motorcycle, a Harley Davidson Road King Classic as they believe in living their lives to the fullest.

www.billiewarrenchai.com

Also Available from Highland Press

Leanne Burroughs
Highland Wishes

Isabel Mere
Almost Taken

Ashley Kath-Bilsky
The Sense of Honor

R.R. Smythe
Into the Woods
(A Young Adult Fantasy)

Leanne Burroughs
Her Highland Rogue

Deborah MacGillivray
Cat O'Nine Tales

Jacquie Rogers
Faery Special Romances
(A Young Adult Romance)

Katherine Deauxville
The Crystal Heart

Rebecca Andrews
The Millennium Phrase Book

Chris Holmes
Blood on the Tartan

Cynthia Owens
In Sunshine or In Shadow

Anne Kimberly
Dark Well of Decision

Jean Harrington
The Barefoot Queen

Jannine Corti Petska
Rebel Heart

Phyllis Campbell

Pretend I'm Yours
Holiday Romance Anthology
Christmas Wishes
Holiday Romance Anthology
Holiday in the Heart
Romance Anthology
No Law Against Love
Romance Anthology
Blue Moon Magic
Romance Anthology
Blue Moon Enchantment
Romance Anthology
Recipe for Love
Holiday Romance Anthology
Romance Upon a Midnight Clear
Holiday Romance Anthology
Love Under the Mistletoe

Upcoming

Isabel Mere
Almost Guilty
Candace Gold
A Heated Romance
John Nieman & Karen Laurence
The Amazing Rabbitini
(Children's Illustrated)
Diane Davis White
Moon of the Falling Leaves
Romance Anthology
No Law Against Love 2
Lance Martin
The Little Hermit
(Children's Illustrated)

Check our website frequently for future Highland Press releases.

www.highlandpress.org

LaVergne, TN USA
17 March 2010
176288LV00003B/105/P